BOSSY *Brothers*

JESSE

NEW YORK TIMES BESTSELLING AUTHOR

JA HUSS

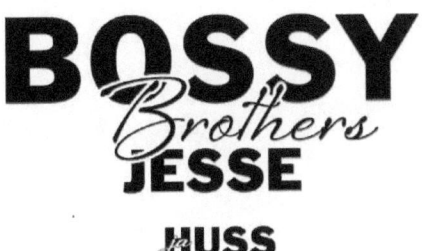

BOSSY *Brothers*
JESSE
JA HUSS

Edited by RJ Locksley
Cover Photo: Sara Eirew
Cover Design by JA Huss

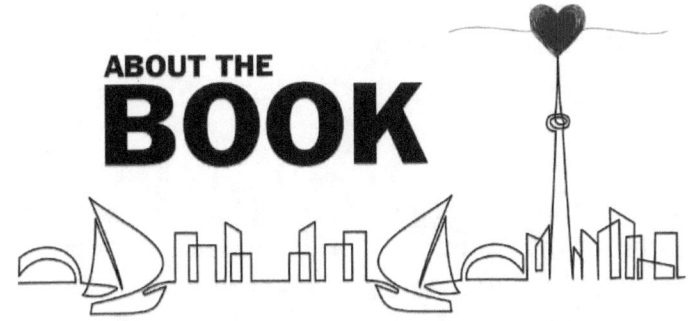

ABOUT THE
BOOK

Thirteen years before Emma Dumas bought me in a bachelor auction to teach me a lesson she stole my heart down on Key West. I fell so hard for this girl I made all the promises. Only with Emma, I really meant them.

And then I disappeared.

But it wasn't my fault. Let's just call my reason "Family Business". I'd tell you what that business is, but then I'd have to kill you. Just kidding. I can't tell you what my family business is because it's so secret, even I don't know.

My point is... I didn't ghost. It was a weird twist of circumstances. And OK, yes. I did hook up with pretty much every girl on the island that week. But after I met Emma, I was ruined. She was the only one I wanted.

It's been thirteen years. I'm a changed man.

I STILL want her. I have ALWAYS wanted her.

But it's kind of hard to tell her that with a gag in my mouth and a hood over my head.

Bossy Brothers: Jesse features a bachelor auction gone wrong, four smart ladies who botch a crazy revenge kidnapping, a power dream date with fast cars, private jets, and expensive yachts, lots of ex-sex, and a happily ever after that proves... sometimes the best man for the job is a woman.

CHAPTER ONE

"Did you ever meet that guy? You know. Like…
the one? And suddenly your ordinary life is so much
more exciting, sunrises are ten times brighter, random
daily sounds become a harmony, and all those revolting
smells you hate about the city suddenly turn sweet?
Yeah. No. Me either."

The audience laughs and I pause to let them.

"I'm still waiting for that fucking prince to show
up, people!"

They laugh again.

I hold up a finger to tell them I'm not quite done
yet and let them settle down. "But listen." I pause here
for dramatic effect. "You don't need a prince to save
you. You just need to find yourself and your people.
That is how you find success."

They don't believe me. They never do at this point. I mean, I get it. You don't turn to independent cosmetic sales because you have a ton of options. Most of these ladies—and a few men—are here because something bad happened in their life. Maybe a divorce or a break-up. Maybe someone died. Maybe they have always struggled. Have always taken all the hits and never caught a break before.

Doesn't matter. They're here now and the only thing they all have in common is hope.

One last spark of hope that they can turn it around. That this shit life they were born into doesn't have to be that way. And OK. I'll admit that independent cosmetic sales isn't most people's definition of success, but when you're in that headspace, when you're in that downward spiral and your options are so limited you cry yourself to sleep at night praying for some magic opportunity to come along and then we show up?

It's powerful.

This group right here have already been through all that struggle and strife. They're already successful. They did it. *They made it.*

And today it's my job to inspire them by allowing them to inspire me.

"Let me tell you a little story," I say. "One day, after a very bad one-night stand gone wrong, I met these…"

I turn to look at my three best friends standing on my right. "These brave, smart, beautiful, sexy women. We were all sharing the same walk of shame." I hold up another hand. "Not together," I say, letting the audience laugh again. "But with the same man. In the same week."

Gasps from our astonished audience. Some scowls too. But scowls aren't for us. They're not judging us, they're judging *him*.

"That's right. He was dating all four of us at the same time. Granted, it was spring break on Key West and we were young and we all wanted to find our prince. And right before these three left to go home, somehow we all ended up in a bar commiserating about all the bad decisions we made that week. Including the name of this particular—very popular—man. And do you know what happened to us that night?"

I scan the crowd of newbies. Mila, Hannah, Natalie, and I have done this speech hundreds of times now and it never loses its effect on our recruits. Ever.

"We bonded over this," I say. "We didn't tear each other down, we built each other up!"

The recruits applaud.

"And two years later we launched our first cosmetics line. And two years after that, we had twenty

9

lines, three hundred and fifty employees, and one of the tallest buildings in the city."

More applause.

"We stuck together, friends! That's what we did. We became a team. And thirteen years later we are here, in this auditorium, asking you to join us. To be a member of our team and climb your own private corporate ladder of success!"

Wild cheers. Total enthusiastic commitment.

I go on like that for another thirty seconds, then hand things over to Mila, CEO of our little venture. Mila is all boss, all the time. She excels at things like social media, and newsletters, and webinars. Actually, she does a little of everything and she's very good at it. Mila is the smallest of us. Just five foot two. Slim, not too shapely, but her cuteness makes up for it. Long dark hair always pulled up in a tight bun, and big, bright eyes. She has two kids—seven and ten—the perfect husband, and scares the shit out of men twice her size when she gets riled up.

She talks about marketing stuff and then hands things over to Hannah, our chemist and chief research officer.

Hannah is almost the exact opposite of Mila. Super tall. Like over six foot. Thin and willowy, Hannah was our face model in the early days. We put her up on billboards and ran infomercials using her as our canvas. But she's super nerdy. Obviously, since she came to this presentation wearing a white lab coat. She's in a long-term relationship with a similar nerdy chemist for a pharmaceutical company on floors five through eight.

And when Hannah's done talking about our proprietary molecular formulas, she hands things off to Natalie.

Natalie is pretty average in every way except for her personality, which is always bubbly and optimistic. Brown-haired, brown-eyed, and about five foot seven, she's our chief operating officer and networking expert. She's the one who talked banks into giving us loans and got us the contract for the first building we worked out of. When we bought this building, she negotiated the price down almost ten million dollars. When it comes to making deals you really want Natalie on your side. She's happily dating four or five men at any one time.

After that Natalie introduces the rest of the sales team bosses and congratulates the room of new recruits for making it to corporate. Every one of them is already a success, but they are here because they are the best of the best. They are in the city because they made a choice to change their lives and leave Kansas, or Idaho, or Alabama or wherever the hell they came from and take a chance on a brand-new future here with us.

We are Bright Berry Beach Cosmetics.

That's how Mila, Hannah, Natalie and I met that night in the bar. Oh, the asshole dude was real. But he wasn't really the reason we became friends, he was just our common enemy over drinks.

It was lipstick that brought us together. We were all wearing the same shade of pink. Bright Berry Beach.

I mean, yeah. It's a lot more complicated than that, but basically… that's really how it started.

Last week we made *Ms. Entrepreneur* magazine's Richest Women in the World list for the seventh year in a row.

We have almost a hundred and twenty cosmetic lines now. We own this whole building and use every single inch of space on the top twenty floors. We employ ten thousand people globally and more than two thousand here at corporate.

We are the definition of success.

And yet… we're still going through with this plan tonight.

There's a part of me that's super-excited about that.

The name of the douchebag man who used us for sex back when we were young and dumb is Jesse Boston.

Oh, yeah. You've heard of him. Youngest of the Boston Brothers. Infamous for their money, and their power, and their bad-boy reputations.

Jesse Boston was our inspiration. Just like we inspire this room filled with recruits to be their best and rise to the top, he did that for us.

We vowed one thing that night in the bar during spring break. We made a pact that we would never fall for a handsome face with a big wallet ever again. Instead, we would make our own future. Our own money. We would write the happy end to our own fairytale.

And we did.

So... why are we bothering with Jesse Boston tonight?

Well, we are women, after all. And we were scorned. Quite simply put, we want revenge.

He should not be allowed to treat women like that. He should pay for what he did to us. And he needs to learn his lesson.

We are the perfect women to teach that lesson.

The room erupts into a standing ovation. The accolades are for each other just as much as they are for us and our team. And then they are split up into smaller teams and the process of assimilation into our corporate community proceeds without us.

We leave the stage, Hannah leading the way. "I have to get back to the lab. I'm cooking up a new scent for the Glow line."

"Go, go, go," Mila says.

"I have to jump too," Natalie says. "I have four new department managers who need a lot of handholding."

"Get them settled," Mila calls. She turns to me. Even though I'm the CFO—finance is my specialty— Mila is the boss of things. She likes to lead and the rest of us really don't, so we appreciate her take-charge attitude. "You ready?"

"As I'll ever be," I say.

"Good. See you at seven. Don't be late."

"I wouldn't dream of it," I say, just as she rushes though the crowd to head back upstairs.

How to describe me?

Well… I'm basically the girl next door. The nice one. The sweet one. I don't have Natalie's firm handshake, or Mila's venomous tongue, or Hannah's brilliant mind for molecules.

I'm just the numbers girl.

The single, not-dating one.

The one who never quite got over her night with Jesse Boston when she was eighteen.

The one who relentlessly follows his tabloid exploits.

The one who came up with this plan.

CHAPTER TWO

"Tell me why I'm doing this again?"

My personal assistant, Zach—who is also my cousin, which is a really long story I rarely have the energy to get into—slaps me on the back and says, "Because people hate you. They look at you and see three things, Jesse. Spoiled, rich asshole."

He pauses to pour a glass of water. I hold out my hand for it, but he takes a sip instead. I narrow my eyes at him and say, "OK. So what if they think I'm a spoiled, rich asshole? What are the other two?"

"No, those are the three things."

"That's all they see when they look at me?"

"Yeah, pretty much," Zach says.

I turn back to the full-length mirror and straighten my bow tie. I don't even remember the last time I put on a tux. I hate this kind of shit. It's not my thing.

"Then this is not going to change anyone's mind," I say.

"You give people too much credit, dude. They will see you go there tonight and stand up on that stage like a fool. They see you get bought for an ungodly amount of money you are definitely not worth, and then they'll see how much that one sale contributed to the end-of-night total charity fund for all those kids, and their stupid little hearts will forgive."

"How come they don't see you as a spoiled, rich asshole? You're the same as me. Worse, actually."

He smiles that charming Boston smile and shrugs. "I'm discreet. You... just never learned to embrace discreet."

It's sorta true. Well, it was true back in my twenties, but I've spent the last five years cleaning up my image and no one cares.

So tonight I'm selling myself at the Billionaire Bachelor Auction.

I can't believe I'm doing this. Because it's also so not my thing. It's actually my brother Joey's thing. It was supposed to be him selling himself tonight, not me.

"Does it ever occur to people that I had nothing to do with the rich part? I mean, what the fuck? How can people hate me because I have money? It's not my money. I was just born into it."

"It's the way you spend it, asshole," Zack says. "Take me, for instance. I'm just like you in some ways."

"All the ways," I say.

"I have the same last name, the same trust fund, the same good looks and charming chin dimple. But I spend my money on things no one hears about. I also work for a living. That makes a difference."

"You work for me, dumbass. I pay you. Way too much, in fact. And your trust fund went missing. I saved you."

"Still," he says, handing me his used water glass and picking up his real drink—a very expensive Scotch that my money bought. "We'll find that trust fund one day. And when I go get that windfall of cash I still won't spend it the way you do. I am humble, Jesse. You... you're... whatever the opposite of humble is."

I set the water glass down and say, "Glad to see that all that fucking money I spent on four years of private college went to good use."

Zack points a finger at me and says, "I appreciate that, by the way. And you know I'm good for it. I'll totally pay you back when—"

"I know," I say. "Once you get that trust fund." I have to roll my eyes. "So how come Johnny doesn't have to do this shit? People hate him just as much as they hate me." Johnny's my oldest brother. The definition of anti-social asshole. And I'm not just saying that. When people look up reclusive, eccentric billionaire in the dictionary there's a picture of Johnny Boston's face.

Zack shoots me a look as if to say, *Do I really need to spell it out?*

He doesn't. I know why Johnny's not here. He's been in his self-imposed exile two floors up from me for the past several years. But Joey, this is totally his kind of thing. He would love to be on stage having women fall all over themselves to pay money for him. Except… he'd probably want that money for himself when the night was over. Or, maybe not. I don't' really know the dude. But he's not any better than me, take my word on that.

Still, I'm the bad brother. I'm the arrogant one. I'm the asshole.

It's not even true. Johnny is definitely the biggest asshole of us three. But somehow he manages to pull off this dark, broody personality and make it all sexy and alluring.

"Look," Zack says, walking over to me to fix the way I straightened my bow tie. "It's gonna work, OK? I know these past five years have been tough for you."

He grabs my shoulder and squeezes. "You've had it the worst, I think. But this is gonna be good for your image. And it makes people happy, Jesse. When people are happy and you're responsible, their hearts and minds open up again. They are able to forgive and forget."

But I'm not buying it. I'm only here as Joey's stand-in. He was the one they invited.

I'm just the one they got.

"Where's Joey again?" I ask.

If Johnny's the serious oldest child, Joey's the troubled middle kid and I'm the spoiled youngest. Even though I'm thirty-three now, they still call me Baby Boston.

Fuckin' hate it.

"He's… I dunno. Tokyo, I think. Not really sure. He just called last week apologizing and asked me to make you do it."

"Last week?" I say. "How come you just told me this today?"

"Because I know you." He laughs. "You'd have disappeared on me if you knew ahead of time."

"But everyone knows I'm showing up in his place, right?"

God, I can't even imagine how people would react if I just popped in out of nowhere. A nightmare scenario plays out in my head of Joey being introduced and me walking out on that stage to glares and gasps. Finger-pointing and accusations.

"Of course," Zach says, pulling me back into reality. "Can you just trust me for once? Jesus. I know what I'm doing."

Goddamned Joey. He's probably gambling over in Japan. Or making dumbass deals with the Yakuza. How come no one cares when Joey fucks up? He does it all the time still. He hasn't spent the last five years cleaning up his act and getting sober, that's for fucking sure. It's only me they hate. It's only ever *me*.

"OK." I sigh with resignation. Because I said I'd do this, so I will. "What time we gotta be there? Should we be leaving now?"

"Punctualality is overrated."

"Punctualality?" I say. "Dude, that's not even a word. Did you even attend those classes I paid for?"

"Yeah, it is."

"No. The word is *punctuality*."

"Whatever. You know what I meant."

"How come no one calls you the dumb one?"

He laughs. "They're too busy calling you the spoiled, rich asshole one."

I exhale. Feeling defeated and already in a bad mood about tonight and the whole shit show hasn't even started yet.

"I'll call for the car if it'll make you happy."

The car isn't gonna make me happy. But Zach doesn't wait for me to protest, just walks out of my bedroom to do his job.

He's ten years younger than me. The youngest of all the Boston Boys. My first cousin, my father's brother's only child. But his father died a long time back when he was just ten, so he came to live here in the building with us.

Zach is really the Baby Boston. Not me. But his side of the fam never caught the public's curiosity like our side did.

I blame my father for that. He's the reason people hate me.

My father died just as Zach was graduating high school and that's when we learned that Zach's trust fund was missing in my father's documents. We knew Zach had one. He has to have one. We all have one. But my father did something with it. Or hell, knowing my father, he got drunk one night and gambled it away, or used it to pay someone off. He was just that irresponsible with his money. When you have so much of it you don't miss a few million going missing you are a breed apart.

We've found cash stashed everywhere after he died. In the walls of the penthouse upstairs. In the goddamned floorboards. In the ceiling. And statements from bank accounts in places like the Cayman Islands, and Costa Rica, and Panama.

But none of it ever had Zach Boston's name on it.

So I took over and paid his way through college. My trust fund is obscene. Whatever our father was really up to, it never touched us. So I guess I can't complain too much about him.

But how come nobody talks about that? How nobody trashed his name? How come no one ever followed his ass around taking sneaky pictures to publish in the tabloids?

Why only me?

Everything Johnny did. Everything my father did. No one ever saw any of it. All they ever saw was me. Fucking up.

I just never understood that. And it got to me. It got to me pretty bad back when I was a teenager. That's how my twenties turned into one long drunken, drugged-up sex party.

But I'm not such a bad guy. I've cleaned up my act a lot since my father's funeral five years ago. A lot. I'm a totally different guy, but no one cares. All they see is the boy in the tabloids. The golden-haired, spoiled, rich asshole.

It's really not fair.

Everyone in my position would've done the exact same thing in their twenties. It's your twenties, for fuck's sake. That's what they're for. Fucking off and fucking girls.

And racing yachts.

I smile. Because I'd do it all again. I wouldn't change a damn thing.

Fuck the public. Fuck all the people. They don't know me. They have no clue what my brothers and I have been through. And anyone who judges someone they don't know is the asshole, not the one being judged.

They see the public persona my father cultivated. They see the yearly listings under Richest Men in the World in those finance magazines. They see our good looks and the tall building we live in, and they hear rumors. Rumors about money and how we spend it. Is it anyone's fucking business how we spend it?

So what if I like yachts? Joey likes racehorses. And Johnny likes to collect art.

But yachts, no. That's what people focus on. That's why they hate me.

I smirk into the mirror. Can't help it.

Because it's possible—maybe even probable—that guys like me give yachts a bad name and not the other way around.

"Stop it," Zach says, entering the room again.

I glance at him in the mirror. "What?"

"I can hear that spoiled, rich asshole voice in your head. You did this to yourself, Jesse. No one did this to you."

"Fuck off. I wasn't thinking that. And besides, I've changed. I'm a totally different person these days."

"So you say," Zach says.

"I take care of you, don't I? You didn't see Johnny or Joey come to your rescue when you found out you were broke."

"I'm not broke. I'm just—"

"Waiting for that trust fund. Yeah, I get it. Is the car downstairs or what?"

"Yup. We're all set."

"Then let's go do this thing."

Change the hearts and minds of the public.

Or…whatever.

CHAPTER THREE

Confession time.

I hired a stylist for tonight.

I've done this before. It's not my first glam-night rodeo. The first time was when Bright Berry Beach Cosmetics was up for an opportunity award. One million dollars on the line and we won it. That was our first big break and while we didn't have the extra money to hire the stylist because that kind of award takes a while to come in and we were on a tight budget, we did it anyway. Just one girl for all four of us. That's all we could afford.

And even though I understand that the winners were not decided that night of the ceremony, I somehow always felt like the reason we won was because we were playing the game of 'fake it till you make it'.

I feel like I'm playing that game again tonight.

I get that it's maybe a little bit ironic that I'm one-fourth owner of the fifth biggest cosmetics company in the entire world and I don't even wear makeup. But that's how life rolls for me most of the time.

Irony is always laughing in my face.

I always get things I'm not really interested in. Big things. Like cosmetics companies. Or cars. Because I don't actually drive. I know how to drive. I have a license. But this is the city. There's nowhere to park. And two years ago a very high-end luxury car company came and asked me to be their spokesperson. I said yes, because why the fuck not?

And they gave me a car.

I paid an ungodly amount of money to park that car in the city for an entire year before I finally came to my senses and had someone drive it out to the country estate we bought for company retreats. So that's where it lives now.

Or the time that tennis racket company called and wanted me to do a commercial for them. Because you know, cosmetics and tennis rackets totally go together.

I don't play tennis but now they send me three new rackets a year.

And somehow I got on a golf club company's list and I get my picture taken with a brand-new set of clubs every spring too.

All that stuff is up at the country estate.

And I just want to say, "What the fuck, people? I don't need a new car, I don't need a tennis racket, and I don't need golf clubs. Why can't someone—for once in my life— send me something I *want*?"

Like Jesse Boston.

Because yeah. I'm just gonna admit it.

I fell for that asshole while on spring break thirteen years ago.

Hard.

Like jumped off a building and crashed my head into the cement kind of hard.

And even though I did find solace in the company of the three women who would become my best friends and business partners, I never got over him.

I stalk him. I do.

I stalk him. I read about him every time he pops up in the tabloids. And that was pretty frequent for many years. All the way up until I was nearly twenty-six he was regular in my life.

But then his father died and I don't know what happened. Jesse... went underground or something. Supposedly cleaned up his act.

His brothers still make the society blogs. But not the tabloids. Mostly Joey. He's Mr. City Bachelor almost every year. Which was why he was invited to be in this charity auction. But Johnny is the one everyone wants to hear about now. He's all dark and broody and mysterious. And no one has seen him in public for like a million years or something.

Or at least since their father died. Whichever came first.

Johnny lives up in that building doing… whatever he does.

He's too dark for me. And Joey is too enthusiastic about his personal life.

But Jesse… Jesus Christ. He's always been the one who floated my boat.

Which is a little inside joke, since he was on the yacht-racing circuit when we met all those years ago.

I've missed my Jesse fix these past few years since he went quiet. So when I found out that Joey cancelled and Jesse was taking his place in the auction, I rallied.

Now the other girls—Nat, and Mila, and Hannah—they're not into the Baby Boston anymore. Their interest waned long time ago. Right around the time we won that million-dollar opportunity award, in fact. Their obsession with him just disappeared. They simply stopped caring. And every time I brought him up they said things like, "Fuck him," and, "I'm so over that asshole!" and, "If I never have to speak his name again it will be too soon."

But that's not how I felt.

I know it's a little bit sad, but I can't help it.

I really, *really* fell for him. And so even though I knew the other girls had already moved on, I took a chance and presented them with this one last way to put him behind us forever.

They said yes. Now maybe I don't have that wicked tongue for sales like Natalie does. And maybe I can't market like Mila or cook things up like Hannah. But I sold the hell out of this plan.

And they bought it.

Anyway. I know this is pretty much a done deal and at the end of the night he will come home with me, because I'm in charge of numbers and I managed to find a way to spare one million dollars to buy Baby Boston for this date. For charity, of course.

For the kids.

And yes, even though I don't regularly wear makeup, I do know how to apply it. I do own one-fourth of the world's fifth largest cosmetic company, after all.

But I hired a stylist anyway. Because this is my last chance to see this man and tell him all those things I've been wanting to say all these years.

Not how I fell for him. Or how he hurt me.

But how much I hate him.

Hate him with a passion.

I don't care if he's the one indirectly responsible for hooking Nat, Mila, Hannah, and me up into this mega-woman company, I want revenge.

I want him to look us in the eyes and *repent*. I want him to feel as horrible about what he did to us that week as we felt after he used us up like *things* and threw us away.

Not only that. I want him to want me.

I want him to fall for me the way I did him.

And then I want to walk away. Forever. Vindicated that I was not trash to be thrown away. He is the trash. He will be thrown away. He is the loser now.

So I get glammed up to the nines. I went shopping after the welcome ceremony this morning for the most fabulous dress.

Red, of course. Long, with one slit up each thigh. Strapless. Hand-sewn crystals on the bodice.

My dark hair is piled high up on my head. My makeup is exquisite and the color on my lips…

Not Bright Berry Beach.

But Woman Scorned Red.

Glossy with an all-night wear guarantee. Courtesy of Bright Berry Beach Cosmetics Heat line.

"Wow," Natalie says when I get in the limo. "You look... just... wow."

"Oh, honey," Mila says. "He does not deserve you."

"He's gonna die when he sees you again, Emma. Just die!" Hannah squeals.

"Please," I say, taking a champagne flute from Natalie as the limo pulls away from my building. "I'll bet you a million dollars each that he has no recollection of us."

"Well, I should hope not," Mila says. "Once we get to the estate no one takes off their ski masks. Got it?"

"Got it," we all say.

"This will be the most efficient kidnapping in the history of kidnappings," Hannah says.

"We're not kidnapping him," I correct. "We're *buying* him."

I have to look away to hide my evil grin.

Because I have been dreaming about a night like this with Jesse Boston ever since he walked out on me.

It's the reason why I pushed us so hard all these years.

Success is the best revenge.

But buying the man who scorned you when you were eighteen and making him regret treating you like trash comes in a close second.

CHAPTER FOUR

JESSE

New revelations about myself always come to me at the most inappropriate times. Like this one, for instance.

I hate being around people. How come I didn't realize this about myself until this very moment? Maybe it was all those years on the ocean that changed me? Or maybe it was the exclusive circle of friends and family I grew up with?

I don't know. But you'd think I'd have figured this out before I was thirty-three years old, standing in a crowd of people who want to buy me for a night.

What the hell was I thinking when I agreed to this?

"Tell me again why I'm doing this?" I lean over to whisper to Zach.

He leans into me and says, just as discreetly, "Because you got busted for drugs five years ago, were stripped of all your yachting titles, and now the only people who will hire you as a yacht racing consultant are criminals?"

I side-eye him and say, "You're an asshole."

"You asked," he says. "I'm just here to tell you the truth, cousin. And that was it."

He's not lying. I did get busted for drugs right after my father died. And then tested for drugs. And then I failed that test, and the yachting association stripped me of every title race I ever won. And even though I didn't have to pay back the winnings, I did.

Which, who cares? No one gets into yachting for the prize money. It's a total waste of resources. And they couldn't legally make me give that money back. I did it to… you know. Plump up my image. It was Zach's idea, actually. I'm joking when I chide him about being dumb. He's not dumb. He's actually the smartest person I know. That's why I hired him. Plus, he's more of a brother to me than Joey or Johnny.

Zach was always hanging out with me when he was a kid. Always wanted to be like me. Except he never made my mistakes. Never got into drinking and drugs. Never got arrested or anything like that.

And it's not like he wasn't around during my racing days. He was on my crew from age fifteen to after he graduated high school. We went all over the world together.

But for me, yacht racing was a passion. An escape. It was the only thing that mattered for so long and then after I got busted for drugs the whole thing was over in an instant.

Until that drug bust, yachting was all I thought about. Every day was filled with sails, and wind, and speed. And after, well. I was reduced to teaching.

Those who can, do. Those who can't, teach.

Isn't that what they say?

It's not fair. Lots of teachers can 'do' just fine. Some of them just get busted for drugs and get kicked out of the racing association.

This is not making me feel any better.

Anyway, I'm not a teacher. I'm a consultant. Big difference. I get paid better, for one. When I actually have clients. But Zach is right. My reputation is shit. The only people who trust my opinion these days are the cheaters.

I took on a few of those clients in the early days after I got busted. But I figured out pretty quick that the more I perpetuated the image, the more it stuck. So I stopped. That was four years ago and I haven't had a single client since.

Four long years of drought.

I still sail. Alone.

And every once in a while I'll meet up with some of my old friends in the yacht club and we'll have an impromptu race.

But it's not the same. One-hundred-and-eighty-degree difference, in fact.

"This is good PR," Zach says, sensing my deteriorating mood. "Trust me. It's gonna be good. You'll see. Monday morning everyone will be talking about you again."

"Yeah," I say. "Because I've basically turned into Johnny over the last four years and just disappeared. I can see the headlines now. 'Bad boy turns good.'"

"That's not a bad headline."

"It is if the article highlights all your past mistakes and not the one good thing you did over the weekend."

"So you'll just do more good things. Just relax. Have some fun. Look at all the pretty ladies here who will bid on you."

But I have since learned that I will go on last.

Last.

Always last. That's me. The last of the Boston Brothers.

"No one's even gonna be paying attention to me by the time I get on stage. I'm gonna get one of the leftover ladies. Like that hundred-year-old grandma over there making eyes at me. What the hell is Old Bat Knottingham doing here anyway?"

"Her great-great grandson is up first."

"First?" I say. "That little puke? He's not even old enough to drink."

"His company just went public. He's the youngest billionaire on record now."

"Fucker. I hope he gets bought by Mean Trish Sellers."

"You know, it doesn't help that you have nasty nicknames for everyone."

"I can't help it that the Old Bat is old and Trish Sellers is mean."

Zach sighs. He's tired of me tonight, I can tell. And I'm being unusually tiresome, I know this. But I really do not want to go up on that auction block.

It's gonna be bad. I can tell. Something really bad is gonna happen. I have such a horrible feeling deep down in the pit of my stomach right now. "Oh, hey. Who's that?" I say, jabbing Zach in the ribs.

The woman is quite stunning. And young. My age. She's wearing a sexy red dress with not one, but two slits up the side. Her long legs peek out with every step and her bosom is practically bursting out of her strapless bodice.

"That's Emma Dumas. Part owner of Bright Berry Beach Cosmetics. Those three woman with her are her partners."

"Emma Dumas. Why does that name ring a bell?"

"Probably because she's on that car commercial they run constantly during the stock reports."

"Hmmm… maybe. But I don't watch stock reports."

"I think she hawks tennis rackets too. So maybe you saw her on one of those ads."

"Possibly," I say, and just when I'm about to disqualify that one too, she locks eyes with me.

I hold her gaze, unable to look away. Her dark hair and red dress are breathtaking. And her face is so… well, I was gonna say, beautiful, because it is. But then I switch to familiar. She is so fucking familiar.

My hand comes up of its own accord and waves to her, but she either misses it, or started turning away before I could finish, because the moment breaks and the crowd surges around her and she disappears.

I groan. "No one is even coming up to me for small talk."

"Uh, so? Just go insert yourself. You're Jesse Boston. Believe me, everyone here wants to talk to you."

I don't think so. Well, maybe Old Bat Knottingham. But I know for a fact she's deaf now and I can't bring myself to go over there and shout in her ear just to convince everyone else I have people to small-talk with.

Eventually the lights dim and brighten, signaling that everyone should take their seats and those of us being sold as meat should go backstage.

"Break a leg," Zach says, clapping me too hard on the back. "See ya on the other side."

"Thanks," I mutter. Then I straighten my cufflinks and get in line behind all the other eligible bachelors to wait my turn.

Backstage isn't any better than out front. There are twenty guys here. I know every single one of them. In fact, I think I know everyone out in the crowd tonight—except for Ms. Dumas and her circle of cosmetic friends—and even aside from the fact that none of them wanted to chat me up before the big show, that's not a good thing because I don't want to go on a date with any of them.

OK, maybe Ms. Dumas. I could actually see myself having a pleasant, quiet dinner with her.

41

Shit. I forgot to ask Zach what my date is. So I don't even know what I'll have to do once this auction is over.

Do I take them home? Out to dinner? Do we make plans another night? How's this work?

"Hey." I elbow Old Bat's great-great grandson, Chad. "What's the deal?"

"What?" Chad asks. He is obviously way younger than me. I was serious when I said he probably wasn't old enough to drink. So we don't *know* each other. We just run in the same social circle. Or would, if anyone invited me in to said social circle.

"You know. Like… what do we do afterward?"

"You planned a date, right?"

"No."

"Yeah, you did," Chad says.

"No, I really didn't."

"It was on the application, dumbass."

"Oh. My brother filled that out."

Chad shrugs, then walks off, calling over his shoulder, "Well, I guess you should ask him then. I gotta go. I'm up first."

Thanks for the fucking help, Chad.

But I decide maybe he's right. Joey has done this auction every year for a while. So I get out my phone and call him up. It's eleven AM there, so he picks up first ring. "Baby bro," he says a little too cheerfully. "Waaaassup?"

"I'm at the auction."

"Yeah, yeah, yeah. How's it going? You going on first?"

"No," I say. "Last, actually."

"Last? I never go on last."

"I'm not you."

"Truth, bro. Truth. So for real, what's going on?"

"How's this date shit work? Like… do I take the winner out tonight?"

"Whole weekend man. I planned a good one. Maybe that's why you're last. People are gonna eat this one up!"

"Weekend?" I say. "No. I'm not doing a weekend with a stranger."

"Yeah. Up in the country house by the lake."

"What?"

"It's gonna be great. Last year Sally Overheim bought me and it was amaaaaa-zing. That's why I put the whole weekend up this time. I was really looking forward to spending the weekend with Sally. If you get her—well, I'm gonna be pissed. But if you do get her, for reals, remind her of what a great time we had last year. She'll treat you right."

"Gross," I mumble.

"OK, I gotta go. I'm being fed sushi by a geisha right now. Little corporate perk from the Osakisan Company."

"Wait!" I say before he can hang up. "What do I do when I get her there?"

"What do you mean? You fuck her."

"Are you sure? What if Old Bat Knottingham buys me? Or Mean Trish Sellers?"

"Old Bat?" He laughs. "She never buys anyone, don't worry. But Trish? Sure, yeah. I'd do her. Don't sweat it, you'll be fine. Talk soon."

Then he hangs up.

I picture being stuck up in the lake house with Mean Trish and almost feel a panic attack coming on.

Why the fuck did I ever agree to do this?

CHAPTER FIVE

"He just looked at me," I say, feeling breathless and dizzy.

"Play it cool. Just play it cool," Mila says.

I turn away from Jesse because my heart is thumping so hard in my chest, if I lock eyes with him again, I might faint.

Why does he have this effect on me? I should not be reacting this way. I am not that eighteen-year-old girl he fucked and forgot about back in Key West.

I am a confident, brilliant, beautiful woman. And I'm filthy rich now too. I am here to buy that asshole and make him pay.

I look over my shoulder again, hoping to get another peek at him. But he's talking to his cousin, Zach, who I have no feelings about at all. He's so much younger than the other Boston Boys, he can't be held responsible for any of their actions.

"Stop it," Hannah hisses in my ear. "You're going to make him suspicious."

"Maybe one of you should buy him?" I ask, still feeling dizzy.

"No way," Natalie says. "There's no way I will be alone with that asshat the whole ride up to their lake house." She does a little shiver. "Gross. I'd rather date a serial killer."

"You're being a little dramatic," I say. "He's not *that* bad."

All three of my friends scoff at the same time. Hannah is in the middle of sipping champagne and almost spits it out.

"What?" I say. "You're comparing him to a serial killer. He's just… a jerk, not a psychopath."

"I beg to differ," Mila says. "Should I tell my story again?"

"No," the three of us say at the same time.

But I'm pretty sure we're not all saying no for the same reason. Hannah and Natalie are truly grossed out at the thought of me being alone with Jesse Boston. That's why they don't want to take this little trip down memory lane or be the one to buy him tonight.

Me, on the other hand... I just... I don't know. I get this weird feeling whenever I think about how they... and Jesse... and they... and then he... yeah. No. I can't listen to it. It makes me feel all rage-y for some reason.

And I have too many emotions running through my head right now, I don't need another one.

Besides, if I hear her story again I'll start thinking about mine.

Not a good idea when you're about to kidnap the jerk who broke your heart.

I need my head in the game. I need all my wits.

I do not need my bloody heart on my sleeve.

Revenge. That's all I want out of this. I want him to feel the way I did.

It's not realistic because I was in full-on puppy love with the infamous Baby Boston. At first it was all jittery, happy nerves and palpating heartbeats. But after I learned about Mila, and Hannah, and Natalie... then it was sleepless nights, and sick feelings in my stomach, and shaky hands.

Also... that ache.

God, just the thought of that ache inside me makes me sad all over again.

Not because I don't have him, either. I get it now. I'm a grown-up who knows a little more about what love is and isn't than I did back then. It's not because I don't have him. I don't want him.

The sadness comes from the humiliation of learning that the person you thought cared for you—even if it was naive to think that—didn't. Not one bit. He spared not one second of thought about me. And, if I'm being honest, I'm like ninety-nine percent sure that he was probably thinking of someone else while we were fucking.

Maybe Mila. Or Hannah. Or Natalie.

That's why I can't listen to their stories anymore. It's just a reminder of how badly I was used.

The lights dim and brighten, letting everyone know it's time for the auction to start. I glance in Jesse's direction one more time, then sigh before I can stop myself.

"Let's go," Mila says. "We've got front-row seats."

"Who'd you bribe to get those?"

"Never mind that. The point is we have them. And there's no way in hell that Jesse Boston won't see all four of our brilliant, beautiful, billionaire faces once he steps out onto that stage."

But will he remember us?

That makes me swallow hard and hold my stomach, because it's churning at the thought of his indifference.

He has no idea who we are. He hasn't thought about us in thirteen years. And the only thoughts he had about us back then were about putting his cock inside our pussies.

Maybe I do need to think about Mila's story? Because all the feelings inside me are sad, and depressed. I could use a little more rage right about now.

We take our seats at the front and a few minutes later the MC of the event comes out and starts talking about the charity.

Kids. We're raising money for an after-school program for underprivileged kids so they don't have to be home alone while their parents are working. Pretty much every inner-city school depends on the Billionaire Bachelor Auction to fund the next school year. So this event is actually super important.

Truth. That's the purpose.

But every woman knows why she's here.

She wants to date one of these handsome, rich men.

Not that all the bidders aren't filthy rich in their own right. Each auction starts at five hundred thousand dollars and most of them go up to—and sometimes, occasionally, over—a million.

I'm pretty sure we're going to get Jesse for the rock-bottom price, but we budgeted a million just in case. Nobody came here for him. He's the loser Boston Brother. They all wanted Joey. Or hell, if Johnny ever made an appearance he'd probably set the record. There's no telling how high the bids could go.

But Jesse?

Nah. He's the joke brother. Like the bad Baldwin brother, right? There is the one everyone loves to hate and the one everyone just hates. The other two are… who cares.

Joey Boston is the one everyone loves to hate. Jesse is the one everyone absolutely hates, and Johnny is… eh. We never see him, so who cares?

I'm pretty sure I'm going to be the only person bidding on Jesse tonight.

After the charity speech the ball gets rolling with the first bachelor. Newly-minted, twenty-year-old Chad Knottingham.

And when it's over the girls and I just look at each other, confused.

It took a while to get people interested in bidding. And his price was pret-*ty* low for being first billed.

But maybe he's too young? Twenty is practically a baby. Maybe people are holding out for number two.

A very handsome, thirty-something heir to a medical supply fortune.

Hmmm.

No. He barely gets above minimum too.

There are a lot of whispers in the room. Lots of shifting in seats as that same scenario plays out over and over again. They are all bought, but can I just say that the enthusiasm in this room is lacking?

Badly?

And the scoreboard keeping track of donations is just barely over five point five million dollars by the time Jesse Boston is introduced.

I mean… I've not been here before but it was my understanding that each bachelor goes for an average of eight hundred thousand dollars. Which should have us up near or over the ten million mark by now.

The moment that Jesse steps out on to the stage, everything changes.

Women stand up, waving their little paddles before the bidding even starts.

I raise my paddle with them. Ready to grab my prize.

But ten seconds in, the bidding is already up to one point one million dollars. And climbing.

"What the hell is happening?" Mila hisses in my ear.

"I don't know. But we're already over budget. We lost."

"We can't lose!" Hannah snaps. "We planned this. This is happening!"

She grabs my hand and raises it in the air.

The auctioneer points to me and says, "Two point seven. That's two point seven. Do I have two point eight? Two point eight from the lady in yellow!"

The four of us turn to look at the lady in yellow and Natalie says, "She can't win! Bid again!"

"You guys!" I say. "It's already at three point one!"

By the time Hannah raises my hand up, the auctioneer is calling out, "Three point eight! Ladies! Surely we can go higher than that for the children!"

And then… I'm not sure what happens. Someone gets knocked over, there's a bit of screaming, and the lady next to Mila gets hit in the eye with a paddle and starts shrieking, "My eye! My eye!"

And by the time all that ruckus is over Hannah is holding my hand in the air and the auctioneer is pointing at me, yelling, "Sold! To the young lady in red for ten million dollars!"

I look at Hannah in shock. "What the fuck did you just do?"

"We won!" she squeals, standing up to clap.

I shoot Mila a look. "We came here with one million dollars. One. And we just spent ten times that much on… on…. *him*!"

I point to him. And Jesse Boston is looking right back at me.

Oh, shit.

I look back at the girls.

Oh, shit. Oh, shit. Oh, shit.

Because Hannah, Natalie, and Mila have already gotten up to leave me here.

The room is in chaos but then the announcer comes on to let everyone know—as if we can't *math*—that Jesse Boston is now the highest-priced Billionaire Bachelor Auction prize ever offered up for sale.

And then he says my name.

In front of everyone.

I watch Jesse's face as Emma Dumas is repeated in the microphone, for the whole room to hear, at least three times.

And not one of those times do I catch even a hint of recognition in his expression.

He just stands up there on that stage with the smuggest, most arrogant, cocky smile I've ever seen in my entire life. Looking like a ten-million-dollar asshole in his bespoke tux, and his opulent watch, and his luxe looks.

And I think to myself... *Yeah. That was ten million well spent.*

Because I'm going to make him pay for his indifference.

I'm going to make him pay for his ignorance.

And when this is all over, Jesse Boston will *never* dump another girl again.

CHAPTER SIX

"Well." *I laugh.* "I can honestly say I was not expecting that."

The whole thing was kinda surreal. At first I didn't fully understand what was happening. I saw the Knottingham kid go for just over five hundred K and figured that was decent. But then someone whispered that's pretty much the opening bid. And then I'm pretty sure someone else said the Old Bat bought him just so he wasn't humiliated. Apparently he's got a fragile ego.

You can't judge a bachelor auction by one dumb kid. But when the second guy—Phil Standard—went for almost the same price, I took notice.

Because Phil is what I'd call a catch. Decent guy. Maybe a little religious for my taste. But he's fucking loaded. And all-American handsome. And a go-getter too. His father refused to pay for anything after college so he started out driving forklifts in one of their medical supply warehouses and it took eleven fucking years of bootstrapping his way up the chain to finally land a position in the executive offices and earn his trust fund.

Still… I was little suspicious that perhaps Phil's religious ties were holding him back from the ladies.

But that wasn't it. All the guys after him went for about the same price.

All the guys but me.

I laugh again, then glance over at my date. The delectable lady in red I noticed earlier in the night. Jesus fuck. I lucked out. I so lucked out. And she paid ten million dollars for me!

She side-eyes me as we walk to the back of the room to make this all official.

"You must really like helping kids," I say. "Or your cosmetics biz needs a big tax write-off this year." Then I laugh because I'm only half joking.

"Mmm-hmmmm," she says, tight-lipped.

I frown. Is she having regrets? Will she refuse to sign the papers?

But no. She signs them. And then they give her a sash that says, *Winner of Jesse Boston!*

Which I love. So fucking great.

"Shall we?" she asks.

"Oh, for sure. We shall," I say, offering her my arm.

She glances down at it. Then up at me. Then back down at my arm. Then back up at me.

I point to it and say, "You can put your hand there if you want." Thinking maybe she's confused? New money? Not sure how to act?

She frowns at me, then sighs, kinda loud, and places her hand on my arm without gripping it. I'm not really sure how one does that, but she manages. "What now?" she asks.

"Uh… well. I'm pretty sure my brother had something really spectacular planned." Then a thought hits me. "Hey, you didn't bid on me because you thought I was Joey, did you?"

"Nope," she says.

"So you knew it was me. Jesse."

She points to her sash.

"Right. I see that. OK. So… thank you," I say, bowing my head a little. "The children certainly appreciate your contribution to help their struggle."

"Mmmmmmmm," she says, again with the tight lips.

Right. Is she not into me? Am I doing something wrong here? I mean, the date hasn't even started yet and she seems kinda pissed off.

"Well, OK. To the lake house, I guess. Should I drive?"

"I think so."

"Wow. Three whole words. That's the most you've said so far. Things are looking up."

I'm kind of a funny dude. I mean, I don't normally have trouble making people who like me laugh. So her not laughing at my easy-going banter gives me the impression she's more of a hater.

But why would a hater pay ten million dollars to spend a weekend with me?

I dunno. See, this is why I hate people. I just don't get them. People are fucking confusing.

"OK. I'm this way, I guess."

I lead her out of the auction room and into the lobby of the hotel and every single set of eyeballs— even Old Bat's—turn to look at us. The whispers start immediately.

She sighs again.

"Don't worry about them. They are obviously jealous."

"Yeah," she says. "Obviously."

Wait. Was that sarcasm? Is she not happy to be with me? I don't understand this. Why pay ten million dollars for someone in an auction if you don't want to spend time with them after?

Joey arranged the transportation so I have to scan the cars in the valet area for a second before I recognize his sleek, black Aston Martin right in front, with a valet standing at the passenger side door. "Good evening, Ms. Dumas. Mr. Boston," he says, bowing a little as we approach. Ms. Dumas thanks him softly as he waits for her to get in, then closes her door.

I hand him a twenty-dollar bill and walk around and get in, trying not to stare at Ms. Dumas as I adjust the seat and pull on my seat belt.

"So," she says, looking out the window.

"So," I say. God, this is awkward. I pull away from the hotel and try for some small talk. "So what do you do?"

"I'm the CFO of Bright Berry Beach Cosmetics." She's still looking out the window. Not at me.

"Right, I think I heard that," I mumble, pressing my foot on the clutch and shifting into a higher gear.

"From who?" she asks, finally turning her head towards me.

"My cousin, Zach. He told me who you were in the lobby before the auction."

"I see."

Then she's silent. So I try again. "CFO, huh? So you're the money girl."

"I'm the chief financial officer."

"Right." Jesus. This is gonna be a long night. "Wanna know what I do?"

There are like three seconds of silence. Then she sighs and says, "Sure. Why not."

Wow. She is tough. But I'm damn charming. At least I was back in my twenties. I know how to do this. And I suddenly feel the urge to charm the pants off this woman.

So I say, "I'm a consultant. For yacht-racing teams."

"How's that working out?"

"Ouch," I say. "Is there something I'm missing here? Because I get the feeling you don't like me. And I'm kinda confused why a smart businesswoman such as yourself would pay so much money for a guy she hates."

"It's for charity."

"Yeah. The children. I've heard that a lot tonight. And I'm sure it's true. I'm sure all charity functions like this one are *all* about the charity."

"Is that sarcasm?" she asks.

"You should know."

"What's that mean?"

"Well, you're pretty good at sarcasm. At least from what I can tell from the past ten minutes we've known each other."

She huffs, clearly frustrated.

But what did I do? I didn't make her buy me. I didn't raise her fucking hand when that auctioneer got up to the ten-million-dollar mark. I didn't even want to be here. I'm just a stand-in.

"Oh," I say, as understanding sinks in. "I get it. You came to the auction for Joey, didn't you?"

"I already told you I didn't buy you by mistake."

"Right. But that's not the same as expecting one thing then settling for another. And it's OK. If you're into Joey and not me, that's fine."

"I'm not into your brother," she snaps. "I'm into…" She pauses. "I just want to go on our date."

"Well, we are on the date and you're obviously not having any fun. So… should I take you home?"

"I paid ten million dollars for this night." She huffs. "I'm not going home. Just… take me to the lake house so we can get this shit show on the road."

Wow.

"OK," I say, giving up. "To the lake house it is."

We drive for a little while. The hotel where the auction was held is up in a sleepy little village nestled in the rolling hills, all surrounded by trees. I've been up here before. Not for the auction, obviously, but there's a big lake nearby and they have a small festival every summer that I went to a couple times with friends back when I was a teenager.

Our lake is about thirty miles north of there and the road is long and winding. Also kinda boring since it's pitch dark out now and there's literally nothing to look at out that window she's fixating on.

But we have to drive through another little village before we get to the little valley where our house is, and while we're passing through a memory hits me.

We came here too, when I was young. Me and my friends. Sometimes we'd have girls with us, sometimes not. But every time we came through on our way to the lake house we'd stop at the Tastee-Freez and get ice cream.

It's such a kid thing to do. I can't recall a single moment after that last time I was up here that I stopped someplace to get an ice cream.

So I change our plans and pull into the nearly packed parking lot, then shut the car off and look at her.

She's very pretty. I will say that. And it's not just the fancy red gown, either. Or her specially styled hair or carefully applied makeup. She's just pretty.

CHAPTER SEVEN

"*What are you doing?*" I ask.

"What's it look like?"

"It looks like you're parking at a Tastee-Freez."

"Nothing gets by you, does it, Emma?"

"Why are you taking me to a Tastee-Freez?"

"Usually people come here for ice cream."

I just blink at him.

"You don't like ice cream?"

"Everyone likes ice cream."

"Exactly," he says, grinning like a foolish, charming bastard. Which makes no sense at all, but wow. I'd forgotten about that smile and how disarming it is. He looks at me. "Come on," he says. "It's a date, right? You paid ten million dollars for this date and now you're going to complain when I do something date-y?"

This wasn't part of the plan. The plan was:

Buy him.

Drive up to his lake house.

Drug him.

Wait for the girls to show up.

Take him over to our lake house.

Tie him up.

Make him regret all his asshole decisions thirteen years ago.

Probably gloat too. Little bit of, "Look at me, so rich and powerful now. And you dumped me, you dumbass. But oh, hey. I'm too good for you now. You could've had all this and now you've got nothing. Sucks to be you."

Which is all pretty childish because he's Jesse Boston. He could get any girl he wants. Just look at how they fell all over him tonight at the auction.

Ten. Million. Fucking. Dollars.

I feel sick. Literally, I feel sick. It's not that we can't afford the ten mil. It's just... that was not the plan. This asshole isn't *worth* ten million. What the hell were all those women thinking?

And us. What the hell were we thinking? This is all Hannah's fault. I'm gonna kill her later.

No revenge plan is worth ten million dollars.

And now he wants to have ice cream with me.

Uggggh.

"So?" Jesse says.

"Hmm?"

"Are we gonna get out of the car? Or are we going to sit here all night?"

"I'm not really in the mood for ice cream," I say.

He grins at me again. Oh. God. Why is he so damn hot? It's not fair. "See, that's the best part about ice cream. You don't have to be in the mood for it. In fact, eating it when you're not in the mood is the best part. Because it puts you in the mood."

And then he does one of those little eyebrow waggles.

I squint at him. "Are you coming on to me?"

"What?"

"Was that innuendo?"

He frowns. "What the fuck are you talking about?"

I point to his forehead. "You waggled at me when you said ice cream puts you in the mood."

"I didn't waggle at you."

I huff. "Dude, you totally did."

"OK, whatever. If you say I did, then I did. But no. It wasn't innuendo. Ice cream is like… that's just what people eat when they're stressed, ya know?"

I just stare at him.

"God, for a woman who paid ten million dollars for me, you sure are a tough crowd."

"I know how much I paid for you," I snap. "Stop reminding me."

"OK," he says, holding up a hand. "Would you like me to take you home? Should we just… end this?"

I huff. "I paid ten million dollars for you. I'm getting my date."

He stares at me. No. He *glares* at me. "Then get your fucking ass out of my car and order a motherfucking ice cream."

And then he gets out, not even waiting for me. Just gets out, slams the door, and walks up to the Tastee-Freez and gets in line.

"Rude," I mumble.

There's quite a line too. Everyone who lives in this village must be here tonight. They are mostly teenagers on dates, laughing and joking as they flirt with each other. A few families with small children. Lots of boys and girls in little baseball uniforms, so a local Little League game must've just ended. And a few old couples who sit quietly as they stare off at the traffic passing on the road and lick their ice cream cones like this is their regular Friday night.

Jesse has his hands in his tux pockets, just studying the menu. And every single female in this parking lot is looking at him with lust in their eyes.

He pays no attention to anyone. Why should he? He's Jesse Boston.

I get out of the car and walk over to him.

He smiles at me. "I knew you couldn't help yourself. What kind of cone do you like? Or do you prefer a sundae?"

"What?" I say. Because I maybe got a little lost in those blue eyes of his. Wow. I'd forgotten how mesmerizing they could be when they're looking right at you. Like you are the only girl in the world.

"Jesus, Emma. What's the deal here?"

"What do you mean?"

"You're so… off. Are you harboring some deep hatred for me or something? Did I say something that offended you? I didn't mean to snap at you in the car, I'm just… frustrated with how this is going. I wasn't expecting hostility."

"I'm not hostile."

"You so are. You want a refund?"

"What?"

"I'll pay you back if you're not having a good time."

"I don't need your money. I'm probably richer than you are now."

He furrows his brow. "Now?"

Ooops. OK. This is going wrong, fast. So I ignore his implied question and stare up at the menu board above the take-out counter. "Vanilla," I say. "In a cone. Dipped in butterscotch."

Out of the corner of my eye I see him look up at the board and grin. "I like half and half." Then he looks at me. "Dipped in cherry."

I smile back, I can't help it.

We move forward a few paces as people place their orders. "So what should we do after this?" he asks.

"What do you mean? We're going to the lake house, right?"

"Sure. I mean, we can do that. But that was Joey's plan, not mine. We don't have to go to the lake house. We can do anything we want. I'm told this is a weekend date. And I don't know what the hell we're gonna do up at that lake house all weekend. We don't keep boats out there anymore. Haven't for a long time because we haven't really spent much time out here since I was a kid. There's no swimming pool and I don't play tennis. But if you want to, I'll give it a go."

Is he serious? What are we going to do all weekend? Who is this man? Because the Jesse Boston I knew would be picturing all the ways he was planning to fuck me.

"I'm sure we'll think of something," I say.

"We could just go back to the city. Maybe hit up a spa for a couples' massage? Or a concert?"

"No," I say, too quick. Because no. This isn't a date. It's a kidnapping, for fuck's sake. And I need him to be at his lake house tonight.

"Yeah. Couples' massage is a bit much for a first date. But I really could use a rubdown." He rubs his neck, illustrating his point that he's carrying some stress.

Hint. Hint. I need a massage. Now that is a typical Jesse Boston move.

The people in front of us are done, and then it's our turn.

"We'll have one vanilla cone dipped in butterscotch," Jesse says, taking a moment to glance at me and grin. "And one half and half dipped in cherry."

And I don't know why I find that kinda of adorable, but I do.

I am out on a date with Jesse Boston and he just ordered me an ice cream cone.

I would've died—simply *died*—for a date like this, with him, back then.

He pays, then places his hand on the small of my back.

I realize then that everyone is looking at us. We are dressed up like celebrities. My red gown, his black tux. A sleek Aston Martin parked nearby.

And every single girl—from six years old to sixty—is looking at me with envy.

CHAPTER EIGHT

I look around and chuckle under my breath.

"What?" Emma says. "What's funny?"

She's kind of uptight. And mean. Which only makes me chuckle again.

"What?" she repeats, kinda flustered.

I place my hand on her arm and pull her closer, then lean in and whisper, "I think every fucking dude here is staring at me. Even those Little League dudes know what's up."

"Wait," she says. And she does this shudder thing. You know, like when you get a chill up your neck and you bunch up your shoulders to make it go away? "What's up?" she says. "What do you mean by that?"

I just shake my head at her. So uptight. But a little less mean.

"Vanilla butterscotch and half-and-half cherry!" the teenager taking orders says from behind the screened-in counter.

I step forward, take the two cones, then nod my head to Emma. "Grab us some napkins, will ya?"

For some reason she sucks in a deep breath. This makes her breasts rise and fall underneath her strapless bodice.

We are so overdressed. And it's a little warm tonight so the first thing I do when we arrive at the only empty picnic table out front is to hand her both cones so I can take off my suit coat.

Emma just stares at the ice cream cones in her hand, like she's never seen one before.

"You don't have to wait for me," I say, slipping my coat off and then taking off my bow tie. I stuff that in the pocket so I don't lose it, then decide the cufflinks need to go too. Because I want to roll my sleeves up.

Emma looks at me, then the cones, then back at me.

She licks her cone, her tongue darting out to swipe the hard sugar shell off the swirly top.

Damn, that was sexy.

In fact, she's sexy. Very fucking hot, this one. And she's so familiar. That feeling that I know her comes back to me.

"Have we ever met before?" I ask, taking my cone back now that my sleeves are rolled up.

"What do you mean?"

"Did we… go to school together or something?"

"Why do you say that?"

"I'm not saying we did. I'm just asking. Because you look so familiar."

"Hmm," she hums, but doesn't answer me. Just takes another lick of her cone.

"Oh, here," I say, placing my coat on the picnic table bench. "You can sit on my coat so you don't get your dress dirty."

She makes a face at me.

"What? What'd I do now?"

"Why are you being so… so freaking *nice*?"

I laugh. "Why wouldn't I be nice?"

"If you remind me how much I paid for you again—"

"I won't," I say, putting up a hand. "Jesus. What do you do, Emma? For real. Day-to-day kinda thing. Because it must be super stressful. You need to relax a little. Maybe we should go get that couples' massage? I think you need it more than I do."

She lets out a long breath, then immediately sucks in another one and holds it. That breath has to come out eventually, so I wait her out. Finally, she exhales and says, "Sorry. It's just… I wasn't expecting you to be so…"

"Nice?" I ask, raising my eyebrows at her. "And that's not a waggle," I say, pointing to my forehead. "It's just a… surprise." I stare at her for a moment. "That you had some kind of preconceived opinion of me before this date."

She turns her head away and mumbles, "Well, you do have *quite* the reputation."

"Yeah," I say, taking a seat on the table and placing my feet on the bench. I point to my coat next to my feet. "Come on. Sit down. You're making me nervous."

She sits. Stiffly, for a moment. Then leans back against the table and begins to lick her ice cream again.

"So what have you heard about me?" I ask.

She shrugs. "I'm sure you know."

"Yeah… but I haven't been that guy for a while now. Not since my father died."

She glances up at me, then quickly averts her eyes.

"I admit I was kind of a jackass when I was younger."

"And now you're not?" she asks, still looking forward. There's a group of little boys in uniform showing off about a dozen feet away. For Emma's benefit, obviously. They roughhouse and joke, laughing as they shoot her shy looks.

Kinda cute.

"Not gonna answer that?" Emma says.

"No. I mean, yeah. No. I'm not that guy anymore."

"It's been my experience that people don't change much."

"Hmm," I say, still watching the little boys.

"So how have you changed?"

I shrug. Eat my ice cream. Think about shit. "I guess, you know. I'm not so angry anymore, maybe."

"Angry? Why were you angry?"

"I get it," I say, not looking at her. "People think that because of who I am, and what I have, and especially what I had growing up, that things are just perfect. But no one's life is perfect. I'm sure you know that, right?"

"My life is pretty perfect."

"Hmm. Well, good for you then."

She turns her body towards me, looks me in the eyes. "No, really. I'm interested. Why were you angry? And what changed?"

"Well"—I chuckle a little—"that's like my life story. Kinda long, and boring, and… personal. But I can give you the bullet points."

"OK. I'm listening."

"Well, give me a second. Because setting up my life in bullet points isn't that easy."

"Take your time. I'll wait." She licks her ice cream. *Almost* smiles at me.

"Let's see... how much can I tell you..."

"Oh, family secrets, huh?"

"Kinda. But also... people, ya know. They would kill to know some of our secrets."

"Our, meaning your family?"

"Yeah. Well, we don't really look the part, do we?"

"What part?"

"White collar. And that's because we're not. Not really. My dad grew up as the son of a plumber."

"Get out of here. Your father was one of the richest men in the world when he died."

Died. He didn't die. He was murdered. But of course, that's hardly first-date material so I don't expand.

"We came from the north side of the city back in his day. My whole family, before my dad and uncle came along, were all plumbers. But my grandfather made them both go to college. It was a change-the-fate-of-the-family kind of move."

"Well," she huffs. "That worked."

"Yeah, it did. But when you come from a blue-collar family and then suddenly you're white collar, living in a huge mansion, buying cars, and racehorses, and"—I nod my head towards the road—"lake houses, it's weird, ya know."

"I do," Emma says. "I come from humble beginnings. You're a generation ahead of me, actually. I guess I'd be your father in this scenario."

"Yeah. So you get it. But maybe your family wasn't so… let's say inclined or maybe just leaning… towards a life of crime?"

She laughs. And this is her first real laugh of the evening. "What?"

"Yeah. We're kinda dirty."

She raises her eyebrows at me.

"Is that a waggle?" I ask. "Are you innuendo-ing me?"

"What? No." And then she laughs again.

"I'm just checking." And then I smile. An honest, genuine, happy smile.

I like her. I know we've met before, I just can't figure out where or when.

"Dirty how?"

"You know how," I say. "Do you need me to spell it out? Because I can't. Sorry. Some things just don't get said, if you get my meaning."

"Family secrets," she says, nodding.

"Right. So as I was saying, my life looked like one thing but it was really something else entirely."

"Your dad, he did dirty deals?"

I nod. "You could say that."

"And did you and your brothers get caught up in it?"

"I guess. I mean, I had it the easiest because I'm the youngest. Johnny knows way more about that shit that happened when we were young than I do. Joey knows some. I only know the outcomes."

She's squinting at me now. "Outcomes?"

"Yeah. When my uncle 'died'—" I shove the last part of my ice cream cone in my mouth and do air quotes, then chew and swallow before I continue. "He didn't just die. Right."

More raised eyebrows from Emma. "Someone killed him."

I nod. Not gonna admit that in words, but yeah.

"And your father? Same thing?"

I nod again.

"Wow." She looks away and says it again. "Wow. OK. Yeah. That's news to me."

"So people maybe jumped to some conclusions about me when I was young. Not that I didn't give them a reason. For sure, I was a dick. Total fucking dick. But I was just caught up in shit I didn't understand and had no power to change."

"So… what did change? You, so you say. But why? How?"

"When my dad died Johnny came down to my floor—"

"I'm sorry. Your *floor*?"

"Yeah. That building we live in? Downtown? Well, the top five floors are like… our house, I guess. My dad had the penthouse, Johnny has the floor below, then Joey, and I'm on the one below him. Then below me was the family floor."

"Wait," Emma says. "You didn't all live together?"

"When I was a kid we did. On the family floor but never the penthouse. That was just my father's offices. But after my uncle died we were all moved to separate floors. My dad said it was for security and then I just never went down to the family floor again."

"What?"

"I know, it's weird. But anyway, Johnny came down to my floor to break the news and I was…" I stop to picture that day. "I was so drunk, so high from the night before that…" I stop and sigh. "I laughed."

"Why?" Emma asks.

"I don't know," I say. "Because I was high and drunk and I didn't understand what he was telling me. And then he beat the fuck out of me."

"Oh," Emma says. "Like a real beating? Or a—"

"No, it was real. My face was so swollen the next day I barely recognized myself."

"What a dick," she says, taking my side.

And I have to admit, that feels nice. "I deserved it," I say. "That was my rock bottom, I guess. Things had to change. Not only because our dad was gone and we had to figure shit out, but because if I didn't, I was gonna lose everything. Not the money, either. There's so much fucking money now, I don't even know if it's possible to lose it all. I was going to lose Zach." I glanced at Emma and frown. "He came home that day and saw me, still all strung out. And he had this look on his face. Like I was the biggest disappointment ever."

Emma nods. Says nothing.

"And Zach is pretty much the only person in the world I never wanted to disappoint. He looked up to me after his dad died and I took over raising him." This is the first time I've said that out loud. Probably the first time I actually articulated that's what I did. But I raised him. "He was the little brother I never had. But he was more than that. I felt like… responsible for him, somehow. And I didn't like that look he gave me that day, so"—I shrug—"I took a step forward and started to learn how to live without the drugs and the drinking."

Emma has turned her entire body towards me now. Practically leaning into my legs, she's so intrigued by this conversation. "Wow."

I nod. "Wow. But that's only half the story. Because this was the second time I tried, but the first time I succeeded."

She shoots me a questioning look.

"My uncle," I remind her. "The day he died I was…" I think for a moment. "God, where was I? That sounds dumb but… I was pretty hungover that day too. Just having a good time and shit. All suntanned and golden fresh from months of yachting, and racing, and partying. I bribed my university to graduate me early. Told them I'd donate a building and they went for it, so"—I shrug—"that whole spring I was just celebrating, you know."

"Yeah," she says. "I know."

And she says it in such a way that I get the feeling she really understands me.

"But Johnny showed up. Found me somehow. Told me Uncle Chuck was dead. Oh, hey," I say, pointing at her. "I know where I was. The Keys! I was on Key fucking West."

Then I stop to think about that for a second. But it's all kinda blurry.

"Key West, huh?" she asks.

I snap out of my memories and say, "Yeah. But a few hours later I was back in the city. Doing my best to sober up fast enough to deal with Zach's realization he was now an orphan."

She stares at me for a few seconds, then whispers, "Holy shit."

"Yeah. Kinda crazy."

And under most circumstances, talking about this shit would send me spiraling into a bad mood. Maybe even a depression. Maybe even the old me.

But talking about it with *her?*

It's different.

Somehow, it's different.

CHAPTER NINE

I think I need a moment.

I might need an entire lifetime to grasp what Jesse just told me.

"Processing, huh?" he says.

"Yeah," I say. "Processing."

"Don't think about it too hard. I did that for way too long and it got me nowhere. Now that I've stopped life has gotten considerably easier."

"How?" I ask.

"Well, I'm not focused on negative shit, you know. And—"

"No. How the hell do you just… not think about it? If someone killed my father and my uncle, Jesus. I'd be scarred for life, I think."

"I take it you come from a somewhat normal family?"

"I guess. Yeah, I guess."

"Your parents still together?"

"Yeah."

He nods. "That makes a huge difference. At least, I think so. If my mom had been around when I was little I probably—maybe, possibly—could've skipped that long asshole, dick-face phase I went through as a teenager and after college."

"What happened to your mom?" I'm almost afraid to ask.

"Just…" He shrugs. "Disappeared, I guess. I have no actual memories of her. Not one. Not even a picture."

"Did your dad destroy them? I mean. I don't understand. Not one picture? Not even when you were born?"

He shakes his head. "We had a few nannies when I was little. But not after I turned five."

"Five?" Jesus Christ.

"Yeah. So that would've made Johnny seven, and Joey six. I guess my dad figured we could handle shit by then."

I just stare at him.

He laughs, then places a hand on my shoulder and squeezes. "Don't look at me like that. It was fine." Then he points to my ice cream cone, which is only half-eaten because I got so caught up in his story. "You gonna eat that?"

I look down at the cone. It's melting all over the napkin. "Nah," I say. "I'm done."

"I'll take it." And then he takes it. And winks at me. And stuffs the whole thing in his mouth. He chews and swallows, then says, "I like butterscotch too, but I didn't want you to think I was copying."

He smiles.

Motherfucking smile of all smiles is what he's beaming down at me.

"You're… not what I expected."

"I guess that's a good thing?" he says. "Seeing as how you were kinda mean to me until I changed our future with ice cream cones."

I try not to smile back. I bite my lip to keep it hidden. It doesn't entirely work. "Sorry," I say, suddenly feeling shy. Shy like the girl I was before Bright Berry Beach Cosmetics. Back when I knew this man and he was just a boy. "I guess I came on this date with a few preconceived notions."

"A few?" he says, raising his eyebrows. "Please. You thought you knew me, didn't you?"

"Maybe."

"Hey, do you know me?"

"What?"

"I feel like we've met before. It's just… I'd have remembered a girl like you. So I don't get where this is coming from."

"I'd have remembered a guy like you, too," I say. Then regret it. Then don't regret it. Then regret it again.

I liked him back then. I really did. Faults and all. But if I had known he was this guy underneath? And he didn't walk out on me with no reason, or warning, or explanation? I would've been way more devastated.

I would not have been angry, I would've been sad.

And I'm not sure sad would've gotten me here. To this place, as this woman, with this company, and enough money in the bank to throw away ten million dollars on a second chance.

Hold up, Emma. What the fuck are you talking about? This is no second chance! This is a goddamned kidnapping!

"So," Jesse says, standing up and tossing our napkins into a nearby trash can. "Wanna continue? Or have I really scared you off now?"

"What?" I say, just staring at him.

"Our date? Or are you done? I won't blame you if you're done. Hell, if some strange dude just told me that story on our first date, I'd be done too."

"First date," I say. "Is there a second one lined up I don't know about?"

He sucks in a breath of air, shrugs, then says, "Maybe? I hope so. Because I don't know what it is about you, Emma Dumas. But I feel like we've been here before. Not this place or time, obviously. But you feel so familiar. And I like you. So…"

"I was mean," I say.

"I know. I like that too. For some odd reason I find it charming."

"I bought you," I say.

He nods. "Yup. You bought me."

"You don't even know me."

He points his finger at me. "I know. *But*. I feel like I do. So what do you say? Wanna go up to my lake house and talk some more? Maybe figure out where we know each other from?"

"You're so sure we do?" I ask.

He nods. "I just know it. We've met before. And I'm dying to know why I walked away. Because that makes no sense to me."

"Me either," I mumble.

He laughs and extends his hand. "Come on. Let's blow this place. I can't take the competition. Those little boys are gonna start pulling your hair and calling you names to get your attention if we stay here any longer."

I take his hand. I know I shouldn't. I know with every fiber of my being that I should not take his hand.

But I do it anyway.

And yup. Sure enough, those sparks I felt back when I was eighteen… they're back. Stronger than ever. It's like the past thirteen years didn't happen. It's like that was some alternate reality. Some other path not taken. And this is the real path we took. Us. Together. This whole time. Never been apart since.

He leads me over to the car, opens the passenger side, and waits for me to get in before closing it and walking around to his side.

When he closes his door he pauses. Then looks at me and says, "Here, let me help you with that, Emma," as he reaches over my legs and pulls my seatbelt across my lap. Clipping it into the buckle.

But he pauses, tilts his head up to mine until our eyes meet.

And then he kisses me.

And I kiss him back.

And we taste like butterscotch-cherry and vanilla-chocolate.

His tongue is cool as he tangles it with mine. And his lips are soft.

And he pulls back too fast, but slowly too. Easing back into his seat. Staring at me.

Then he smiles, turns on the car, puts on his seatbelt, and backs out of the Tastee-Freez.

CHAPTER TEN

Everything is different now.

Funny how that can happen. One pit stop at the Tastee-Freez and a little bit of truth goes a long way toward earning goodwill.

Zach has been telling me this for ages. Hell, everyone has been telling me this for ages. Not the ice cream and truth, but the act of being genuine, I guess.

I just never really saw it in action before tonight.

Because for sure, Emma Dumas had a chip on her shoulder when she first got in my car and now... I glance over at her. She's staring out the window again, but everything about that stare is different. For one, she's smiling. Just a little. Just barely. But it says a lot.

Now... everything is better.

This lake where all the city rich people come for the summer is huge. Very, very big. But every house comes with a pretty nice bit of land too. Ours has twenty-five acres attached to it. I think most of the lots are that size. Some of them are only ten, and there's a few that have sixty or more acres. So even though there are like two hundred homes on this lake, they are spread out and well-treed. You can't see anyone from our backyard but the glimmer of lights across the way.

And sure, everyone's got a telescope so we would all spy on each other when the summer festivities really get rolling. But it's early June right now and most people don't show up until the week before Fourth of July. So it's pretty quiet tonight when I pull onto Lake Road and start winding my way through the trees to our house on the far west side.

Lake Road is really just a big loop. And it's a pain in the ass to get anywhere by car around here, which is fine. Because everyone has boats. There's a floating restaurant in the middle of the lake. Busy as fuck during the summer. There are even live bands out there sometimes. And there's a little—not quite town, but area, I guess—on the North side of the lake that has a bait shop, and a little grocery store, and a bar. Shit like that.

We're like our own self-contained community out here.

Like the Hamptons, I guess. Except there's a whole different vibe. Sure, everyone's rich here, just like there, but it's different. Everyone out here is mostly new money. People who aren't so full of themselves yet that they think they're above swimming and boating on a lake.

"Damn," I mutter.

"What?" Emma asks.

"I wish we still had a boat. I could take you out on the boat."

"I have a boat. I have a house here too."

"You do?"

"Why are you so surprised?"

"I… don't know. I guess I never thought of that. But yeah, makes sense. When did you buy out here?"

"A few years ago. It's not just mine. My partners and I got it as a retreat house for the company."

"Cool. So are you inviting me onto your boat?" I ask.

"Umm… well. I guess I'd have to make sure we… had insurance."

"What?" I laugh.

"For non-employees," she says.

But then I glance over and catch her shaking her head and then notice I can see her face in the reflection of the window and see her mumbling something.

"Something wrong?" I ask. "You're not mad because I kissed you, are you?"

"No," she says, turning to face me. She touches her lips unconsciously, then catches herself and puts her hands in her lap.

"No, there's nothing wrong? Or no, you're not sorry I kissed you?" I ask, teasing her for more information.

"The kiss," she says, smiling at me.

"So there is something wrong. But not the kiss."

"No, I meant—"

"It's fine," I say, reaching over to grab her knee. That makes her jump and squeal a little and I have a flashback to another girl I did that to once. Long time ago. Can't remember when, and don't really want to. Back then, all those girls I dated—shit, 'date' isn't even the right word. 'Fucked' is more like it—I don't want to think about them and Emma in the same breath.

She brushes my hand off, but I can tell it's not a rebuke. She's ticklish.

I just grin and grin as we weave our way along the dark Lake Road.

Finally, we arrive at the gate to our property. "Shit," I say.

"What's wrong?"

"I hope I can remember the code. Totally fucking forgot about this and I haven't been up here in years." I pull up next to the intercom and start punching numbers. None of them work. I look over at Emma and say, "I'm gonna be so fucking embarrassed if I can't get in."

She laughs, and then there's a crackle on the intercom. "Mr. Boston," a man's voice says.

Emma and I look at each other with raised eyebrows.

"Mr. Boston?" the voice says again. "Is that you?"

"Uh, yeah. Who's this?"

"I'm Stan. Joey's butler for tonight. He told me you might not have the new code. I'll let you in. One moment."

"Butler," Emma says, waggling her eyebrows.

I point at them. "More innuendo."

She laughs again. And damn. That laugh comes out easy now. "You're funny, you know that?"

I grin, then pull forward as the gate opens for us. "I do my best."

Our driveway is long and winding because most of our acreage is out here between the house and the road. The house is right up alongside the lake and when we finally come around that last bend and see it all lit up and pretty, Emma and I both say, "Wow."

"What are you saying 'wow' for?" she says, pushing me on the shoulder. "It's your house."

"I know," I say, pulling up in front, underneath the huge porte-cochère canopy of massive wooden beams. "But I forgot how amazing it was."

Fucking Joey. He must've been taking care of this place all these years because it wasn't me. And it sure as fuck wasn't Johnny.

There's no valet—not that I expect one—but when we get to the front door it opens automatically and Stan, wearing a typical butler face frown, stands aside and says, "Welcome home, Mr. Boston."

"Thanks, Stan. This is my date for the weekend, Ms. Emma Dumas."

Stan bows at the waist and says, "Very nice to meet you, Ms. Dumas. Would you like to start with champagne on the back patio, Mr. Boston?"

He winks at me. "Sure," I say. "Sounds pretty nice, actually." I turn to Emma and say, "Shall we?"

She's looking around nervously and I wonder if it's too much? The gate, the driveway, the house, the butler. Maybe it's too much?

"Emma?" I say. "You all right?"

"Sure." She rallies, wiping her hands on her dress. "Yes. Drinks on the back patio sound fabulous."

I offer her my arm, and unlike the first time I did this back in the city, she accepts it with grace and maybe, possibly, even eagerness.

The grin on my face just gets wider and wider as we make our way through the house and out the back French doors.

"This is quite lovely," Emma says as I lead her down several stone steps to the covered patio area behind the house. It's really an outdoor living room. Has a kitchen and everything.

"Thanks. I can't take credit for it though. This is all Joey, I guess. Someone obviously spends a lot of time out here. And no way is Johnny keeping up with the landscaping and shit."

There's a small table set up in the center of the room. Not a patio table though. Round but made out of raw-edged wood. And the chairs aren't plastic or that resin you typically find outdoors. They are plush and deep. Like living-room chairs you'd find indoors.

I wave my hand at one, waiting for Emma to take her seat, then walk around to the other one and sit.

"Nice," she says, leaning back into the cushions. "You really know how to impress a girl."

"Again," I say, picking up the bottle of champagne from the ice bucket to check the label—it's a good one—"I wish I could take credit. We'll have to send Joey a thank-you note on Monday."

I pop the cork as she chuckles, then pour her a glass and pick up the other bottle.

"We're not having the same drink?" she asks. Confused.

"No,' I say, twisting off the cap on the bottle of sparkling cider. "I quit drinking almost five years ago."

Her face goes a little pale.

"Don't worry," I laugh. Pouring my cider into a flute. "I'm not a buzz kill. You enjoy yours. I'll enjoy mine

She takes hers and I hold mine up, thinking up a good toast. "To the best ice-cream date ever." I stare into her brown eyes a little longer than I should. Then add, "I hope it's the first of many," and it doesn't even sound like a pick-up line.

Because it isn't.

Yeah.

I like her.

"To many more," she says, taking a sip.

Then her phone buzzes. Which is a little bit confusing, because she's not carrying a purse.

"Oh," she says, feeling up the skirt of her gown until she produces a phone from a hidden pocket. "One sec. It's just the office."

She texts back quickly, then shoves the phone back in her dress. "Now where were we?"

CHAPTER ELEVEN

Shit. Shit. Shit.

"Everything OK?" Jesse asks.

"Sure. Yes. Absolutely. Why?"

He chuckles. God. How did I get here? I mean, two hours ago I was fuming at this man. He was number one on my hate list. I loathed him. With a passion. So much of a passion, I put together this ridiculous kidnapping scheme to 'teach him a lesson'.

I'm an idiot. For so many reasons.

One, kidnapping is illegal and comes with prison time if you get caught. What the fuck was I thinking? This is the dumbest plan ever. How could four super-smart, super-capable, super-logical fucking women ever think that this was a good idea?

And two, he is nothing like I expected. Like not even a little bit. Not one teeny, tiny fucking morsel of that asshat he used to be is present and accounted for tonight.

And that story.

Jesus Christ. He comes from a mob family? Or something? I don't know. I'm not really sure. And his father and uncle were murdered and his mother just… like… fucking *disappeared* after he was born. Just what the hell was I thinking?

We're going to be killed for this. Fuck prison time. Johnny Boston is gonna show up at Bright Berry Beach next week with a shotgun and blow our heads off!

"Emma?" Jesse asks.

"Hmm?"

"Are you sure you're OK?"

"Yup," I say, smiling. Then take a sip of my champagne. Then down the whole thing and grab the bottle because I need another one.

"Was that bad news in the text?"

Bad news? Only if a message stating that my best friends and partners in crime are on their way across the lake in a boat to make moving his body easier is bad news.

"Nope," I say, forgetting about the drink. I probably do not need another drink. "All news is good news. But can I say… or ask you… will that butler be here all night?" I crinkle my nose at him.

Jesse looks over his shoulder at the butler, who is standing sentry at the edge of the outdoor living room.

"Stan should take the night off, don't you think? I mean, we're fine, right?" *And,* I don't add, *I need him to be gone by the time my crazy kidnapping partners pull up in a boat in ten minutes.*

"Oh," Jesse says, leaning forward in his chair a little. "Sure. Yeah. I don't know him either. No big. I'm sure Stan would appreciate a night off, wouldn't you, Stan?"

"Whatever you wish, Mr. Boston. The food is ready. I can serve it before I leave."

"No, no," I say quickly. "Totally unnecessary." Jesse is squinting his eyes at me now. He has to know I'm acting weird. "We did just eat," I say.

"Just ice cream," he says. "You're not hungry?"

"Are you?" And I have this feeling. I just know he's going to say, *Starved.* So I waggle my eyebrows at him. And this time there is no way to mistake that this waggle is pure innuendo.

"Oh." He smiles, then chuckles. "Oh. OK. Hey, Stan. Do a guy a favor and beat it, will ya?"

"If you wish, Mr. Boston."

"I do wish." Then he leans across the table and takes my hand in his. "Ms. Dumas and I would like to be alone."

And even though I know this whole night, from top to bottom—with the exception of the ice cream—is wrong on every level possible and I should not lead him on or let him hold my hand, I do lead him on and I do let him hold my hand.

My heart actually thumps in my chest. Three times. Real hard. And my head goes a little bit swoony.

Because I'm falling for him. I'm falling for Jesse Boston all over again. Like I'm eighteen years old. Like I'm still that same innocent, naive, gullible girl who fell for him thirteen years ago.

"Hey," he says, giving my hand a squeeze.

"Hey," I say, a chill running up my spine as my hand slides inside my dress pocket and plays with the two roofies. We weren't sure how many to use, so we decided on two. But now I'm pretty sure zero is the correct answer.

Yup. Zero roofies is definitely the way to go.

My phone buzzes again.

"You're popular tonight. You don't have a boyfriend, do you?" He lets go of my hand and sits back in his chair as he rakes his fingers through his thick, dark-blonde hair.

"Boyfriend? No," I say. "It's just… work. My partners, I mean. They're just texting to make sure I'm OK."

"Ah," he says. "Yeah, I get it. You were less than thrilled about coming on this date with me."

"But... I'm thrilled now. Really. I'm actually having a good time with you."

"I hear another 'but' coming. What is it?"

"It's just... um... well. Maybe I am a little hungry. Are there any hors d'oeuvres?"

"Oh," he says, looking for Stan.

"No, don't call Stan back. I don't need them that bad." And then, as if on cue, and the whole world is plotting against me—because of course it is, that's how shit like this shakes out when you're stupid enough to plan a kidnapping and then chicken out at the last possible minute—my stomach growls.

Loudly.

"Oh, shit!" Jesse says. "No, you gotta eat. Let me go get the tray. I'm sure there's a tray. Joey thinks of everything when it comes to dates. Be right back."

I check my phone once he disappears from view.

We're here!

Dammit! How the hell did they get across the lake so fast? I strain my eyes, peering out over the water, searching for the little boat.

And yup. There it is. Silent. No motor, as we discussed. Bobbing just past the long, Boston Brothers dock.

My phone buzzes again.

Did you do it?

No, I text back.

Do it now!

And just by the tone of the text I can tell it's Mila talking to me.

I don't think we should.

Too bad! We voted. Everything is in place. Now drop those pills into his glass. He's already coming back.

I look up towards the house, but I can't really see it. There's a hill in the way. But then I see the top of his head and my phone buzzes again, and I don't know what comes over me, but my fingers have the roofies and then I'm dropping them into his glass, which, unlike mine, is still full.

I grab the champagne bottle and fill my glass back up so we can have a toast when he gets back. And then I just stare at the pill at the bottom of his glass… and… and I can't do it.

I switch glasses just as Jesse comes into view.

"You're in luck!" Jesse calls as he skips down the steps towards me. "I found a whole tray of meatballs on a stick!"

He's laughing so hard at this I forget that we're in the middle of a kidnapping and start laughing too.

"What's so funny?" I ask, as he sets the tray down in front of me.

And then he sits, picks up his glass and takes a sip.

Spits it out. Looks at the glass and makes a face.

Fuck.

He was not drinking champagne. How did I forget that? He just fucking told me like five minutes ago he's sober!

"Oops," he laughs. "Wrong glass. I picked up yours by mistake." And then he takes mine—which is his—raises it to his lips, and downs it all in a single gulp.

I'm reaching for his glass, consumed with second guesses, and hedged bets, and regrets when he sets it back on the table.

He looks at my hand and I withdraw it quickly. "What are you doing?"

I just shake my head. Because it's too late. "Um... the meatball story?"

"Oh, fuck! Fuckin' Joey. Sometimes you can't help but love that dude. He came up with meatballs on a stick back when we were kids and my dad still had parties on the lower living floor in the building. I know, I know. Inside joke. Not so funny. But... whatever. I think it's funny that he was gonna serve his date meatballs on a stick. And oh shit!" He laughs again. "I just did serve my date meatballs on a stick!" He sighs. Loud and long. Smiles at me like he's never seen a woman before in his life. And says, "Goddamn, Emma Dumas. Where the fuck have you been?"

"What?" I say. Because for a second I think he's remembered me.

"My whole life. I don't know what it is about you. But I just… feel like we know each other. Where did you go to school?"

"Um… for high school?"

"Any school. Tell me. Tell me everything about you. I'm fucking dying here."

"I went to…" And I pause and wonder if he'll figure it out and remember me. And do I want him to remember me? Or don't I? "I went to Key West High."

His head backs up in surprise. "Key West. Really?"

I nod. "Born and raised down there."

"I was there once. Did I tell you that already? I can't remember."

"Yeah," I say. "You said you were racing boats down there when your uncle died."

"Yachts," he corrects me, smiling. "And I wasn't racing. I was on a break and just taking it easy." Then he sinks back into his chair.

And holy fucking shit. Do those roofies work that fast? Because he definitely looks dizzy.

"What year did you graduate?" he asks.

"Long time ago," I say.

"How long?" he asks. And now he's not smiling.

I shrug. "Like thirteen years."

"Like thirteen years? Or exactly thirteen years?"

"Does it matter?" I ask.

He narrows his eyes at me, then sits up and leans forward, his elbows on the table. "Yeah. It does."

"Exactly then. Exactly thirteen years ago. I was eighteen," I say. Because he does remember me.

"And I was twenty," he says. "That's the year…" But he doesn't finish.

"That's the year what?" I ask.

His eyes flutter and then close. He opens them just as fast. Stares at me. "We did meet before, didn't we?"

I nod my head. Slowly. There's no point in pretending now. I already did it. I can hear the boat just off shore as the girls paddle it up next to the beach.

We're going through with this whether I want to or not.

CHAPTER TWELVE

KEY WEST - THIRTEEN YEARS AGO

Her name is Emma. I asked a friend of a friend to find out for me and that's the answer he came back with.

Local. Working a shaved ice kiosk down in Mallory Square. Her parents own a dive shop, she has three brothers, and she plans on going out of state for college after graduation.

I must've been too drunk that first night we arrived. That's the only explanation I can come up with for why I didn't immediately see this little pig-tailed siren of a girl with the plump pouty lips calling me to my death on her rocky island of shaved ice.

I missed her. I've been here two whole weeks already. Two weeks I could've been spending with her, and only her. And instead I've settled for stand-ins and second-bests.

How? How did I miss you?

"What can I get for you?" she says.

It's hot as fuck today and the sun is blazing down on me with the heat of an eternal hell I will surely end up in once I get this sweet siren of a girl back to my yacht.

She's wearing a white tank top that hugs her bronze skin, a pair of Daisy Duke cut-off shorts, and those goddamned curly pigtails bob and bounce around her heart-shaped face like we're floating underwater.

"Hello?" she says. "I don't have all day here. There's like fifty people in my line. What flavor do you want?"

"You," I say.

She makes a face. She has this perpetual frown, I've noticed. My friend calls it her resting bitch face, but that's not right. That's totally wrong. It's a pout only one girl in a million can pull off. Her mouth is small and perky. Her lips are bright pink and plump. And just the outer corners turn down. Not like she's mad or sad.

But like someone disappointed her. Someone let her down.

"Oh, God," she says. "Look. I've got pineapple, I've got berry berry, I've got piña colada, cherry vanilla, banana cream, and key lime pie. And just so you know, there's no cream in the banana cream. It's just a name."

I smile at her.

"OK, piña colada."

"No," I say, snapping out of my trance. "Cherry."

"Cherry vanilla. Very original. What size?"

"I don't care."

"Good. Large it is. In a souvenir cup. I get a bonus every time I sell ten of those. That'll be twelve fifty."

She turns her back to me and starts scooping ice into a large pink plastic cup that says Mallory Square on it. I should be looking at her ass. Or the way her back moves underneath the thin white tank top. Or her pigtails, still bouncing and bobbing around her head as she places my cup of ice underneath a vat of cherry-flavored sugar juice.

But that's not what I see at all.

I see us. Tonight. Maybe watching the sunset from the upper deck of my yacht. Or down below, doing other things.

She turns back around and smiles.

And holy mother of God. The smile is even better than the pout. "Uh," she says. "You're cute and all, but it's not free. Twelve fifty."

I reach for my wallet in the back pocket of my board shorts, pull out a twenty, and say, "You can keep the change."

She sucks in a deep breath of air. Looks at my bill. Then takes it and says, "Whatever," as she punches buttons on the cash register and the drawer pops open.

"So… tonight," I say.

She frowns at me. "Tonight what?"

"What time do you get off?"

She glances nervously over my shoulder at the people waiting in line behind me, then says, "Are you serious right now? I'm working."

"What time?" I say again. Because I'm not walking away from this girl without a date.

"Seven."

"I'll be back at seven."

I take my pink cup and walk away. And I swear to fucking God, I have never grinned so big in all my life.

The only thing I really remember about later was on the deck of the yacht. I didn't have my team with me because I wasn't racing, I was down in the Keys fucking off. No reason, really. Just ended up there. I hooked up with a few guys from the racing circuit and that's who I was bumming around with.

But that night with Emma it was just her and me under the stars. We missed the sunset. Didn't care. There was plenty to look at up there after it was gone.

She was standing at the railing and I was behind her.

Every time I touched her she said, "No."

But it was the sweetest fucking no ever. And eventually I had my arms around her. My hand between her legs. She never even took her shorts off and I made her come with just my fingers.

After that I was pretty sure she was just gonna bail on me and never come back, but she didn't. She took off her shirt, then her shorts, and placed both hands on my bare chest, pushing me down onto the cushions of the top-deck couch. And the next thing I knew she was climbing into my lap.

She stayed the whole night.

I remember that because I was surprised. Every minute that ticked off, I was surprised. I kept thinking, *Any second now. She's gonna get up and leave and I'll never see her again.*

It hurt. Thinking that fucking hurt. Because I liked this girl. She was the first girl—the only girl—I'd ever longed for.

But all those minutes kept passing by and she was still there. I don't think we slept. I know I didn't. If she was gonna sneak out in the middle of the night I wanted one last chance to talk her out of it before she disappeared from my life as quick as she blew into it.

And the funny thing is… I'd been high and drunk for weeks at that point. So high, so drunk, I didn't even know the difference anymore.

But that night we didn't even drink. Not one joint. Not even a fucking cigarette. I had one tomato in the fridge and a slab of good mozzarella. And that's what we ate. Sliced tomatoes with cheese.

That was it. And it was enough.

She was enough.

For the first time in my life, I felt… full.

And then the next day Johnny showed up and I never saw her again.

Until tonight.

There are brief periods when I know I'm in a boat. My mind doesn't have to be awake to be aware of the water underneath me. This is just something I feel.

I hear them too. Little bits of this and that.

"His suit is ruined." And, "Jesus Christ, he's fucking heavy." And, "He's such an asshole."

But none of it makes sense because the words just float there like a dream. Then there's a moment when everything rushes at me, all at once. Like I'm being blown over by a cyclone of words and suddenly—I'm awake.

My eyes are open, but I can't see anything but the inside of a black hood over my head. I can hear and I'm breathing. So two out of three isn't bad.

"He's coming around," a female voice says.

And the only thing I can think of is… *How fucking ironic is this?*

I haven't talked about my father in years. Hell, I haven't even *seen* Johnny since the goddamned funeral. So how the fuck does it happen? That I get kidnapped on the one night I decide to tell a girl these secrets?

"Slap him," another girl says.

"Why?" a third asks.

"Just… make him wake up already. It's getting late."

"What? You got a hot date?" the second voice says.

"Don't be dumb. I just want to slap him."

Two separate chuckles at her admission. Both female.

One of them kicks me in the shin and I moan.

117

"He's awake. Are you awake?"

Who are these bitches? Who sent them? And why now? After all these years? Was it the auction? And then I remember what I was doing last night. "Emma," I say, surprised at how weak and faint my voice sounds. "What did you do with Emma?"

Silence from them.

"If you hurt her, I'll fucking kill you," I say.

More lingering silence.

My head is still very fuzzy. If I could see, if this hood wasn't over my head, I'm pretty sure the whole world would be spinning.

I was drugged. Who did that? What happened to Emma? Where am I? And was I really on a boat? Or was that just some leftover feeling from—

Shit.

I know her. It comes back to me in an instant. I know her. I knew it. I fucking knew it.

Emma Dumas was the girl back in Key West.

The hood is ripped off my head and the world comes into a sort of blurry focus.

Three people stand in front of me. All dressed in black, ski-masks over their faces. And even if I didn't hear them speaking a few minutes ago, I'd know they were female because of their black Catwoman costumes.

Fucking girls.

My eyes narrow down into slits trying to get used to the light. "Where the fuck is Emma?"

They look at each other, but say nothing.

I'm tied to a chair. My legs to the chair legs. My arms twisted behind me at the shoulders. Hands behind my back.

"Who are you?" I ask. "And what the fuck do you want?"

They say nothing.

"You'd better start feeding me answers real fucking fast—"

"You'd better shut up real fucking fast," the shortest one says. "For once in your life, Jesse Boston, you're not in charge here. We are."

"So get the fuck on with it and tell me what's happening."

The tallest one walks around me in a circle, face turned towards me, scowling underneath her ski mask. "You don't remember us, but we remember you."

"We remember the way you lied to us," the third one says. I recognize her voice from the one earlier telling them I was coming around.

"What the hell are you talking about?" I say.

"What are we talking about?" the tallest one says. She's completed her circle and stops right in front of

119

me. So close I have to tilt my head up to see her hidden face. She places both her hands on my shoulders and leans down. "We're talking about how you used us. Got what you wanted and then threw us away like trash. How many girls, Jesse? How many, over the course of your pathetic lifetime, did you treat this same way?"

I almost laugh.

"Is that funny?" the short one asks.

"You're... ex-girlfriends?" I say. "Really?" Then the whole thing is too much and I do laugh.

"Ex-one-night-stands," the third one says.

"And you know," the tall one says, "it's not even that, is it girls? Who cares if everyone is getting what they want? If expectations are set, and met, then who cares if you fuck around, right?"

The others agree.

"But *you*," she seethes. Like I evoke some deep-rooted hated inside her. "That's not how you do it, is it? You lead people on. You tell lies."

"Lies like... 'I've never felt this way about anyone before,'" the short one says.

"Lies like... 'I think we have this deep connection,'" the third one says.

"Lies like... 'I don't want you to leave but I have to meet some friends. Promise me you'll come back later. Because now that I've met you, I can't live without you,'" the tall one finishes up.

All this is ringing a bell. I will say that. Because I have said those things to possibly dozens of girls. Maybe even more than that.

But that was a long time ago.

Long time ago.

"Who the fuck are you?" I ask.

They look at each other. Come to some kind of conclusion. Then the tall one begins to speak.

"Key West. Thirteen years ago."

My stomach sinks. My heart gets this immediate ache. Because she's telling me about how we met in a bar on Key West, and I took her back to my yacht and we fucked on the upper deck, and then I may or may not have said all those things they just ticked off and moved on to the next one.

Who is now talking. Telling me how we met on the beach and then I took her into a nearby alley and fucked her against a wall. Again, with the promise of more to come. A promise of a deep connection.

And then the third one is going on and on about how I followed her around Mallory Square telling her how beautiful she was and how my whole life needed to come to a complete stop so she could get on this ride and take it with me.

I promised her a life on the ocean. Sailing around the world on my yacht.

And all three of these encounters all have one thing in common.

That was when I met Emma.

This is why my heart aches and my stomach sinks.

Emma.

She's not hurt. She's not in trouble. She's not tied up in some mob boss' basement as punishment for some long-forgotten transgression.

She *did this*.

CHAPTER THIRTEEN

It's hard to listen to this. I mean, the whole thing is hard. The realization that I'm partly responsible for drugging and abducting a man and then holding him captive in the basement of our lake house. The whole boat ride over here from his place.

I thought he was dead like sixteen different times. And I couldn't take my eyes off him. I was so worried and I wanted to go back thirty minutes and change things. Never let him pull into the driveway. Never tell him to send the butler home. Never respond to Mila's texts.

Because this night—this stupid ice-cream cone date—this was the Jesse I wanted all those years ago.

And he's different now. I tried telling that to the other girls, but they had settled into this plot and were in it to win it.

But as soon as he woke up he asked about me. Then threatened them.

If you hurt her, I'll fucking kill you.

Like we were a thing. Like I was his. Like he... *cared.*

I'm so fucking stupid.

Because he didn't care.

All their stories of him are just like mine.

The way he pursued them. The way he convinced them that they were special. The way he promised them things.

He said those things to me too. So all these new feelings tonight are just bullshit. Just lies. Just... *stupid.*

He never cared about me back then and he doesn't care about me now.

Really doesn't care about me now. Because he has to know I did this to him.

The door I'm leaning against suddenly opens and I back off as the girls rush through and close it behind them. Mila points to the stairs and we follow her up into the large kitchen.

They rip off their ski masks as we enter, their faces all flushed and hot.

"So he shut up pretty quick, don't you think?" Natalie says, then gets a coffee cup out of the cupboard and places it under the coffee maker, presses the button and the machine stars whirring to life.

She just makes a cup of coffee like this is no big deal.

"Now what?" Hannah says. She leans against the counter and pulls out her phone, stares at the screen, then smiles and starts texting.

"We should leave him here," Mila says.

"What?" I say. "For how long?"

"Well, I have to run Stephanie to ballet in the morning. And Donny has a baseball game. So I could probably get back here around one-ish? But we have to be quick because tomorrow night is the new-recruit dinner and I'm in charge this time." She looks at me like this all makes perfect sense.

Let's just leave the abducted billionaire in the basement overnight and then after I finish mom-ing tomorrow, we'll pick this back up and finish it.

Hannah bursts out laughing.

We all look at her.

"Sorry! But Devin just sent me a chemistry joke."

Natalie takes a sip of her coffee, then says, "OK. Well, I've got two dates tonight so I'm good with leaving him overnight."

"What?" I say. "Like what is happening right now? And how do you have two dates tonight? It's nearly two AM!"

She shrugs. "Well, the first one is just a quick look-see. The second one is sex and breakfast. And they both live within two blocks of me. God, I love it when it works out like that."

"You guys!" I say. "We just abducted a man and he's tied up in our basement!"

"He's not going anywhere, Emma," Hannah says, fingers furiously tapping away at her screen as she smiles.

"We cannot just leave him here."

"Well, what do you wanna do?" Mila asks. "It's a long drive home and I have to be up by nine to drop Stephanie at ballet."

"Who cares about fucking ballet?" I say.

"First of all," she says, using her mom voice on me as she holds up a finger, "Stephanie has worked her ass off this year and tomorrow are the auditions for the summer production of *Alice in Wonderland*. She really wants to be the caterpillar's face. And second, fuck this guy! He deserves this!"

"He so does," Hannah mumbles, still texting.

Natalie sets her coffee cup down and grabs her purse off the counter. "Yeah, let's go. I have to change before I meet up with date number one. You wanna ride with me, Ems?"

"No," I say. "We're not leaving him down there. He doesn't even have water."

"He doesn't deserve water, Emma," Hannah says. "He's a dick. A total dick."

Mila says, "We'll just come back tomorrow, drug him up again, and then drop him off back at his place tomorrow night like this never happened. He has no idea who we are."

"Hello!" I say. "I bought him at the auction. He knows I'm involved!"

"He thinks you were kidnapped," Natalie says. "Plus, he's super disoriented right now. Maybe we should drug him tonight too?"

"No," I say. "No more drugs."

"OK, it's settled then," Mila says. "Let's go. Emma, how are you getting home? I'd offer to take you, but your place is totally out of my way and I really need to catch some z's before Stephanie's audition."

Hannah stuffs her phone in her back pocket and grabs her purse off the counter and starts heading for the door.

"I'll drive the Land Rover home," I say. That's the car we keep out here.

Mila shoots me a look.

"What? I'll bring it back tomorrow."

"That's not what I'm worried about. You do not go down there. You hear me?"

"Why the hell would I go down there?" I ask. "The last thing I need is for him to figure out I'm the stupid mastermind of this shit show."

"Good, let's go," Natalie says.

We all file out of the house. Mila last, so she can arm the security system. Hannah takes off without another word. And by the time I back the Land Rover out of the garage, only Mila is left. Sitting in her Mercedes, waiting for me to pull in front of her. Like she doesn't trust me to leave Jesse here overnight.

I shake my head at her as I drive past, then exit the gate and follow the long Lake Road back to the highway.

But the whole time I'm driving back to the city Mila stays behind me. Not taking her eyes off my car until I have to exit onto another freeway and she has no choice but to let me go my own way.

I watch out the side window as she keeps cruising straight and then I get off on the next exit and turn around.

I have to go back. I can't leave Jesse Boston tied up in the basement.

I need to know things.

Things like… was any of it real? Or was it all lies?

CHAPTER FOURTEEN

There is a vent in the basement that must connect to the room where they are talking upstairs because I hear every fucking word of their conversation.

And now I know who they are.

Bright Berry Beach Cosmetics.

Then the realization kicks in hard.

I dated/fucked/lied to all four of them.

Well, not Emma. I didn't lie to her. I liked her. I fell hard for that girl in the pigtails. And now that I know who she is I can't stop seeing her face in my mind.

The last thing I need is for him to figure out I'm the stupid mastermind of this shit show.

That lingers in my head as well.

This was all her plan.

After they leave I just sit in my chair fuming. So pissed off. They really are going to leave me here all night, then drug me again tomorrow and… what? Hope I'll just forget this all happened? Be so riddled with guilt about how I used them I'll let it go?

No. Fuck that.

As soon as I get out of this mess I'm calling Johnny. I will ruin them. Every single one of them.

I doze off for a while, the drugs still swirling around in my blood, then wake up abruptly when the familiar sound of a garage door opening rumbles through the house.

Then listen as somewhere upstairs a door opens and closes. Then another. And footsteps on the stairs.

Maybe they changed their minds on the way home?

The door to my room opens and Emma appears.

We stare at each other for a few seconds.

"Well," I say. "What the fuck do you want?"

She leans against the doorway and folds her arms across her chest. She's still in the pretty red gown from the auction. Her hair—which was up a very sophisticated up-do when this night started—is falling all over the place, kinda framing her face and reminding me of the pigtails she wore back when we met at the beach.

"I'm letting you go."

"So do that," I snap. "Untie me. Right the fuck now."

"Do you know who I am?"

"I know," I snarl.

"So you remember now?"

"I remembered back at my house. I was just about to bring it up when the drugs hit my system."

"Were you?" she says, furrowing her brow. Then she frowns and all those memories of her perfect, pouty lips threaten to overcome my anger. "You were not. This is just another lie, isn't it?"

I sigh and shake my head. "Fuck you. You drugged me, Emma. Do you have any idea how long I've been clean? How long it *took me* to get clean?"

"What?"

I laugh. Kinda loud. "Oh, never thought of that, did you? I cannot fucking believe you did this."

She frowns. Then pouts. And damn. I know I hate her but… I really, really like that pout. "I'm sorry," she says.

"What the hell? Just what the actual fuck? How long have you and your little friends been plotting this bullshit plan?"

"You used us! You lied to us!"

"Oh, yeah. Totally makes sense now. Oh, and by the way?" I nod my head to the vent in the ceiling. "I heard everything you guys said upstairs. That one friend of yours? She's using men too. What would you think if that first guy she meets tonight drugs her? Abducts her? Ties her ass to a chair and leaves her to rot overnight with no water?"

Emma purses her lips.

"Not so funny now, is it? And what if he and his friends—all *her* used-up boyfriends—just stood around talking about how they had to take their kids to ballet? Or meet other girls for sex? Or joked around sending texts? Those guys would be labeled sociopaths!"

"You're right," she says.

"I know I'm goddamned right! Now un-fucking-tie me!"

She walks forward towards me. Then behind me. She must have a knife because she slips something cold between the tight zip tie and my skin, and then the pressure releases. I bring my hands into my lap, sighing with relief as my stretched-tight shoulders relax.

She does the same for my ankles and I stand up and look down at my suit. I am covered in leaves and dirt. "What did you do? Drag my ass on the ground?"

She presses her lips together and says nothing.

I rub the welts on my wrists as I look at her, wondering how the fuck she could even think of a plan like this. "Did I ruin your life, Emma? Is that why?"

"No," she says. "My life is fine."

"Yeah, I know. You're a huge success story. Own your own billion-dollar company, pretty as fuck, and smart. So what the hell were you thinking?"

She shakes her head at me, then turns with a swing of her dress, and starts to walk out.

I grab her by the arm. Maybe a little bit too tight, but fuck that. She's not walking out on me. "I want an explanation."

She turns slowly. Looks me in the eye. Lips pursed in defiance. Eyes blazing with anger.

"How bad do you have to hurt someone to pull a stupid stunt like this?" I ask. "Did I hurt you like that? Because I liked you, OK? A lot. And tonight, when I finally figured who you were, when I finally figured out you were *that* girl—the one I fell for all those years ago and then got ripped away from... you can't even imagine how fucking happy I was. For like five whole seconds I thought to myself, 'Finally. Finally something good happens to me. Something natural and not contrived. Something special.'" I stare at her as her pout falls into an even deeper frown. "And then I realized it wasn't good at all. It was just the same old shit all over again."

"You liked Mila a lot too," she whispers. "All those things you said to me that night. I played them over and over in my head for years. Wondering if they were true or not. But you said them to her too. You said them to all of us. What am I supposed to believe?"

"They were true," I say.

"You were drunk. And high."

"Yeah, I was. Because I had a problem back then. But I thought about you too. Every fucking day for weeks."

"But you left anyway."

"I didn't leave, Emma. My uncle died and my brother came and got me. I was on a plane less than an hour after I last saw you." I throw up my hands and sigh. "Why am I even bothering? I told you this right before you fucking drugged me and it made no difference. You and your friends have already made up your minds about me. I'm the asshole. I deserve this. I deserve to be drugged, abducted, and left to rot in some dark basement with no water. What if I died?"

"You weren't going to die." She huffs. "And I came back for you. You're free, aren't you? Just... go. Get the fuck out of here. I never want to see you again."

I just shake my head at her. "You know what sucks the most about this night?" She looks at me but doesn't offer anything up. "I like you. I lik*ed* you. And you… well," I say, throwing up my hands. "You got what you came for, I guess."

I walk past her and come out into another room. Look around, find the stairs, and then take them three at a time.

I come up in a kitchen, spy the door, reach for the handle and pull. Only to realize… she locked me in.

When I turn around she's behind me.

"What now?" I ask. "Is there a second phase to this plan?"

She says nothing.

"Open. The fucking door, Emma."

She presses her lips together and shakes her head. "Not yet. I want to know something first."

"What?"

"Back in Key West… did you mean any of it?"

I stare at her. See her. The new her, the old her. The new me and the old me too. Her little shorts and that tight, white tank top. Her red strapless dress with the form-fitting bodice. Her tanned legs then and her pale ones now. Peeking out from underneath the slits riding up the side of her gown.

Her pout. Then, it was perpetual disappointment in others. And now... it's different. It's disappointment in *herself*. She's the one who let herself down this time.

I say, "Every fucking word."

She looks down at her feet. "I'm sorry. I really am. I wanted to stop it." She looks up at me. "At first, I was mad. So angry at you. I have harbored this hate for you for so long, this felt... reasonable. But..." She sucks in a long breath and lets it out. "I changed my mind."

"Why? When?" I don't even think about these words. They just come out automatically.

"The ice cream."

And I smile. I can't help it.

"Your story... I didn't know any of that."

"But you went through with it anyway? What the fuck, you know? Just what the actual fuck?"

She shrugs. Swallows hard. "The other girls didn't have that moment with you. They were still angry and I was... not. That's why I came back. Not just because it was wrong, but because I wanted to see if you really meant it."

Is she fucking kidding me right now? Is she asking me to... what? Explain my *feelings* to her? After what she did?

I huff out some air. So angry. So pissed off at her.

But she looks very vulnerable.

And maybe it's the drugs? Or maybe deep down inside I'm just *that guy*?

I don't know. And I don't even care at this point.

I want to fuck her. Right now.

And then I want to leave her all over again.

Just like last time.

Only this time I'll be walking out of my own accord.

It won't be Johnny dragging me away.

CHAPTER FIFTEEN

He takes a step towards me and I hold my breath. Now what?

I picture him spewing insults at my face. Threatening me with legal action. Calling the police and having them drag me away and then one by one going to my friends' homes and arresting them.

The headline on Monday. *Bright Berry Beach Executives arrested for kidnapping.*

Our lives falling apart in an instant over what?

Hate? Hurt feelings?

But the look on his face isn't one of hate. It's… could it be? Am I crazy? Is that… longing? Is he… does he want to… no. I'm making shit up now. He's angry and vindictive. A known liar and cheat.

But people can change, right?

I sure did. I don't even recognize myself right now.

"Emma," he says, once the distance between us is closed. He tentatively places a hand on my hip. Grips it.

And when I don't push him away, he places the other one on my other hip. Tugs me towards him.

Am I crazy? Is he coming on to me?

Surely not. After what we did? No.

"Emma," he says again. "I'm sorry I left you back in Key West. I explained this to you before I even knew it was you. I didn't have time to think it through, and I was high back then. I *couldn't* think it through. But I thought about you for so long afterward. You were my one regret. The only real regret I've ever had with a woman. And if I could go back in time I would've just talked to you that night. Built something real first. So that when the moment came and I had to leave, you'd know something was *wrong*. And it wasn't you, it really was me."

I realize I'm holding my breath and let it out. "Really?" I say. Because I can't help myself. When I fell for him, I really fell for him. And I never got back up.

"Really," he says, leaning into my neck.

His lips are so soft. So tender, a chill runs up my spine and makes me shudder and suck in a breath.

"Like that?" he asks, nibbling on my ear.

"Mmm," I manage to moan.

140

"Because I do," he whispers. "I like it a lot. I'd like to nibble you all over."

Jesus Christ. I feel like a teenager again. My stomach is tied up in knots and there's a heat between my legs that's been missing action for so long now, I almost can't control myself.

But then I get a hold of myself and pull away.

"What?" he asks.

"What are you doing?"

"What does it look like?" he asks, leaning in again.

But both my hands immediately come up to his chest and push him back. "Why are you doing this?"

"Uh… because I *like* you."

"I drugged you. I had you kidnapped. That was me. That was my plan. I did that. So what the hell are you doing?"

"For fuck's sake, Emma. I just told you I've been missing you all these years and tonight we reconnected and I felt that all over again. Why can't you just accept that I like you?"

"See points above," I snap. "You're doing it again, aren't you?"

"Doing what?"

"Playing me!" I say. It comes out a little shriek-y.

"OK," he says, pulling away, removing his hands from my hips so he can hold them up in the air like he's surrendering. "Let me spell it out for you. We," he says, pointing first to himself, then to me, "had a little connection back in the day. Do you agree? Or not?"

"I only know what I felt. I have no idea what you felt."

"Listen," he says, rubbing his temple. "I'm telling you right now what I felt. Either you believe me or you don't. But"—he holds up a hand when I open my mouth to protest—"if you don't believe me, then that's on you. OK? Not me. I didn't know who you were at the Tastee-Freez. But I did tell you, several times, that you felt familiar. Remember that?"

I nod. Because it's true. He did.

"And that was before you pulled your little stunt. So what's it gonna be? You wanna do this? Or walk away?"

I narrow my eyes at him. It just can't be that easy. "So you forgive me?"

"Sure. I forgive you. You wanna know why?"

"Why?" I ask, so softly.

"Because for me, forgiving you is nothing. It costs me nothing to forgive you. But you will have to live with this for the rest of your life. You will have to forgive yourself, Emma. And take my word on this, OK? I was a guy who had to look at myself in the mirror after I cleaned up my act. I had to see him for what he was. I had to learn how to forgive myself for all that shit I did when I was younger. And it's not as easy as you might think."

I want that to make so much sense. I want this to be his reason for suddenly becoming reasonable, I really do. Because I do not want him to leave me again. I'm so pathetic. So fucking pathetic.

"So what do you want to do? Part ways enemies? Or try for a second chance?"

I want this second chance so bad. So fucking bad.

"OK, I'm outta here."

"Wait," I say, grabbing onto his arm. "Just… give me a second to catch up, will you?"

He steps away. Leans against the wall. Folds his arms over his chest. Glares at me.

What is that glare? What is it telling me that he's not?

Because I think I see hate in that glare.

Which means everything he just said is a lie. Just another Jesse Boston lie.

"I'm waiting," he says.

"OK," I say. Because I can't walk away from him. Or let him walk away from me. Not without finding out for sure if he's for real.

"OK what?"

"OK, then…" I suck in a deep breath, gather myself, remember *who I am*, and say, "Please continue."

He grins. And even though I know it could be a trick—that all of this could just be him playing me again—I relax when he beams that grin at me.

He takes a step forward, hands on my hips, mouth leaning into my neck, and commences nibbling.

I am going to regret this, I know it. The minute we're done, I will be kicking myself for falling all over him like an idiot.

But I don't care. That's at least twenty minutes in the future and all I want is the here and now.

So I place my hands on his hips. Then pull his shirt out of his pants.

He laughs a little in my ear as he continues to kiss me. "That's better," he whispers. "Just give in, Emma. Find out what you've been missing all these years."

I have ten comebacks to that on my lips. Things like, *You mean, what you've been missing.* Stupid teenage girl things.

But I just stop caring about the scorecard. I don't have energy for hate and suspicion right now. Because I'm unbuttoning his shirt. And just a few seconds later I'm popping that button on his pants too. Unzipping that zipper just as his hands reach down and slide underneath the slit of my dress.

And that's it, folks.

Show's over.

Because we are going to *fuck*.

But he says… "I could fall for you, Emma. If I let myself, I could really fall for you."

Something snaps in my brain when I hear these words.

Something electric. Some kind of charge running through my body.

At first I think it's desire.

But then I realize it's not.

His words are an echo of mine.

I fell for him. I fell for him hard.

Things I've been thinking about all week since we started putting this plan in motion. And the fact that he's now parroting them back at me means… I must've said them out loud tonight. At some point he heard this come out of my mouth and now he's just telling me what he thinks I want to hear.

Because how perfect would it be if I kidnapped Jesse Boston, got him in this vulnerable position, took all his power away—and then gave it all back because he knows how to lie like a champion?

I don't think so, asshole.

CHAPTER SIXTEEN

Oh, she is eating this up. It's so easy, I almost feel guilty. No wonder I did this so much back when I was young. Girls, man. They believe anything.

But when her hand slips down inside my pants I suck in a breath of surprise at just how good that feels.

Back when we knew each other—if what we had even counted as knowing each other—we were kids. Everything on her part was a little hesitant, a little uncertain, and she had a shyness about her that's definitely not present now.

"Do you like that?" she asks. Her hand is fully wrapped around my cock and she squeezes it hard as she says this to me.

"Mmmm-hmm," I groan. Because whatever we're doing, I can't pretend I'm not enjoying myself.

"I like it too," she purrs into my ear. "Put your fingers inside me."

Holy shit. Fuck yeah. "Don't have to tell me twice," I murmur into her mouth as I kiss her.

Her tongue responds, twisting up against mine as I slide her panties aside and begin to play with her clit. She's nice and wet for me too. So nice and wet. I want to do everything to this girl right now.

Last chance, right? Because when this is over, we're done. She will never talk to me again.

And good. I'm so through with her. I did like her. Both back then and tonight before she fucking abducted me.

"You're thinking too hard," Emma purrs, taking her kiss to my neck.

Holy fuck, that feels good.

"Sorry." I chuckle. "I just want you," I say.

"So take me," she coos. "Right here, right now."

And then she pulls back and looks me straight in the eyes. For a second I think, *Oh, shit. She's on to me. She's gonna walk out. Get my dick all hard and ready then just... disappear on me the way I did her, all those years ago.*

But that serious look on her face fades and then... it's just her. The girl I remember. The sweet one at the shaved ice stand. The one who captured my attention like no other girl ever had before, or has since.

She backs up until she hits the kitchen island. Places both her hands flat on the edge, and pulls herself up until she's sitting.

I'm transfixed on her face for a few more seconds. But my eyes wander down to her fingertips, which are pulling the middle part of her dress aside to reveal her black lace panties.

I lick my lips.

"Yeah?" she asks, pulling her panties aside and flashing me her pussy.

"Yeah." I nod. And I completely mean it too. To hell with the games. I'll think about that shit later.

"Then come here," she says, beckoning me with her finger. "Come closer, Jesse."

Oh, man. She said my name. That is so hot. Hell, this whole thing is hot.

I press myself up against her, opening her legs with my body and easing my hips forward until I'm pressing my hard cock right where it needs to be.

"Oh," she coos. "Not so fast, mister." Then she places a hand on my head, grabbing my thick blond hair in her fist as she pushes down.

"Oh, you little sexpot, you," I growl. But hey, I'm game. I'll eat her pussy if that's what she needs.

I place my hands flat on her knees and bend down. All the while my eyes are locked on hers. Unable to look away.

She smiles and tips her head back as my mouth eases in. I inhale her sweet scent, then lick her as she continues to hold her panties to the side.

"Yes," she moans, closing her eyes and clenching her teeth. "That's perfect."

"I'm just getting started," I say. "It only gets better from here."

"Shut up and keep going," she says.

Which makes me chuckle a little. Fucking Emma Dumas. After all these years. Finally, I have her right where I want her.

My tongue darts out and swipes over her sweet spot. She grips my hair tighter and closes her legs on my head.

Jesus. I dive in and begin licking her like crazy. My teeth nipping at her little nub, making her squeal and squirm.

I grip her knees and open them up as wide as I can, then say fuck it and lift them up and out, so she's spreadeagle above my head. I need access. Because I'm going to eat this woman's pussy like dessert.

My tongue laps and licks. I suck on her, unable to get enough. I'm out of control as she wiggles her ass on the smooth granite island and finally has to fall backwards and just give in. I reach across her body and grab her tits, squeezing with both hands. Then grip the seams and pull her bodice down. She's braless, so her spectacular breasts spill out.

I stand up and lean over, taking one nipple in my mouth. Nipping at it, then swirling my tongue around until it's just a tight little nub.

"No," she says, pushing on my head. "Go back. Keep going. Don't stop now!"

Oh, shit. OK. I dive back down and pick up where I left off. Only this time I slip two fingers inside her and her back comes up off the countertop, bucking with pleasure.

"Yeah," I say. "Come for me, Emma. Just let go. Spill your sweet come all over my fingers so I can stick them in her mouth and make you lick it off!"

She moans and then goes rigid and stiff. I smile. Just grinning like a fucking kid as she comes all over my fingers. Then my tongue darts in and laps her up.

And I want to die.

No. I want to stick my hard, throbbing cock inside her and fuck her until she comes again.

I stand up, pull my pants down just enough to release my cock, and then start forward. Ready to rock her world.

But that's when she sits up and says, "Hey, thanks."

"Yeah, no problem." I grin. "It's my pleasure." I fist my dick, priming it with a few pumps before I aim it right at her sopping wet pussy.

But she places a hand on my chest and says, "No. I think you misunderstand. Thanks for the good time. It was super fun. But I'm done now."

Then she places her stiletto-heeled foot up against my chest and pushes me back as she stands up, pulls her bodice back up and straightens her dress, and smiles.

"What the hell?" I say. "What the hell is this?"

"This?" she says, twirling a finger in the air. "This is what's called the *classic hate fuck*, Jesse."

Then she grabs her keys off the counter, punches in the security code, and walks out the door.

I follow her out, buttoning my pants back up. "Where the hell are you going? What the fuck is happening?"

She whirls around pointing her finger in my face. "You. Asshole."

I slap her hand away. "I'm the asshole? You drugged me, abducted me, tied me up, and then talked me into eating you out until you came and now you're going to walk away from me? You're the fucking asshole!"

"Wrong!" she seethes. "I might not be the most clever girl in the world when it comes to men, but there's one guy—just one—I know pretty well. And that's you. You were gonna do this to me. I could practically read your filthy fucking mind back there!"

"You bitch!" I say.

"I'm the bitch? So you meant all that bullshit? 'Oh, Emma,'" she says, in a fake voice. "'Forgiving you is nothing. Blah, blah, blah. But you will have to live with this for the rest of your life. Blah, blah, blah. How about a second chance?'" She sticks a finger in her mouth and pretends to gag. "Just how stupid do you think I am?"

"I can't fucking believe you right now! You are such a fucking—"

"No," she says. "I just did what you've been doing your whole life, asshole. How's it feel to be lied to, huh? How's it feel to believe those lies and then wake up and realize you're a fool?"

"You're the fucking fool!" I say. So pissed I'm seeing red.

"Really?" She laughs. "Which one of us got what they wanted and which one was left hanging this time?"

And then she turns, walks over to her car, gets in, and starts it up. She flips me the finger as she backs up, and then screeches her tires as she peels away.

"Fuck you!" I yell. "I'm totally pressing charges!"

But she sticks her hand out the driver's side window and just flips me off again.

I stand there in shock as her brake lights disappear into the thick grove of trees. Then turn around, seething with anger.

And decide… I'm gonna steal her boat.

CHAPTER SEVENTEEN

"*I cannot believe* you let him go!"

Mila is furious with me.

"Yeah, well. I think it was for the best. We shouldn't have done it. I was cutting our losses."

"You know he's totally gonna press charges. What do I tell my kids when the cops show up to arrest Mommy?"

"First of all," I say, "he's not going to press charges."

"How do you know?"

"Because men like Jesse don't call the police when girls take advantage of them. And second of all, your kids don't even call you Mommy, you make them call you Mila. So cut the crap."

"Jesus. What's up your ass?"

"I bought a billionaire last night and then I drugged him, abducted him, and tied him up in a basement. That's what's up my ass. And you're welcome, by the way."

"For what? Screwing up our whole revenge plan?"

"For shutting this down. And besides, we got our revenge. Trust me. I don't think Jesse Boston will ever look at a one-night stand the same again."

"It wasn't enough. Drugging him? Half a night of tied-up submission?" She huffs. "That's nothing compared to what we could've done."

"It wasn't just that."

"What do you mean?"

"Never mind. Just... I ran the numbers and we came out ahead."

She blows out a breath of frustration.

"So how was Stephanie's audition?"

"She got the part she wanted."

I smile. Because I can hear the smile on Mila's face. "Good, I'm glad. Just believe me, this was for the best. We should forget all about Jesse Boston. Hell, the whole Boston family can just fuck off."

"Yeah," she says. "Did you tell Hannah and Nat?"

"Yup. I called you last. I knew you'd be the toughest."

"He hurt me, Emma."

"I know."

"I fell for him."

"I know. I did too."

"He actually ruined me for years. I never trusted another man again until Lance came along."

"That's because Lance was your one."

"I know, but... now I'm worried about you."

"Why?" I ask.

"Because I don't think you ever moved past it. You don't even date anymore. At least Hannah is in a committed relationship and Natalie is always putting herself out there. She asks you to double with her all the time and you always say no. You're not even trying anymore. Why wouldn't I worry?"

"Natalie dates five men at once. Don't you think that's her acting out her insecurities too?"

"No. I think that's her version of taking charge. Something you never do."

"Ha." I laugh, then catch myself. Because I sure the fuck took charge last night with Jesse. But I'm never going to admit I let him lick my pussy until I came. Not to Mila, not to anyone.

"So how did he get home? Ew, you did not give him a ride, did you?"

"Hell, no," I say. "I dunno. Walked, I guess."

"You really don't think he's gonna call the cops? Because if someone did this to me, I'd definitely call the cops."

"I'm telling you. He spilled some secrets last night while we were eating ice cream and—"

"I still can't believe you stopped on your way up to the lake to have ice cream with that douche."

"Anyway. Long story short, he and his brothers aren't exactly... on the up and up. He practically admitted they were mob bosses. Or something. He's not calling anyone."

"What if they put a hit on us? Oh, God. Do I have to hire bodyguards?"

"Just relax. Play it cool. I'm willing to bet a million dollars he just forgets this ever happened. It's in his best interest. I mean, what guy wants to admit to something like this? We'll probably never see or hear from this asshole again."

My phone buzzes in my hand. I look down at the screen and see 'blocked number' flashing at me.

"Shit," I say.

"What?"

"Oh... just my mother on the line," I lie. "I'll call you later. Tell Stephanie congrats. And tell Donny to hit a home run, or whatever. Bye!"

I let the call to go to voicemail, then tap my fingers on my leg as I wait for the message to chime.

No chime. No message.

OK. Probably just one of those robocalls. Nothing to worry about.

But the call comes in again. Blocked number.

Now who could this be?

My bets are on either some jerk's lawyers or the jerk himself.

I take a deep breath, tab accept, then say, "Emma Dumas," as I let it out.

"Missing anything this morning?" The jerk himself. And he sounds like he's eating something. Because he's chewing like a caveman.

"Who is this?"

"Hm. Funny."

"Should I be missing something?"

"Oh, I dunno. Maybe your boat?"

I smile. "Nicely played. But that boat was a piece of shit anyway. You can keep it."

"Oh, you mean that one by the dock?" He laughs. "No, I didn't take that one. In case you forgot, I know a thing or two about boats. I took that one in the boathouse. The million-dollar one."

Asshole. But what do I care? One stupid boat I never use isn't enough to piss me off this morning. I won last night and we both know it.

"Can I help you with something, Mr. Boston?"

"No, Ms. Dumas. I'm calling to help you with something."

"What's that?"

"Wanna know what's on the agenda for today?"

"Excuse me?"

"Our date? Remember? You bought me? Now you have to show me a good time."

"That's not how bachelor auctions work."

"It actually is. You pay to take me somewhere."

"No, I pay *them* so you can take *me* somewhere."

"Exactly. So I made all the decisions."

"What are you talking about? I'm not spending the day with you. I'm never seeing you again for as long as I live."

"Well, unless you want to live in a six-by-six prison cell, then I suggest you rethink that plan."

I huff. "You're kidding me."

"I am abso-fucking-lutely one hundred percent dead serious."

"Why are you doing this?"

"To get even, of course."

"What happened to forgive and forget?"

"In the light of day, and not under the influence of roofies, I find it highly overrated."

"Ha! I knew that was all bullshit!"

"It wasn't bullshit. I just decided to rethink my new code of ethics after you had your happy little hate fuck last night. Which, by the way, doesn't count."

"Oh, no?" I laugh.

"No. Because we didn't fuck."

"I got you. I got you *good*."

"Yeah, maybe. But I'm the one who got you *off*."

"Pig."

"Oh, that reminds me. I'll pick you up in an hour and don't forget to wear the pigtails. I really—like really—dig that look on you. See you soon."

The call drops and I just look at it in my hand for a moment. He wishes. I am not going anywhere with him. And if I was, I certainly wouldn't be wearing pigtails.

My phone buzzes an incoming text.

"Now what?" I mutter. But when I glance down at the screen I see a pic. I pick up my phone to get a better look, because it's a piece of paper with lots of little writing on it.

I zoom in and read the top of the page.

City General Hospital Lab Results.

Shit. Then I say it out loud. "Shit." Because there it is. In black and white.

Patient Jesse Boston.

Blood tested positive for flunitrazepam.

Dated this morning, time-stamped at seven AM.

My phone buzzes again.

A text from the jerk:

Unless you want to watch me tell my harrowing story of how four cosmetics moguls lost their minds on TV tonight, I highly suggest you be outside your building in one hour. Wearing pigtails.

CHAPTER EIGHTEEN

I'm outside. Where are you?

That's what I text to Emma once I pull up in front of her building. She's testing me but I'm ready for her today. I am willing to overlook the drugging and the kidnapping—but no one walks out on me the way she did last night.

No one.

So am I being petty and childish by demanding that she spend the day with me learning her lesson?

Absolutely.

Do I care?

Absolutely not.

I don't even know what we're going to do today. I have no plans other than monopolize her day. Make her waste time with me. Make her _hate_ me.

This is what's called the classic hate fuck, Jesse.

Her words are burned into my mind forever. I will never stop hearing her say that to me. Ever.

The balls on this woman. Giant, motherfucking bull-sized balls on this woman.

My phone dings in my hand just as a horn honks behind me.

I glance down at the screen and read her message. *I'm right behind you.*

Then I glance in the rear-view and see her waving at me from a... what the fuck?

She's smiling broadly from the driver's seat of a matte-black Lamborghini Huracán, her curlicue pigtails bobbing around her face.

She honks again. My phone dings. The text reads. *Get in. I'm driving.*

Oh, I don't think so. I came here in a motherfucking Ferrari Portofino. Red. So I text back. *You get in. I'm driving.*

My phone rings. "What?" I ask, so annoyed. Because while the Portofino was an excellent choice, I do have to admit the Huracán has sex written all over it.

"I'm driving. Get in."

"You're not driving," I say. "I'm the man, I do the driving."

She revs her engine behind me. "We're taking my car. If you're a good boy maybe I'll let you drive it."

"I could buy my own Huracán, Emma. I don't need to drive yours."

I catch her smiling even bigger in the mirror. "We can compare dicks all day long if you want. But I'm not getting out of this car until we arrive at our destination. So. I suggest you pick and choose your battles carefully, Mr. Boston. Because as you can see, I'm sporting pigtails. And what you can't see is that I'm wearing the same outfit I was that day at the shaved ice stand all those years ago."

"Hmm," I say.

"Hmm, indeed. This is your fantasy, right? You want to make me look like that teenager I was back then. Fine. I'll play along. If you let me drive my car."

"I don't know where you got this car, but it's definitely not yours."

"It is now. I had it delivered fifteen minutes ago."

"You bought a two-hundred-thousand-dollar car to impress me?"

"Two-seventy-five with upgrades. But who's counting? And I didn't do it to impress you, Jesse. Don't be dumb. I did it to make you feel inferior."

"So that's how this is gonna go?"

"I have no idea what you're talking about."

"You're trying to hate-fuck me with a car."

"I… don't really know if that's a thing. But sure."

I hesitate.

"You know you want to drive it."

"I really don't have a thing for fast cars, Emma. You miscalculated."

She revs her engine again and it sounds like a fucking lion. Or a lion ready to fuck. One of the two. "Everyone has a thing for *this* car. Don't you want to see the interior? I wish I had time to customize it myself, but oh, well. Listen to the sound system—"

The chorus of *Smells Like Teen Spirit* blares out into the city. Everyone within a hundred yards turn to look at her.

I check the mirror again and find her banging her head and laughing hysterically, her pigtails flying back and forth.

I text, *Stop it. You're embarrassing yourself.*

She pauses her head-banging to text back. *Get. In. The. Car. Now. Or I'll roll down the window and ask that hot-as-fuck jogger to get in instead.*

I glance at the jogger. He's shirtless, sweaty, and not bad-looking—OK. No. He's hot, even I can see that—and he's also smiling at Emma like he wants to throw her down on the hood of that Huracán and fuck her right here in front of the whole city.

I get out, toss my keys to her building valet, and intercept the jogger with a hand in the air. "Back off, asshole," I say.

He sighs, shakes his head, then continues on his way.

The valet dude gives me a ticket just as the Huracán's passenger window slides down. Emma turns the music off and says, "Aww. He was interested, wasn't he?"

I open the car door, slide in, and… holy fuck, this is a nice car. The seat hugs my ass and shoulders like it was custom-made for me and the whole thing feels like the cockpit of a very nice private jet.

"Told ya," Emma coos. Then she shoves the gear shift into reverse, backs up squealing her tires, and zips around my Ferrari like she's Danica Patrick.

She giggles as we ease our way down Broad Street towards downtown, glancing over at me every few seconds to see if I'm intimidated.

I'm not.

Pffft.

"So where were you planning on taking me?" she asks as we pull up to a stoplight.

"Breakfast," I say.

"Where?" she insists.

"The Champion Hotel."

"A hotel," she scoffs. "Come on. Are you serious? Were you hoping that I'd be so impressed by your little Ferrari and their overpriced eggs and bacon that I'd beg you to take me upstairs so you could get what you missed out on last night?"

"It's a very nice restaurant," I scoff back.

"Hmmm," she says. "I guess. If you're into boring. Too bad I'm not. And anyway, I already planned our whole day."

"Did you?" I ask.

"Mmmm-hmm. So we're going to skip the Champion and go with option B."

"Which is what?"

She looks at me and winks. "You'll see."

Option B is the airport. More specifically, the small one only private jets use, and not the giant commercial one everyone else uses. I raise an eyebrow at her.

She just smiles like a fucking Cheshire cat.

"We're at the airport, Emma."

"I can see that."

"What are you doing?"

"Taking you on the dream date. I did pay ten million dollars for you. And you seem to think I owe you a good time. So… good times are coming your way, buddy. And it all starts here."

Then she shifts gears and we shoot forward onto the tarmac. I grip the dash and yell, "You can't drive on the fucking tarmac!"

She laughs and laughs. Then turns the wheel, the Huracán slides to the right, and we stop in front of the biggest corporate jet out there on the market today.

Hot pink in color and Bright Berry Beach splashed across the body.

"Good fucking God," I say. "Where the fuck are we going? Australia?"

"Oh, we're not taking that one. They just needed to move it out of the hangar to get my personal jet out."

"You have a personal jet?" I ask.

"Don't you?" she counters.

"What the hell are you doing? Are we playing Who's Got More Money? Because that's so juvenile."

"You wanted me to look like a teenager today, right?" Then she shrugs her shoulders, gets out of the car, and walks towards a valet.

I get out and meet up with her just as the valet says, "No problem, Ms. Dumas. Your jet is just about ready.

The crew is preparing breakfast now. Why don't you and your friend board and grab a bite to eat as we get clearance for takeoff?"

"Sounds wonderful, Benjamin. Thank you for coming in on short notice today."

"It was my pleasure, ma'am." Benjamin bows to her like she's some kind of foreign dignitary, then backs away and heads towards the Huracán.

"Jesse!" Emma calls over her shoulder as she walks. "We're this way, sweetie."

I have to suck in a deep breath of air to hold my tongue, because she's treating me like man candy. What the fuck?

Where is she taking me? And why is she doing this?

Oh, I know. She wants to get even. She's not satisfied with simply drugging me and tying me up, then walking out after I make her come. No.

This is a power grab. The ultimate power grab.

I follow her to the other side of the pink monster jet and find a much smaller Gulfstream. Black. With a hot pink stripe down the side.

Subtlety isn't one of her strong points.

There's a red carpet laid out in front of the airstairs and what I can only assume is a flight attendant bowing to her as she approaches. She greets him with both hands in hers, then laughs and tosses her pigtails.

I have to suck in a deep breath of air because she does look like the girl I met all those years ago.

And just for a second I forget that this is a game. Just for a second I forget that she's one-upping me. Just for a second I wonder what it would be like to date Ms. Dumas for real.

And then she opens her mouth and says, "This is Mr. Boston, Miles. I bought him at an auction last night so we're spending the weekend together." Then she looks at me and smiles before turning back to the jet and climbing the stairs.

I watch her. Mostly focused on her ass cheeks, which look fantastic in those shorts. But then her eyes, because she stops at the top and looks over her shoulder to say, "Hurry along, Jesse. I don't like to be kept waiting." And disappears inside the cabin.

Oh. That's enough.

I climb the stairs after her thinking… *OK. I'll play. You wanna play, lady? I'll play.*

Before this day is over I am gonna hate-fuck the fuck out of you and show you who's boss here.

Me.

I'm gonna be the bossiest motherfucking Boston Brother there is.

CHAPTER NINETEEN

Even though this jet is one of the smallest on the mainstream luxury market, I had it customized to my exact specifications.

I figured if I had to fully immerse myself in this corporate life, I was going to do it in style. As CFO, I'm the one who makes the most trips. Hannah almost never leaves the corporate office and neither does Mila. It's Natalie and I who jet-set all over the globe striking deals and forging new relationships.

When we go together we take a whole staff with us, which is why we need the Bright Berry Monster, as we affectionately call her.

But I go alone a lot too. And it's not environmentally responsible to take the Monster in those situations so a smaller jet was a necessary expense.

Still, it's quite impressive.

The cabin has been divided into three sections—
the galley and seating for the two staff, then the middle
section, which is workspace, and finally the aft cabin
which is for resting.

Yes, I have a bed in my jet. But I deserve to look
fresh when I arrive in Europe for a quick meeting.

I glance over my shoulder at Jesse once he enters
the cabin and smile.

Take it all in, asshole. You think you're rich?

I'm rich, motherfucker.

*I don't need to be wheeled around town in your stupid red
Ferrari or brunched at your favorite posh hotel.*

Welcome to my life.

*I missed out on nothing when you ghosted on me thirteen
years ago.*

He wants a date? He wants to force me to spend
time with him over threats of prison?

Fine.

We're on a damn date.

I'm gonna date the hell out of this man today and
show him who's boss.

"Come in," I say. "No, don't sit there. That's for
the staff. Come this way, Jesse."

He's glaring at me. Which is so perfect.

The work station in the center section has been
transformed into the dining experience configuration.

174

Fine china with napkins folded into the shape of swans on top, heavy silverware gleaming in the sunlight pouring through the windows, and no fewer than three crystal glasses each.

"This is… a bit much, don't you think?" Jesse says, feigning indifference.

"Is it really?" I ask. "Or is it just that you're not the one going over the top?"

"Emma," he says, unbuttoning his jacket. He's very smart casual today. Brown sport coat over an untucked, dark-blue button-down shirt and dark jeans.

"May I hang up your coat, sir?" Miles asks him.

"Sure," Jesse mumbles, removing the coat and handing it over.

"Would you like coffee this morning?" Miles asks as Jesse takes his seat across from me.

"No, thanks. Just water for me. I'm dehydrated from last night." He glares at me when he says this. Like I need reminding that he was drugged.

"I'll have water as well," I say, brightly.

Miles disappears into the forward cabin, drawing the pocket door closed behind him so we can have some privacy.

"Where are we going?" Jesse asks.

"Where do you think we're going?"

"I have no clue, Emma. But wherever it is, I need to be home tonight."

I shrug. "My wish is their command. I can have you home whenever you'd like. In fact, we don't even have to go. We can call this charade off right now and just go back to our regularly scheduled Saturday mornings."

"And get you out of this ridiculous trip?" He laughs. "Not a chance."

"Good. I'm looking forward to our ridiculous trip."

"You didn't answer my question."

"You'll see when we arrive. Isn't this how the billionaire date is done? The rich guy comes in and sweeps the poor girl off her feet with promises of fantastic food and exotic trips inside pretentious flying machines?"

"You forgot the most important part."

"Which is what?"

"Hot sex in my bedroom at the end." He grins like he's so charming. Like this is a fantastic joke.

"You mean hot sex in *my* bedroom. Since I'm the one in charge of this date."

He smirks again, then looks down at the table, shaking his head. "I don't give two flying fucks where we have the hot sex, Emma."

"You presume a lot, you know that?"

"Do I?"

I nod.

"I wouldn't call it presumptuous. Not after the way I made you come on my face last night."

I open my mouth with a surprised, "Oh, really."

He shrugs. "I'm just really good at it. Nothing to be ashamed of."

"You cannot shame the CFO of Bright Berry Beach Cosmetics with a little dirty talk, Mr. Boston."

"Funny. Because you're blushing a bright berry shade of pink right now."

I take a deep breath. And luckily Miles appears and tells us to get ready for takeoff, then disappears behind the pocket door just as the plane begins to taxi across the tarmac.

But Jesse is on a roll now. Because he says, "I like the outfit, by the way. And the pigtails too." Now he's really grinning. And the worst part is that I am blushing. I can feel the heat creep up my cheeks.

"It's not like I had a choice."

He rubs the day-old stubble on his chin. "Everyone has a choice, Emma. You didn't have to buy me last night, but you did. You must have really fallen hard for me back in the day if you were willing to spend that kind of money on revenge. Especially revenge that backfired."

"It was a group decision," I say. "It was actually Hannah who bought you, not me. The CFO in me said you were a poor investment."

"Then why are we doing this?"

"Because you threatened me with prison if I didn't show up when you arrived."

"And the feminist inside you couldn't handle that?"

"Fuck you." I laugh. "You're just pissed I showed up with a better car. And now you're feeling insecure because you know there's nothing in this world you own that can impress me."

He stands up, grabs his cock through his jeans, and says, "Wanna bet?"

I can't help myself. I look.

He's not hard but I swear to God, he gets hard as I watch.

My eyes dart up to his and he's grinning wide. "Told ya."

"Just sit down."

He sits, still smiling, and then reaches across the table and grabs both my hands before I even realize he's doing it.

I try to pull away.

Mmmm… that's a lie. It's a half-hearted effort at best. But he squeezes them anyway, just to make sure.

"You're gonna regret this game you're playing."

"You think so?"

He nods. "Yeah, see, I've got something else you want."

"Let me guess, you have two cocks hidden in those tight jeans?"

"Are they tight?" he asks, looking down at himself, then back up at me. "Nah, that's not it. I have your… *attention*, Emma. You're completely under my spell."

I laugh. Loud.

"Maybe you forgot about me all these years, and maybe you didn't. Doesn't matter. Because now that I'm back you'll never get me out of your head again. And if we don't finish what we started last night you'll spend the rest of your days wondering what if."

I'm just about to say something snide in return when the plane picks up speed and we jet down the runway. Jesse squeezes my hands again and I make the mistake of looking into his eyes.

Mesmerizing blue eyes that bring back memories of those two days we spent together long ago. His hair is neater now. Not tousled from the beach wind. His jaw has more stubble, and his shoulders are broader.

But it's still him.

179

The plane lifts up off the ground and my stomach becomes light and filled with a million fluttery butterflies.

And he's right. I am under his spell.

Because that feeling in my gut isn't due to rapid acceleration or altitude change.

It's all the what-if's and could've-beens.

He lets go of my hands and leans back, frowning now as the plane levels out and then I realize I've been holding my breath and let it out. But that anxious feeling doesn't go away. It actually gets worse.

"Why are you looking at me that way?" I ask.

He just stares at me for a moment. Miles opens the pocket door, ready to take our breakfast order, but Jesse stands and says, "You know what, Miles? We're gonna hold off on breakfast." He shoots me a cunning grin. "In fact, come back in an hour. By then we'll be ready for breakfast in bed."

CHAPTER TWENTY

It's a bold move. One that definitely comes with a high probability of backfiring.

But I'm nothing if not bold. And besides, all of life's greatest rewards come from taking audacious risks.

Miles looks at Emma. She stutters out, "Ummm… well… thank you, Miles. That's all for now."

Miles then looks at me and I swear to God, there's a gleam in that dude's eyes. He backs off and says, "Very well. I'll check back in an hour, Mr. Boston."

Which only bolsters my confidence. So I extend my hand to Emma and say, "Shall we then?"

Emma looks at my hand, then my face, then glances at the closed pocket door where Miles disappeared.

She's all bright berry pink again.

Man, I almost feel guilty.

Almost.

She left me hanging last night. And that shit cannot stand. I got in her stupid Lamborghini, I got in her stupid jet, and I'm going along with her stupid date.

But I'm only doing it to prove who's in charge here.

Me. And she's about to figure that out real quick.

"What's wrong, Ms. Dumas? Afraid you'll like it?"

She huffs, then takes my hand and stands up. "Well, people don't come back for seconds if they didn't enjoy the first plate, Mr. Boston. So I'm happy to give you another shot at pleasing me. It's the least I can do after ruining all your best-laid plans to control me today."

"Oh, honey." I laugh. "I'm just getting started."

I turn before she can respond and lead her to the back of the cabin. I admit, I have never seen a bedroom on a jet this small before. And then I have an unreasonable surge of jealousy, wondering if she takes all her bossy men on impromptu control-freak dates like this.

I step inside, maneuver around the double bed so she can enter behind me, then pull the door closed and press her up against it. "Ready?" I ask.

"Let's play," she quips.

But before she even gets that very short retort past her lips, I'm kissing them.

Both her hands come up to my chest and for a moment I think she's going to push me away.

She doesn't.

She kisses me back and I swear to God, a tingling sensation runs through my whole body when her mouth opens and her tongue begins twisting with mine.

I grab her hair, realize she's got it up in those adorable, but ridiculous pigtails, and drag the elastic down one of them, tossing it aside.

Now I can really kiss her. I slip my fingers through her hair and hold her in the palm of my hand.

Unexpectedly, my heart begins to race inside my chest. And my cock, which was semi-hard from my little display back in the middle cabin, becomes ready in an instant.

Then her hands do come up to my chest. She flattens them out, pressing me backwards.

But oh, no. *Oh, no, Little Miss Control. Not this time. I'm the bossy one here, not you.*

I turn my body, taking her with me, and a moment later I'm pushing her backwards. Her knees hit the bed and she falls, breaking our kiss.

She laughs, quickly sits back up, and begins unbuckling my belt.

Wasn't expecting that, but OK.

I watch her fingers pull the leather out of the buckle, and when she tips her head up to smile at me, I maybe even get a little lost in her brown eyes.

The ripping sound of a zipper going south redirects my focus on what she's doing and then—

"Holy fuck," I mumble.

—she pulls my cock out and gives it a nice, tight squeeze.

I close my eyes for a second, feeling a little unsteady and lost, wondering why this woman makes me feel this way, then forget about that when she begins jerking me off.

"Like that?" she coos. Pumping harder, squeezing tighter, and scooting forward so her breasts are pushing against my thighs.

Oh, but I see her evil plan. I'm on to her now. She thinks she's gonna jerk me off and then say, *Thanks, but no thanks.*

I think not, you little tease.

"I will be fucking your pussy," I say. Then realize I didn't actually mean to say that.

"You sure about that?" she asks, easing her face forward, gearing up for her next move.

184

Mmm-hmm. Gonna take my mind off the endgame with a blow job, are ya? Get me all worked up, maybe let me come on your tits, then walk out and tell Miles to bring you some pancakes and a coffee?

I'm one step ahead of you, lady.

I push her head away and bend down. Two seconds later I've got her tight little cut-offs unbuttoned and unzipped and I'm dragging them down her legs. Two seconds after that I'm tossing them into the corner.

I grab her thighs, push them forward, and lick her pussy through her panties.

Take that, Emma.

She groans and pushes my head down. "Yes," she mumbles. "Just like that."

I pull back, suddenly realizing I just gave up a blow job to eat her out, and say, "Oh, no."

"No what?" she innocently coos.

"You're doing it again."

"Less talking, more licking, Jesse. Chop, chop."

I stand back up and run my fingers through my hair. "You're totally doing it again. Forget it," I say. "I'm not eating you out."

She slips a hand between her legs and her fingers take up where I left off. "I offered you a blow job," she reminds me. "You wanted to do this, Mr. Boston. So what's the problem?"

"The problem is you're going to get off and leave me hanging. Again."

She stops playing with her pussy and instead leans back, propping herself up with her elbows. "Wow. You really give yourself a lot of credit, don't you? You're not even that good. I only came so fast last night because my vibrator broke two weeks ago and I haven't had time to replace it."

"Is that right?" Then I point at her. "And fuck you. I'm not gonna fall into that pathetic trap and try to prove you wrong."

"Jesse?" she asks.

"What?"

"Do you want me to suck your cock or not? Because I'm totally willing." She pauses for an answer, but I don't know. I just don't know what the right move is. "OK," she says. "So you wanna keep licking me?"

"No."

"So we're done here?" she asks, rolling over on the bed to retrieve her shorts. She lies back on the bed, bends her knees, and pulls them back on. And the whole time I stare at her wet panties until her shorts obstruct my view. "Good. I'm hungry and I'm dying for some bacon."

She stands up and heads towards the door behind me, but I slip in and block her.

"Now what?"

I shake my head.

"Use your words, Jesse."

I point my finger at her face and say, "We're fucking or nothing."

"Or nothing?" She laughs. "Then I choose nothing."

"I'll turn this fucking plane around," I threaten.

"I'd like to see you try," she growls.

We lock eyes and glare. Daring the other to blink first.

"Get back on the bed and take off those shorts," I command.

She lifts her chin and narrows her eyes, then runs her tongue across the edge of her top teeth and grins. She only has one pigtail at this point, so the whole display is absurdly cute and horrifyingly hot at the same time. "So you can continue?"

"So *you* can continue," I say.

"You choose blow job, then?"

"Fine," I say. "I choose blow job."

She taps my chin once with the tip of her finger and laughs. "I win."

"Hey, I'm the one getting a blow job out of this."

"You sure are."

"And I *will* fuck you later," I say.

"You think so?" she adds.

OK. I've had it. I'm taking charge of this woman right now. I lean forward and kiss her mouth, one hand tugging on that stupid pigtail. I press her back into the pocket door and slip the other to the button of her shorts, repeating all my hard work from two minutes ago.

"It's a promise," I whisper into the kiss.

"Challenge accepted," she whispers back.

CHAPTER TWENTY-ONE

EMMA

Hate fuck, round two.

Except there's no fuck. And there won't be later, either. He even knows this. He called me out just a few moments ago. But look how quick his mini-man brain forgot what was happening.

God, men are just too easy.

I don't even feel guilty about this. I won't. I refuse. Jesse Boston has this coming.

My hand finds his cock just as our eyes meet. He's grinning when I squeeze him.

You arrogant prick, I muse, just as I begin sliding my palm up and down his shaft.

"Do you like that, Jesse?" I coo. Plumping my lips a little, the way the models do it in the glossy magazine cover ads for our lipstick.

"Oh, I like it," he growls. "But I like this more."

He places his hand flat on the back of my head and urges me to kneel.

I don't even resist and my hand never stops tugging on his dick as I lower myself down and settle in front of his legs.

My smile creeps across my face as I tilt my head up to lock eyes with him.

"I'm telling you," he says. "You're not gonna win. You know I'm better at this than you are. You're about to give me what I want. You're on your fucking knees with my cock in your—"

He doesn't get any farther. Because I take my pouty little mouth right up to the tip of his cock and plump my perfect lips around his head.

He closes his eyes for a moment. Then opens them real fast like he didn't mean to do that.

But he totally did that.

It takes some concerted effort on my part not to laugh.

Was this my plan when I came up with the idea to out-power-date him today?

No. But so what? He put me here, he's refusing to back down, he's being cocky—so this is what he gets.

A little blow job is a small price to pay to see the look on his face when this is all over and he realizes— *this is all over.*

I take him a little deeper. My hand still working its magic. In fact, I double-hand him. Two fists around his fat cock.

Hmmm. I lower my eyes from his to get a better look at it.

It is kinda fat. Nice and thick. And long.

I'd forgotten how nice and thick and long, actually.

But so what? That's just good for me, isn't it?

Wait, no. I'm not going to fuck him. *Eye on the prize, Emma.* And the prize is…

"Oh, fuck yeah," Jesse moans. He's got both hands on my head now and he's rocking his hips with the rhythm of my motion. Pushing his cock a little bit deeper with each forward thrust. And I have to admit, this is kinda hot.

Wait, what was the prize again?

Yeah. I remember. I'm the boss here. Not him.

"Put your hands on my legs," he says.

I glance at his legs. Notice the muscles of his thighs through his tight jeans. Jesus, he's got nice thighs too.

"Do it," he says.

I don't do it because he tells me to. I do it because I just want to feel those muscular thighs for myself.

Oh, God.

"Yes," Jesse says. "Rub them. I like that."

I am rubbing them. His jeans are soft, but I suddenly wish he wasn't wearing them.

He fists my hair and starts to thrust forward with a little more determination. And now that my hands aren't in charge of how deep he enters me, he takes advantage of his newfound power and makes me gag.

I press on his thighs, pushing him back a little to give myself some space. But he doesn't yield to my subtle hint and I just barely gain enough distance to stop his cock from sliding down my throat.

OK. Fine. I see what he's doing. It's hard to get the upper hand when you're giving a blow job, but certainly not impossible.

I might not be a blow job expert, but I'm no amateur.

My eyes lock with his, daring him to give me what he's got.

"Oh, you're going to regret this," he says, smirking like the bossy baby Boston brother he is.

"Mmmm-mmmm," I hum, letting my vocal cords vibrate around his cock. We lock eyes again and if I didn't have his monster dick practically down my throat, I'd smile.

But he gets the idea. *Bring it*, my look says.

He grips my hair, pulling on the one pigtail I have left, then forces my face all the way to his stomach.

I gag hard this time.

Fucking asshole.

But I refuse to give in and let him win. I will not. I take it like a champ. I open my mouth as wide as I can, let him push himself inside me as far as he wants, and I will myself to hold it together. Staring up at him. Daring him to try it again.

He doesn't relent. Just holds me there. Doing his best to force me to give in.

But I don't.

I breathe through my nose and narrow my eyes.

"Oh, fuck," he says. Glaring down at me. "Fuck."

Take that, you cocky asshole.

He eases up first and I suck in a huge breath as saliva spills out over my lips.

"Jesus Christ," he says. And I'm pretty sure he's impressed. I'm pretty sure he wasn't expecting me to be so adept at this blow-job stuff.

But I don't even take a moment to relish his surprise. I swipe the spit off my chin and slap it on his cock with both hands, then give him a two-fisted hand job as I ease my head forward once more.

I don't wait for him to make me do anything.

I take him deep. I take him deeper than I've ever done before.

I make myself gag this time. But I hold it in. Breathing through it.

He's moaning things like, "Fuck." And, "Jesus Christ." And, "Emma, my God. My *God*!"

I come up for one quick breath and then dive back in, giving it my all. I bob my head back and forth, both hands still pumping, my lips, my mouth, my chin all slick with the wetness of my own saliva. His belt buckle jingles with the motion of my take-charge attitude. He bends his knees a little and his cock suddenly hits the back of my throat.

But I hold that gag in. I refuse to give him that kind of control.

I will win this little blow job battle, my friend. You just watch me.

I reach for the hem of my tank top and whip it over my head and suddenly my nipples bunch into tight peaks and pull my spectacular breasts up right along with them.

"Holy fuck," he groans.

"Mmmm-hmmm," I hum, still working him with my mouth. *That's right, motherfucker. Enjoy them while you can.*

My hands are really getting into it now. I squeeze, and slide, and pump, and tug and—

"Fuck!" he yells.

I'm pretty sure Miles heard that yell all the way up in the front cabin, over the thrumming jet engines, with two closed pocket doors between us.

And I do not care.

I am about to win!

His cock slips out of my mouth and I jerk it hard. Looking up into his eyes. And I say, "Come on my tits, Jesse. Come on them right now."

He doesn't want to.

I mean, of course he does. But he knows. He now knows just how bossy I am. Just how out of control he is.

Because he grits his teeth. Clenching his jaw. Trying his best to hold it in.

But my hands. Oh, my hands are magic right now. And his dick is slick with my saliva so they slip and slide along his shaft. Gripping tight.

"Do it!" I say. "And next time I'll let you come on my face."

Shit. That kinda slipped out. There's not going to be a next time. But whatever. It works. Because he opens his mouth, and pulls my hair, and the next thing I know his milky-white come is spurting all over my breasts.

I bite my lip to stop the smile.

195

He bows his head and closes his eyes. His cock still jerking and trembling from his release. His come still spurting out in small bursts.

I lean forward, grab a fistful of his shirt, and wipe my mouth.

He doesn't even care.

Not now, anyway.

But he will.

Take that, you arrogant bossy brother.

"Fuck," he says, sitting down on the bed and flopping backwards.

This gives me a really nice, long look at his cock. Because it's still hard and it flops back with him. Flat against his stomach. Lying to the side a little, accentuating the cut muscles of his hips.

Damn.

Why does he have to be so hot?

"Emma," he says, extending a hand.

I squint my eyes at that, but his are closed so he doesn't even see it.

"Come here," he says, when I don't speak or move.

"Why?" I ask, standing up so I can look down on him.

He's unbuttoning his shirt.

"Oh, no, motherfucker," I say. "We're not—"

"Shut up," he says, eyes still closed. "You fucked up my shirt already." He says this as he twists and turns to take it off. "Might as well use it to wipe your tits too."

I frown.

He throws it at me. Still, those eyes are closed. Like he's beat.

I catch it and shrug. It's probably a two-hundred-dollar shirt. So what the hell. I wipe his come off and throw it back, making sure it lands on his face.

He laughs, fucking eyes still closed, and tosses it aside. "Come here," he says. This time his fingers do that little beckoning motion. "I don't want to fuck you. I just want to hold you."

"What?" I snap.

He opens one eye. Grins. "That was amazing. I honestly—fuck. Was not expecting you to be so…"

"So what?" I growl.

"Just come here." He sighs. "I'll get you off while I doze."

"You asshole!"

But a moment later he sits up, grabs my wrist, and pulls me so hard, I land on top of him.

"There," he says, humming the words into my neck as he wraps his arms around me and holds me tight. "See. That's better."

And even though this is not what I was expecting or wanting, and being wrapped up in his arms implies I'm under his protection and that's not what I was going for…

I relax and let him hold me.

Just for a moment, I tell myself. *Just a few moments. Then I'll get up, put my shirt back on, and walk out the winner.*

CHAPTER TWENTY-TWO

The rumble of waves and the sweet, rocking motion of the yacht wake me up from a deep, heavy sleep. Damn. I sigh. It's so great to be back on the yacht.

"Are you awake, Mr. Boston?" an unfamiliar voice asks.

I crack open one eye, realize I'm lying face down on a bed, have a moment of panic that I'm not on the yacht and actually have no clue where I'm at. Then spy the portholes in the side of the cabin and relax.

"Ms. Dumas wanted me to serve you breakfast and let you know we'd be landing in about thirty minutes."

"Aw, fuck," I groan as I turn over.

My belt jingles as I do this and… I realize, my cock is hanging out. I squint both eyes up at the man standing over me with a concerned look on his face, and suddenly recognize Miles.

His eyebrows are raised when he glances down at my dick.

"Sorry," I mumble, then fumble with my pants and tuck the boy away. "Now… what the fuck is happening?"

I feel drugged. Did that little succubus drug me again?

No. I think this is just the hangover from last night's drugging.

"Breakfast is served, sir. I'm sorry I'm late. You said one hour, and it's been two and a half, but Ms. Dumas insisted I let you sleep it off."

"Did she now?" I ask, forcing myself to sit up so I can rub my hands down my face and take a deep breath to collect my thoughts.

"Would you like me to wash this?"

I remove my hands from my eyes and squint up at Miles. "What?"

"Your shirt, sir. It's…" He's holding it up with tiny, silver pastry tongs. "Soiled."

"Sure," I mumble, then look around and say, "You have a fucking laundry room on this thing?"

"No, sir. But the jet club has facilities."

"Jet club?" I ask. Still half in my sleep dream. My heart aching a little about not being on the yacht.

"Yes, sir. I'll have it washed and pressed for you when you return."

"Where are we going again?" I ask, looking down at the fold-out tray that hovers over the bed.

"I'm afraid I'm not allowed to tell you that," Miles whispers. "Ms. Dumas wants it to remain a surprise."

On the tray there's some kind of fizzy drink in a champagne flute, a tall glass of ice water, a miniature bowl of blueberries, and three teeny-tiny cinnamon rolls. I feel like Barbie and Ken will be joining me any minute now. I pick one up and hold it between my fingertips. "What the fuck is this?"

"A mini-roll," Miles says, as if these things actually exist. "They have exactly thirty-five calories and one net carb in them."

I drop it back on the plate. "I'm gonna need three of these in super-size, please."

"Yes, sir."

"I'm kidding," I say. "Wait. No. I'm not. If you've got grown-up cinnamon rolls I really would like a few."

"Very good, sir."

"And what's this?" I ask, pointing to the champagne glass.

"Sparkling orange juice sir. Non-alcoholic."

"OK." I sigh. "Where's Emma?" I'm pretty sure she didn't ditch me since we're still in the air. But you never know with this chick. She is one insane surprise after another. For all I know she took the parachute exit two hours ago and left me here just to prove she can walk out any time she wants.

"Working in the middle cabin, sir. She said for you to take your time and meet her out there when you're ready."

"Cool," I say, picking up all three mini-rolls and popping them in my mouth. "Mmm, these aren't bad."

"Would you like a dozen more?" And did I just detect a smile on Miles' smug face? "Or would you like me to bake you man-sized rolls?"

I point my finger at him. "You're cool, you know that."

"I do, sir."

"Sure, I'll take a dozen of the little fuckers if you've got them ready."

"I always make a full batch," Miles says. "She always eats them all." Then he winks at me and leaves. I catch a glimpse of Emma in the middle cabin before he closes the pocket door, but then she disappears.

Damn. The whole blow-job thing comes back to me. Who knew sweet, pig-tailed little Emma Dumas had that skill lurking deep inside her?

But shit. She did it again. No fucking.

I chuckle a little. But this time I got my reward and she got nothing.

Point goes to me.

I think.

Maybe not. I don't know.

I drink the entire glass of water, then the fizzy juice, then dump the entire bowl of blueberries into my mouth and chew as I stand up, button my jeans and buckle my belt.

I have no shirt.

But fuck it. I feel a little better. I didn't sleep at all after Emma left me last night. I had to get Zach to Photoshop me a fake drug test report, then plan my revenge.

Which is not really working out the way I imagined.

But I was tired. She did drug me. No sleep, no food except one and a half ice cream cones. And I was angry.

I'm on my game now, son. On. My. Game.

I pull the pocket door open, ready to make my grand re-entrance into Emma's boring little life, walk through, and lean against the cabin with my arms folded in that way that pumps up my already spectacular biceps. I even flex my pecs when she glances up at me through a pair of adorable nerd-girl glasses.

But she looks away, uninterested, and says, "OK, get me those reports when you have them. I need the final numbers ready for Natalie by Monday so we can plan this next trip."

What a faker. There is no way she didn't appreciate what I just gave her.

She fixed her hair. And did she get rid of the pig-tails? No. They are bouncing alongside her face as she pulls the earbud out and places it on the table.

In front of her is the *Wall Street Journal*, a glass of orange fizzy, and two Barbie and Ken mini-rolls on a tiny little plate. She picks one up, still ignoring me, takes a bite—a fucking bite? Are you kidding me? The thing is only a bite big!—then sets it down on the plate.

"Did you get some rest?" Emma asks, peering up at me from behind those adorable glasses.

"I did," I say, flexing my pecs again.

She doesn't even glance at them. But she saw. I know she saw. "Did you eat?"

"If you can call that eating. What the fuck is up with your Barbie townhouse food?"

"What are you talking about?"

"Those," I say, pointing to the two crumbs of mini-rolls.

She glances down at them. Then up at me. "You have a problem with my cinnamon rolls?"

"You didn't eat the ice cream cone either." I slip into the chair opposite her then pick up her plate and dump the crumbs into my mouth and chew. Then I point at her. "I'm gonna challenge you to an eating contest."

She guffaws so loud I lean back in my chair. "Is that the only game you feel prepared to win today, Mr. Boston? Haven't you learned your lesson? I win everything now. I'm not that girl you once met." Then she cocks her head at me and narrows her eyes. "Didn't you see the way I ate your cock?"

"What?" I laugh.

She wants to smile. But she presses her lips together to tuck it away.

I nod my head. And I guess I don't have her self-control, because my grin is big. I don't know. I might like her. I mean, I did like her. Would like to like her still. But she's not letting this one-up bullshit go.

I do like that dirty talk though. So I say, "Well, I had my eyes closed for half of it. Maybe you could give me a play-by-play?"

This time she not only smiles, she laughs.

Got you.

"Where are we going anyway?" I ask.

"You'll see."

The door opens and Miles appears with a whole shitload of little rolls on a bright silver tray. "Your rolls, sir," he says, placing the plate down in front of me. Then he looks at Emma. "We're in descent now, Ms. Dumas. We'll be on the ground in ten minutes."

"Thank you, Miles," she says sweetly.

Why doesn't she talk like that to me?

I'm not a bad dude. OK. I was a bad dude. But I'm not anymore. "You should give me a chance," I say.

She narrows her eyes. "A chance to do what?"

I shrug. "You know. Date you."

"Date me?" she huffs.

"Yeah," I say, sitting up a little straighter. "If Johnny hadn't pulled me away from you all those years ago, we'd have been a thing."

"A thing? What kind of thing?"

"You know. We'd have fallen in love, and broke up a million times by now. Been in more fights than we could count. Hate-fucked so many times we lost count."

"So romantic," she says.

"We'd be... *that couple*. You know?"

"No," she says. "I don't know."

"That couple," I say again. "The one everyone hates because they're so in love, but all they do is fight. And break up. But then they can't live without each other, so they always get back together, even if they're not together."

"You mean… they have ex sex? And no one wants to be around them because they're so annoying. "

I point at her. "Yeah. There you go. *That* kind of couple."

"Why would anyone want to be that couple?"

"Because," I say. "It's true love."

"Sounds more like true hate. Definitely an emotional contradiction I want no part of. Quite probably a severe psychological condition that results in decades of misery."

"Or," I counter, once again pointing my finger at her. "Love is a battlefield and they're just both generals."

"You're insane." Then she finishes her fizzy drink and folds her paper. Takes out her phone and pretends to be busy so she doesn't have to talk to me.

But I sit there for the next few minutes just gazing at her with a new sense of awe.

Yeah. That's what this is. Love is a battlefield— thank you, Pat Benatar—and we're just both generals.

"I'll prove it," I say.

"I'm sorry?" she says, glancing up from her phone. "What's that mean?"

"You'll see."

I was gonna say, *Just wait till we fuck.*

But I decide that's what she wants me to say. She wants me to want her like that, just so she can say no and keep the game going.

But guess what?

I didn't get to be a general on the battlefield of love by accident.

A few minutes later we're landing and I'm looking out the window. Something I should've done earlier, I decide. But I was pret-*ty* distracted.

"Palm trees," I say. "Blue-green ocean. Beach."

Emma just grins and says, "Welcome to Key West, Jesse Boston. You wanted to take me back in time? Here's your chance."

And all I can think, when I walk outside and let the hot, summer, Florida sun hit my bare chest, is, *Well played, Ms. Dumas.*

Well played.

CHAPTER TWENTY-THREE

He's smiling.

That wasn't the plan. I didn't start this little adventure to make him happy. "Why are you so happy?'

"What?" He chuckles. "Why wouldn't I be happy? I'm in Key West with the girl who got away. Fucking sun. Fucking ocean. Fucking beach. This is my jam, girl."

I can't help it. I laugh.

"Besides, you're happy too."

"I didn't mean to laugh. It's just... your *jam*?"

"That's what all the cool kids say now."

"No, it isn't."

He shrugs. "I'm cool. You know it. I know it. Let's just stop pretending."

"Arrogant, that's what you are."

He points at me and grins. God, why does he have to have such a sexy grin? "I wish I had grown up here. You're so fucking lucky." And then his smile falls. Just a little as he looks out the window at the ocean. "God, I miss it."

"The beach?" I ask.

"All of it. The wind. The salty air. The rocking motion of the yacht." He looks at me. "The idea that you could set sail and end up on the other side of the world, ya know?"

"So. Go do that. No one's stopping you, right?"

"No," he says. "No one is. It's just not the same anymore."

"Why not?"

"I don't even own a yacht right now."

"So go buy one."

"And then what?"

"Sail it, of course."

"To where? With who? Why?" I don't know what to say to that, so he says, "The racing circuit was my excuse. That's why people came with me, why I had a destination, why I had direction. But they kicked me out for drugs."

"So race yourself."

He shakes his head. "It's just not the same."

"Hmm," I hum. Because I don't really get it.

We're in the limo on our way to the beach where my parents still run their little dive shop. Except it's a lot bigger now. I have three older brothers, none of whom went to college like me. And all of whom still live here doing their beachy thing, courtesy of me.

Not entirely true. But I did lend them money to get started in their respective businesses. My parents still own and run the dive shop I grew up with. Same little place near the marina. But I bought all the buildings next to them. So now the Dumas family owns and operates Dumas Diving, Dumas Boat Tours, Dumas Deep-Sea Fishing, and Dumas Water Adventures. We also own an entire block of cottages a few blocks away. Nothing super nice because my family is forever middle-class, no matter how much money they make. So we cater to middle-class people who just want to have a good time on the island and not kill their savings account.

"So…" Jesse says. "Where are you taking me?"

I thought this was a good idea when I came up with it. But now I realize… what the fuck was I thinking? I planned a day of water sports. Diving, of course. Because I'm a rock-star diver. Been doing that my whole life. So I was pretty confident I could show Jesse who's boss by taking him diving. He might not even be certified and then I could make a big deal about how we have to snorkel instead.

But going to the dive shop means meeting my parents.

Just what the fuck was I thinking?

"Emma? You gonna answer me?"

"You probably don't have a diving certification, do you?"

"Fuck yeah, I do. I don't have it with me. But you'll vouch for me, right?"

Of course he does. "Sure," I say.

"You're disappointed, aren't you?" He smirks.

"No, I'm not."

"Yeah, you are. You planned this whole day to out-date me."

"Well, I'm winning so far."

He leans over in the backseat of the limo and says, "I'll come in last every day of the week for that little surprise you gave me on the jet." Then he waggles his eyebrows at me, points to them, and says, "Yes. To be clear. That was innuendo."

I sigh.

"Seriously, you should let it go now. We're having fun."

I side-eye him.

"Liar," he says. "You are having fun with me. I'm a fun guy."

He is fun. I will admit that. And he's kinda been a good sport about the whole drugged-up kidnapping. I did feel pretty guilty about the drugs after he mentioned how hard it was to get clean. But he hasn't brought it up again. And he's not like… jonesing for coke, or meth, or whatever his drug of choice was back in the day. So, dodged a bullet there.

But again, my fucking parents.

The limo stops and Jesse looks out the window and up at the sign. "Dumas—oh, shit." He looks at me. "You brought me… *here?*"

I nod.

"Your parents' fucking dive shop?"

I nod again.

"Emma," he says. "I have no fucking shirt on."

I laugh. I can't help it.

"What? I can't meet your parents for the first time with no shirt on." He leans forward and taps on the window just in time to catch the driver before he gets out to open my door. "Dude," Jesse says, once the glass rolls down. "Take us to… somewhere to buy clothes. I need to change."

"Yes, sir. Mr. Boston," the driver says.

213

And I wonder, how the hell does the driver know who Jesse is? He's *my* driver.

We go back towards the shops and double-park alongside a beachy clothing store.

Jesse opens the door, looks at me, then says, "Just drive around the block a few times. I'll be out in five minutes." He jumps out and slams the door before I can even answer.

True to his word, he is standing at the curb five minutes later when we make our fifth trip around the block.

But it's what he's wearing that makes me suck in a deep breath of air and hold it.

I put on these shorty-shorts and the tank top because he asked for the pigtails. This was what I was wearing when we met. I didn't do it to flirt or make him want me. I really didn't. I just wanted to piss him off.

But he's waiting to be picked up wearing something very similar to what he was all those years ago now too.

My heart aches a little as he smiles and waves when we pull up. Because he's wearing tan board shorts, a white ribbed tank that shows every single hill and valley of his amazing muscle-y chest and stomach, a pair of dark sunglasses, and skater shoes on his feet.

He is twenty years old again and I am lost in time.

Falling. Just… falling and falling. The same way I did when he came up to my shaved-ice stand the first time we met.

He opens the door and jumps in, grinning like a boy. "OK. I'm ready now. Probably not the best choice for meeting the parents, but this here outfit was my *jam* back in the day."

He laughs at his joke. And I can't help myself. I laugh too.

Then I realize… I don't think he did this to play a game. He didn't choose these clothes to one-up me. This really is just him. The one I met. The one I loved and hated in the span of three days. The one who inspired me to spend ten million dollars on a second chance and commit more felonies than I can count.

"What?" he says. "Why are you looking at me like that?"

"These clothes," I say.

"I know. But… your parents are still cool, right?"

"What do you mean? Still cool?"

"You told me."

"When?"

"You know. Back then."

"I told you about my parents?"

215

"Yeah. Dive shop. Grew up there. Swimming with dolphins. Mom"—he points to me—"Silvia. And Dad, Jack." His eyes are bright now. Like he's really happy with himself. "And your brothers." He squints his eyes. "Alonzo." Pauses. "Tony. And…" He snaps his fingers. "Luke." Then he pauses again. "Weird fucking combination of names. Where the hell did Alonzo come from?"

"My grandpop," I say. "But we call him Lonz."

"Yeah," Jesse says, leaning back in his seat. "Yeah. I remember that now. Your grandpop. And fuckin' Lonz. Never met a Lonz before."

"You looked me up in there, didn't you?"

"What?"

"You Googled me."

"No," he says.

"Then how do you remember all that? Last night you had no idea who I was."

"I dunno. It just all came back, I guess."

"Liar," I say. "I'm totally gonna Google your family and be all, 'Hey, Johnny. How's Samantha doing? Hey, Joey. How was your trip to Easter Island?'"

He laughs. "You're insane."

"What? That's what you just did."

216

"There's no Samantha. And I'm one hundred percent positive Joey Boston doesn't even know where Easter Island is."

"Not the point. You're cheating!"

He leans over into my personal space. Way too close, in fact. But he slides his sunglasses up onto his head, places a hand on my cheek, and says, "Emma."

"What?"

We stare into each other's eyes. Those goddamned blue eyes look like the ocean outside my window right now.

"I'm not cheating," he says. "I just remembered, that's all. You made a big impression on me. That's what I've been trying to explain."

I start shaking my head, but his palm is firm on the side of my cheek. And then he leans in even closer and says, "Besides." He kisses me. Softly, right on the lips. Little bit of tongue. Just the right amount to encourage that tingly feeling building in my stomach. And whispers, "I can't cheat. Because this isn't a game," right into my mouth.

He pulls back, slides his sunglasses down over his eyes, and says, "Let's do this."

CHAPTER TWENTY-FOUR

I don't know why I'm not nervous about meeting the Dumas clan, I'm just not. I have this weird feeling. This strange new belief that I'm right where I'm supposed to be.

I get it. I get it. Last night this crazy bitch bought me in an auction, drugged me, kidnapped me, tied me up, released me, and then roped me into this entire day of mysterious jet travel and Barbie and Ken mini-rolls.

But I'm having a blast.

Serious fucking blast.

Just being here again. On Key West. The beach, the ocean, the sand and maybe… just maybe we find a sailboat and… nah. I won't even go there yet. It's not even necessary.

I have Emma. And I'm gonna meet her fam.

I'm fully prepared to throw with her brothers. That's what brothers do, right? I'm pretty sure it is. Hell, if Zach was a girl instead, I'd be throwing with every goddamned asshole who tried to date him. Her. Whatever. My point is, I'm ready to prove I'm down with those Dumas brothers. That's all I'm saying.

Did I ever come back here? No. I didn't. Never came back. And sure, part of that was because after my uncle died I had Zach around and I was partying almost every day. The missing trust fund. Johnny and Dad whispering secrets all the time, Joey... well, I have no clue what Joey was doing but I'm pretty sure he was fucking girls.

"This is a bad idea," Emma says when the limo rolls to a stop in front of her parents' dive shop.

I'm about to tell her to chill, I got this. But a woman comes rushing out of the dive shop waving her arms and yelling something I don't catch until I open the door and start getting out of the car.

"Emma!" the woman says. "Where did you go?"

Emma gets out behind me, looking cute as fuck in her little Daisy Dukes and pigtails. "What are you talking about, Mom?"

"You pulled up and then left! I thought you were kidnapped!"

"Mom, I was in my own car. You can't get kidnapped in your own car. I wasn't kidnapped."

I laugh. "Actually, you can get kidnapped in your own car, Emma."

She shoots me a look that says, *Don't,* then says, "We had to make a stop before we got out. That's all."

But... Emma's mother isn't looking at her anymore. She's looking at me. "Who is this?" she asks, eyebrows waggling at me in what is clear older-woman innuendo.

I wiggle back because that's what you do. "I'm Jesse Boston. Emma's boyfriend." And I do not have one ounce of guilt when I say it.

"He's not my boyfriend," Emma says quickly. "Just a friend. We're on a day trip."

"Day trip?" her mother asks. "No. You're staying the weekend now, missy."

"Mom, I wish I could but—"

"We'd love to stay the weekend," I say, then take Emma's hand. "But we don't have a room and—what?" I'm looking at Emma and she's making one of those slicing motions across her throat with her other hand. Like she's totally gonna kill me.

"Room?" Mrs. Dumas says. "We have a whole street full of cottages just a few blocks over. You can stay there."

221

"Oh," I say. And I get it. Emma was telling me to shut up with that gesture. Not that she's gonna cut my throat.

Though she might do that next. Because Mrs. Dumas is pulling me inside, yelling, "Jack! She came back! Don't call the police!" Emma trails behind me, helpless. And for a second I think... maybe I should've been worried?

Nah. Then I laugh.

"This isn't funny," Emma hisses.

"It was your idea," I mutter back.

"Emma?" Her huge father appears from a back room on the other side of the counter. "You're not kidnapped."

"Funnily enough," I say, "I was kidnapped last night."

"What?" everyone says.

"Kidding," I say, extending a hand to her dad. He's like six foot five, two hundred fifty pounds, easy. And his hand makes mine look like a child's.

I'm not a small dude. I'm almost six two. Little bit leaner than the head of this clan here. But I can hold my own.

I think I can, anyway. Until the screen door swings open, bangs against the wall, and three leaner, let's just call them super-muscular, Dumas clan members barge in.

"Who kidnapped Emma?" the first one says. Then stops. Because obviously no one kidnapped Emma. He's got to be a full inch taller than his father. Tattoos all up and down his well-tanned arms and chest. Did I mention he has no shirt on? He doesn't. He's also holding—wait for it—a barracuda. Yup. I'm pretty sure that's a barracuda.

While I'm picturing myself being beaten to death with a dead barracuda, the other two, equally as muscled up and mean-looking as this here first one—who I predict is our friend Lonz—stand next to him and fold their arms across their chests in a way that makes their biceps pop out like cannons.

I wait for the pec flex. The way I did back in the jet. But they are not fucking around. They are dead-ass serious.

OK. Yeah. I definitely cannot take the Dumas brothers. Maybe if Johnny and Joey were here, and Zach, and five or six of their closest friends… we might have a chance.

"She's fine," I say, laughing nervously and holding up both hands in surrender. "Just a little mix-up."

"Who the fuck is this?" the big one asks.

"Mouth, Alonzo," Mrs. Dumas chastises.

223

How did I know he was Alonzo? Um, maybe because he's just what an Alonzo looks like?

Anyway, there's like twenty minutes of bumbling explanations. Alonzo, Tony, Luke, and good old Jack decide they will not kill me, or beat me with a barracuda, once Emma and I explain—several times— that we just needed to pop over to the shops because I needed to buy a shirt.

That was awkward.

But ten more minutes of sidestepping the fact that their sweet, little pigtailed sister sucked my dick like a fucking porn star in her jet bedroom and then used my shirt to wipe my come off her tits, and we're all back on the same page.

In fact, we've agreed to stay the entire week in one of their cottages. Emma just nods at her mother as this arrangement is made, all the while waggling her eyebrows at me. And I can't figure out if she's innuendo-ing me for a whole week of sex in this cottage, or telling me that we'll be back on that jet tonight and to just play along.

Either way, I am bulldozed over by these people. Completely flattened like a pancake.

And I love it. I love every fucking minute of it.

But something else becomes abundantly clear during all this craziness.

She wins.

I cannot compete.

Emma Dumas's bossiness blows mine out of the water.

It's not her huge, overreacting, overprotective family, either.

I'm just... I'm falling, man. I'm falling fast. Hard. Like just jumped off a two-hundred-story building kinda hard and fast.

And getting kidnapped by her last night might be the best thing that ever happened to me.

"OK, listen, Mom," Emma says. "I will come back in a few days but I really do have something important to do on Monday, so—"

"What's more important than visiting your family? You never come home anymore. It's like you abandoned us."

"I was here two months ago."

"Two months." Her mother sighs. "You should be here every weekend for Saturday dinner like your brothers. Look at their busy lives. And they still manage to come over for Saturday dinner."

"You guys all live on the same street."

"What's your point?"

"I'm in the city. Three hours away by jet. I think my point was pretty obvious."

Her mother looks at me. "Saturday dinners have always been sacred in our house."

I nod at her. "Sure. Yeah. I think everyone should have Saturday dinners."

"Oh?" her mother says. "Does your family do Saturday dinner? Or Sunday dinner?"

"We don't do dinner."

Her mother, for serious, gets this really confused look on her face.

"You know... well. My mother... disappeared when I was a kid and my father did his best, but... yeah. We don't do dinner."

Emma's doing that little slicing-her-throat motion again. But her mother says, "I'm sorry, did you say your mother disappeared? Who took care of you?"

"Oh, mostly my older brother, Johnny."

"Well, we've had a nice chat," Emma says, interrupting. "But we've got plans today on the water. So we gotta get going."

But her mother isn't done yet, because she says, "Would you like to come for Saturday dinners, Mr. Boston?"

I brighten. "Uh... OK. Sure. Yeah. Actually that sounds fun."

"No," Emma says. "We're not even dating, Mom. He's just... ya know. A *thing*."

Emma's mom side-eyes her for a moment, frowning. Then looks at me again. "Does she always boss you like that?"

"Mom," Emma starts.

But good ol' Mom puts up a hand and continues. "She's always been so sassy. Don't let her scare you away with her sass."

I glance at Emma and beam her a smile. "I kinda like her sass."

Emma's face goes a little Bright Berry Beach Pink as she shrugs. "What can I say? I'm sassy."

"She's bossy too," her mom continues.

"Really?" I ask. "I hadn't noticed." Emma shakes her head.

"Yes," her mother says. She's just not letting this go. "She's very bossy, Mr. Boston." Then she hesitates and laughs. "Oh, that's cute."

"What's cute?" Emma asks.

"Mr. Boston?" her mother says. "Sounds a lot like Mr. Bossy to me. Maybe you've finally met your match, Emma?"

I glance at Emma and take her in. All the ways I've seen her over the past twenty-four hours or so. All the ways I remember her back when we were here, on this island together. She is quite something. She was always quite something.

"It's a pretty even match," I say. "In fact, the very first time we met she was working the shaved ice stand in Mallory Square and she bossed me into buying a souvenir cup."

Emma stares at me for a moment. That perfect pout of a mouth—the one that always looks like someone is perpetually disappointing her—lifts up just the slightest bit. She says, "How do you remember that?"

"I told you. You made quite the impression on me." We lock eyes for a moment. In fact, we *have* a moment. One of those memorable moments. One I might want to think about forever. One that might just change my life.

But it's interrupted by Emma's mom. "Now you don't have to come every Saturday night like my boys, Mr. Boston," Emma's mom says. "But I would appreciate it if you could have a regular schedule so I know how much food to make. So would you prefer the first and third Saturdays? Or the second and fourth? Sometimes there's a fifth, but not often. So I'll let those slide."

"Mom," Emma says. "This is Jesse Boston, for fuck's sake."

"Mouth, Emma," her mother snaps.

"He's not gonna fly down here twice a month to have dinner with a strange family."

"Uh," I say, holding up a hand. "I'd actually love to come. Thank you, Mrs. Dumas. I'll take second and third, if that's OK."

She walks towards me, pats my cheek as she beams me a smile, and says, "That's perfect. And you're very welcome. You should bring your brother Johnny too. I bet he'd like a nice home-cooked meal."

I take a moment to picture Johnny down here having dinner with me and then unexpectedly laugh. "Sure," I say. "I'll bring Johnny."

CHAPTER TWENTY-FIVE

After that awkward moment, I usher Jesse outside the dive shop and say, "This way."

"What are we doing?" he asks. "We didn't even grab equipment."

"Would you just let me handle things?" I say.

"Would I just let you? You've been handling them all freaking day."

"I am the boss," I say, then glance at him to see if he finds that funny or annoying.

He catches my look, so I quickly shift my eyes, and grin. Funny, I think.

"I'm gonna call you Little Miss Sassy from now on. You sassy little—"

"Oh, my God. Shut up already."

"—bossy girl," he finishes. "Which, by the way, I can't find it in me to hold that against you."

231

"No?" I ask, looking both ways so we can cross the street to the marina. "Why's that?"

"Because holy fucking shit. Your whole family is nothing but a bunch of bossy bossers."

I can't help myself. I chuckle at that. "You only got a spoonful, buddy. I hope you don't really plan on showing up for dinner because you're gonna get a heaping helping if you do."

"I kinda liked it."

"Which part?"

I glance over at him just in time to see him shrug. "All of it, I think. You forget, I didn't have a family like that growing up. Hell, I don't have a family like that now. Joey is always off doing—whatever the fuck it is he does. Parties, I guess. Fucks girls. But he's always doing it somewhere else. Ya know? Trying to avoid the tabloids, maybe. Not that he has to worry about that. They only care about me for some reason."

"And Johnny? You told my mother you were gonna bring him with you. She takes everything literally so in two weeks when you show up for Saturday dinner, he better be with you or you'll get an earful, mister."

"I honestly don't even know if he's alive."

I scoff.

"I'm fucking serious. I haven't seen him in forever. Years, actually."

"Jesus Christ, Jesse. You need to go check on him."

"I think he's OK. I was up on Joey's floor yesterday morning looking for a tux for the auction and I heard noises up there."

"What kind of noises?"

"Like pounding and shit."

"And you didn't go check?"

"No. It's Johnny."

"What if someone got into his place and they were like… fighting to the death?" He laughs at me. "I'm serious."

"It's Johnny. OK? He can take care of himself."

"Well, you guys are weird."

"That's my whole point. I'm weird and you're normal. I wanna try normal for a while."

I scoff again. "Jesse, you just committed to Saturday dinner in Key West two weeks a month for the rest of your life. Good luck getting out of it now. And by the way, I'm not coming with you. So if that was a plan to have two dates a month with me, it's gonna backfire."

"Fine," he says. "I don't need you."

"I don't need you either."

"Where the fuck are we going?" he asks, just as I lead him onto a long dock. "And how did you make all these arrangements, anyway?"

"Pfffffft. You slept forever on the plane. I had plenty of time to plan this." I side-eye him as we walk down the dock. Not turning my head because I don't want him to see me side-eyeing him, but I'm curious to see his reaction.

He's looking around. This is the dock for the big boats. I was just trying to show off when I made these arrangements. Show him who had the bigger boat in their pants. But now that I think about it, this will actually be a nice surprise for him.

He lets out a sigh as we walk up to the trimaran. "Jesus Christ. You're taking me out on this?"

"You don't like it?" I ask.

He shoots me a look that says, *Are you on drugs? I love it.* "Corsair 970. Is this yours?"

"Do you think it's mine?" I chuckle.

"You did buy a Huracán this morning to one-up me."

I poke a fingertip into the center of my cheek and say, "I did do that, didn't I?"

"It's yours then?"

Should I lie? Nah. "It's my brother Luke's personal cruiser. He said I could use it today. Dive equipment

234

all stowed, wetsuits down below, and there's even some fishing poles if we want to give that a go."

He stares at me for a moment. I can't see his eyes because of the sunglasses, but I know he's squinting them at me. Wondering what I'm up to.

"What are you up to?"

I chuckle. "Can't I just plan us a nice date?"

"I was threatening to put you in prison this morning, so call me suspicious. Maybe you're going to throw me overboard. Or strand me on some tiny sandbar."

"Well, you can think what you want. And sure, I did make this arrangement to show off. Maybe even convince you that walking out on me thirteen years ago was your loss, not mine. But"—I shrug—"now it just sounds like a nice time, don't you think?"

We stare at each other for a few seconds. Then he lifts his sunglasses up so I can see his blue, blue eyes, and says, "I didn't walk out. I keep telling you that."

"And I heard you," I say back. "I'm over it, OK? This is just like I said. A nice time, that's all."

We continue to lock eyes. Then he lets out a breath, drops his sunglasses down into place, and says, "Do you know how to sail?"

"I've done it enough to help you out, if that's what you're asking."

He looks at the sporty little trimaran and sighs. "Thank you."

"You don't need to thank me."

He looks back at me. "No. Really. I do. Because this"—he pans his hand towards the yacht—"this is me. This is what I do. And now I get to do it with you."

My stomach does this weird fluttery flip thing as he stares at me and suddenly I'm at a loss for words.

"I told you back then I'd take you places. Take you across the ocean and show you places. And I never did. But now…" He looks back at Luke's sailboat. "Now I can."

I nod. Smiling as he returns his gaze to me. Maybe even turning my trademark shade of Bright Berry Beach Pink. Because he's looking at me like… like I'm his best friend and his best girl. And even though I had no plans beyond showing him who was boss when this day started, right now I wouldn't mind being bossed around by Jesse Boston.

He hops onto the deck. Pauses, taking it all in. His gaze wanders up the very tall mast, then down to the sails, all packed away. I don't know him well. Hardly at all, in fact. But I can feel his mind whirling and twirling with ideas and plans for those sails once we get out of the marina.

"Where will you take me?" And then I realize I just said that out loud and didn't mean to.

He grins. Grins big. Then extends his hand and says, "Join me and see."

CHAPTER TWENTY-SIX

Home.

That's the only word that comes to mind once we motor out of the marina and Emma and I raise the sails. When the wind fills them and the ship lurches into it. When the spray from the salty sea air hits my face and the sun beams down on my bare shoulders— everything about my overturned world uprights itself again.

It's not that I don't sail anymore. I do.

But I haven't done it like this in so long, the last time I felt this free actually eludes me.

Certainly haven't sailed in the tropics since before my father died and I've never done it with a girl like Emma. Ever.

I have so many regrets about that weekend we spent together when we were young. Because I wasted it. Sure, we kissed and fucked. We stargazed and dreamed. But I could've done it so different. I could've done it better.

I set a heading for one of the eastern islets and just stand in the wind and let the stress and tension of more than a decade evaporate.

Never in a million years could I have predicted this day.

This morning I was angry. Fuming that Emma and her friends got the best of me last night. Embarrassed about the whole mess and eager to show her who was in charge. I was going to force her to spend the day with me. Make her miserable. Drag her to places she didn't want to go.

Maybe it would've turned out like this. I like her. I knew I liked her before I found out who she was and the history we shared. So maybe we'd have found this kind of peace with my plan back in the city. Have breakfast, and then... I don't know. I'd buy her shit she didn't need. Expensive shit to prove I could. But of course, that would've just perpetuated the hostility.

She has too much money to be impressed by *things*.

So I don't think so. I really don't.

I don't think I'd have come up with such a perfect way to impress her as she did me. And here's the thing. This didn't cost her much. Oh, the jet is expensive. The fuel, and Miles, and the crew. Not to mention the hangar fees. But that's just side money, really. Besides, I really don't think she was trying to impress me with the jet as much as let me know she and I are equals when it comes to that kind of shit.

But this yacht. This day trip sailing around the tropics. This is something else. It's not the money, because again, it's costing her the price of fuel and nothing more.

It's the thought that went in to it. And maybe… the fact that this is just something she can whip up by asking a few favors of her family.

And her family. God, what I wouldn't give to have her family. All that boisterous bellowing and macho posturing tempered by her mother's monopolization of everyone's Saturday night with the promise of a well-cooked meal.

Her day is purposeful. Not the way mine was planned. Different.

Maybe I'm making that up. Wishful thinking and shit like that.

But she planned this day for me. Only Jesse Boston would be so impressed with such an experience.

I glance at her now, her pigtails blowing in the wind, her eyes scanning the deep blue ocean. Every once in a while she points at something and says, "Dolphins." Or, "Sharks." Or, "Jellyfish."

She is at home here with me on this yacht as anyone could be.

When we get close to the little islets I'm heading for she helps me lower the sails and we motor in towards a sandbar.

There's other people sailing today, but no one close. It's just us when I drop the anchor and look at her.

"What do we do here?" she asks. And not in a snide way, either. More of an eyebrow-waggle way that comes with innuendo. I realize that's our thing now. We have a thing.

"Everything," I say.

Here is a sandbar. Small. Maybe forty feet long and twenty feet wide. There's is literally nothing to do here and yet my answer of 'everything' still rings true.

"Let's dive first," she says.

And then we take our time putting on the wet suits and gear. I listen attentively as she muses about her childhood. About all the things she did out here with her family. She actually knows where we're at. Which shouldn't surprise me, but does.

Everything about her is a surprise.

Then we're falling backwards into the ocean and everything goes silent except for the sound of underwater breathing and bubbles.

I am home and she brought me here.

Even though above the water there is nothing to see but the ocean lit up with the afternoon sun, below is something else entirely.

There are a few scattered patch reefs nearby. Nothing big or extraordinary. But we see a small octopus, and a few rays, and the bright-colored coral wave in the wind of water.

And every time I look at her pigtails floating weightless around her face, I feel every moment I've missed since that weekend thirteen years ago.

What would my life have looked like with Emma in it from the beginning? Would we really be that couple by now? The ones who argue and hate with as much passion as they laugh and love?

I don't know. There's a part of me that wants that. Wants to know someone so well that the fights are mostly meaningless and no matter how ugly they get, you know it's just temporary.

But there's another part that says this is better. We lived lives that were our own. She got her chance to shine and succeed and I found a way to be a better man. And we did that separately so we could come back together today, ready for what comes next.

What does come next?

I can't even begin to imagine. Because Emma Dumas is no ordinary woman and I am no ordinary man.

But somehow I think it could work.

I think we only get better together.

We don't resurface until we're out of air. We drop our masks and mouthpieces and laugh. I pull her along as I swim back towards the boat or she takes a turn pulling me.

Getting out of the water is always a bummer. You're so free and weightless in the ocean and then your buoyancy disappears and you realize you've got fifty pounds of equipment strapped to your back and a whole world of problems up here above the surface.

We flop down on the tarp between the main and outer hull, breathless, tired, and happy. She gets up first, peeling off her gear until she's down to her shorts and tank top. Then helps me, because I just lie there transfixed, watching her with a smile.

She sits down next to me, then lies down, propping herself up on one elbow. "Now what?"

I turn my head to look at her, pretty exhausted but not looking forward to the approaching sunset. Because I don't ever want this day to end.

"Now," I say, turning my face back up to the sky, "we be still."

"Did you like the dive?"

"Fuckin' loved it," I say, smiling.

"Me too," she says, turning over on her back. "I haven't done it in a long time. Been too busy with my city life to think much about Key West."

"You don't miss it?" I ask.

"Almost never." She turns back on her side again. Beams at me. "Until now, that is." She huffs out a small laugh. "I've never been on a dive date before."

"Me either."

"That's weird, right? I mean, I grew up diving. You're the big boat guy. And yet, it took all these years and this weird day to finally make it happen."

I turn now too. I just want to stare at her. Her pigtails are curling and drying in the late afternoon heat and sideways beams of sun. She got a little glow to her that only a day in the tropics can bring on so quickly. And she smells like a perfect summer sea.

"I've missed you," I say. Not really appropriate and kinda stupid, but I say it anyway because it suddenly feels true. Like this was the elusive emotion bubbling up inside me since I first saw her at the auction last night and I just now figured it out.

She starts to shake her head and laugh, but I don't let her brush off like that. Not this time. I lean over, positioning my body over the top of hers, and kiss her.

We sink a little deeper into the bouncy tarp in this moment. Like the weight of the world is on top of us, but disappears at the same time because we are still floating. Still suspended above reality, hovering in mid-air above the calm water below and the endless sky above. Rocking with the up-and-down motion of a moving sea.

"Now's your chance," she whispers into our kiss.

I know what she means. Now's my chance to get that fuck I've been wanting. Now's my chance to take control.

And I take it. I take all her control away and say, "Yeah. But I'm gonna pass."

"What?" She laughs.

"I'm gonna pass," I say again, still kissing her. "I don't need that right now. I just need this."

She must understand because she doesn't object. And we lie like that for a good long time. We watch the sun set and the stars come out. And I feel like I made good on those promises I made her all those years ago.

I will take you places and show you things.

And I have. At least… I've started to.

The night air grows chilly after a while and both our stomachs start rumbling. We motor back to the marina and ease up to the dock well after midnight.

I have a moment of regret that we missed Saturday night dinner with her family, but only a moment. And then we're back on the jet being served an elaborate meal of steak and lobster by Miles, who still looks as fresh as he did this morning.

My shirt is even waiting for me. Clean and pressed, just like he promised.

Emma drinks champagne and laughs as she tells me about how her mother will be monopolizing two of my weekends a month from now 'til eternity. And I listen, and smile, and picture it in my head as I down some fizzy orange drink.

I picture a whole life spent with Emma and the diving, fishing, boating Dumas clan down in Key West and everything in my world is right again.

CHAPTER TWENTY-SEVEN

"*Do you want to come up?*" I ask, just as he pulls the Huracán into the valet of my building. He didn't ask me to drive the Lamborghini, just took the key from the parking attendant at the airport and opened the passenger door for me.

Who gets to drive my shiny new sports car wasn't a battle worth having. Besides, I have this new urge to be under his control.

I've thought about this question for hours now. We're both exhausted and it's nearly dawn. But I have an unreasonable urge to keep him here with me.

It was a dream date. And while I kinda planned it that way, the entire thing was so perfect and beautiful, and unexpectedly real there's no way it could've been planned.

Except… we didn't have sex. And I really wanted to have sex. I'm hoping he's feeling the same way. I'm hoping he reads between the lines and says yes to my offer.

"No," he says.

I shoot him an open-mouthed look of shock.

"I want you to sleep for as long as you like. Then text me. Our weekend date isn't over yet, ya know. I have one more day with you, Ms. Dumas."

"Oh." I laugh, then suck in a deep breath of air. "OK. That sounds like a plan."

"Wait right there," he says, holding up a finger. Then he gets out of the car, leans in to the valet to say something as he palms him a tip. Then walks around to my side and opens my door.

When he extends his hand to help me out I take it, feeling slightly shy, then slightly foolish for feeling shy, and step out.

He doesn't let go of my hand. "What's going on here?" I ask. Because even though I can sense that something has shifted between us, I'm just not entirely sure what that shift means.

He doesn't answer me. Instead, he closes the car door, drops both his hands to my waist, and urges me backwards until I bump up against the car door.

Then he kisses me.

It's expected and unexpected. Yes, I figured he'd do this. No, I didn't think I'd feel this way when it happened.

I swoon for this man's kiss.

My head goes drifty and light, my legs go weak and shaky, and my stomach flutters with the wings of a million tiny butterflies.

Everything around us disappears. Nothing else exists when the tip of his tongue sweeps up against mine. He tastes like fizzy orange. Everything about him is cool and refreshing. He is some kind of new promise. Or maybe the disappearing memory of old regrets.

"Do you remember what I want you to do?" he whispers, pulling out of the kiss.

I open my eyes and nod my head.

"Say it back to me."

I know he's being bossy, I just don't care at the moment. "Sleep. For as long as I like. Then text you," I say.

He grins as his eyebrows lift up. Innuendo, I realize. "Perfect," he says.

And now he's backlit by the pink and orange of the rising sun stealthily forcing its way into the city between a maze of tall buildings. A beam hits my face, blinding me for a moment until I turn my head.

He turns my head back, positions himself between me and the sun, and kisses me again. This time I don't close my eyes. I watch his lips. Notice they are very nice, and soft, and—"Hmmm," I mumble. Because he put one hand behind my neck to hold me in this kiss a little longer.

He murmurs, "Gonna let me boss you today?"

And I say, "Sure." Which comes out very breathy, and sexy, and erotic. Kinda like a purr. Which I didn't mean to do, but ends up being totally appropriate because he chuckles a little and kisses me again.

"Good," he says. And this time when he backs out of the kiss I know our date is officially over because the valet pulls his little red Ferrari in front of my Huracán.

Still, he holds my hand in his. Takes two steps towards his car—and for a moment I think, *Holy shit. He's gonna take me with him.* Would I go? I'm totally going.

But then he lets my fingers slip through his hand and he turns and thanks the valet driver, then disappears inside the car.

I stand there like a love-sick teenager as he pulls forward. Then catch him waving at me in his rear view and wave back.

I don't know how I get up to my apartment. I have no clue at all. I just know I'm inside, peeling off my clothes, reluctant to change because I smell like the beach.

No, I smell like him. That's him all over me. The sun, and the wind, and the sand, and the sea. Every bit of it is him.

I sink down into my couch cushions and sigh just as my phone rings in my pocket.

Mila.

I stare at the screen, debating if I should answer it or not, then decide nope. Not gonna have that conversation right now. I just want to rest and... think about him.

I turn it off so there's no more debate, place it on the coffee table, and then flop over on the couch and close my eyes—my body still rocking with the motion of planes, and boats, and...

When I wake up it's almost evening.

I still smell like Jesse's day and that thought evokes an automatic smile. When I turn my phone on the home screen states I have nine missed messages. Eight texts from Mila and the girls, and one, a voicemail, that's from Mr. Bossy Brother himself.

I press play:

"Hey. This is Jesse Boston. You know, that guy you drugged and kidnapped because I was a dumbass drug addict back when we first met thirteen years ago and I didn't have the good sense to call you and explain why I had to be a douchebag and bail out so quick? Yeah. Me. Hard to forget, easy to miss when I'm gone. Oh, no, wait. That's you."

Holy shit. Drifty, flighty, light-headed butterflies in my stomach.

"I hope you got some sleep. I did. Couple hours, at least. I'm taking this no-pick-up as a sign that you enjoyed yours more than I did, but you could also be ignoring me. I'd say there's a sixty-forty chance that you're ignoring me. But I'll take those odds. You might also be asking yourself, *Hey, did I ever give this asshole my number?* The answer is no. I called myself from your phone while you weren't looking. Always one step ahead. Really, almost never one step ahead, if I'm being honest. But. I give it a go every once in a while. So… wanna know what I dreamed about?"

Oh, man. I just fell all over again. So hard.

"We swam with the dolphins but then we turned into mer-people."

I laugh.

"And Johnny and Alonzo were like… warring mer-kings? Or some shit. I'm not totally clear on the mer-people political hierarchy, but Joey and your middle bro, Tony, traded sides, I guess? So Tony was working for Johnny and Joey was working for Alonzo. And then Johnny threw this sissy-girl fit about family loyalty and then your mom called everyone to Saturday-night dinner and made us leave our spearguns and tridents at the door. And then the dog said—I didn't see a dog at your dive shop, so I don't know where he came from—but he said, 'No dogs allowed,' when the dolphins tried to join us."

I can't stop laughing.

"It was a pretty cool dream. I think it means I miss the beach. And sailing. And I had fun yesterday. And you totally won our little bossy game. Which is now

255

over, by the way. And I might want to marry you and your crazy family because how many families could keep up with the Bostons, ya know? Not many. And... yeah. It all makes so much sense in that context." He takes a deep breath and says, "So. Don't bail on me, Emma. Don't pull a Jesse. Call me when you get this. I would like to take you out on a date tonight. I'll even let you drive."

I want to listen to it all again. Maybe even memorize every word, but I want to call him back more.

"Ms. Dumas," he says, picking up my call. "Did you have an excellent rest?"

"I did," I say. "And I listened to your message."

"Shit, what did I say? I can't remember."

"Seriously?" I huff.

"No. I wrote it down and recited it word for word before I called."

I laugh but I can't tell if he's kidding.

"I'm kidding," he says. "I winged it. Was it OK?"

"It was... pretty damn adorable, actually."

"Pretty. Damn. Adorable. I'll take it. So would you like to date me tonight?"

"As opposed to tomorrow night?"

"Tomorrow night we could be married."

"Oh, man. You're a funny guy."

"I'm a fucking joy. But really. Can I pick you up? Or," he says, "you can pick me up. How 'bout that?" I swear, I can hear his eyebrows waggling at me.

"Your innuendo is showing." I giggle.

"I try," he says. "I do my best."

"Yeah. I'll pick you up. Should I... I don't know, buzz your butler when I arrive? Or how does one pick up a Boston Brother from that monstrous building you live in?"

"His name is Zach and he's my cousin, remember? He'll meet you downstairs and bring you up. That way I can maintain my image as mystery man, you know?"

"Sure," I say. "I get it. One must not give up on their mysterious persona too quickly."

"What time?" he says.

"Give me two hours."

"I'm counting the seconds, Ms. Dumas."

"I might be early."

"I wouldn't object to you coming now. That was not innuendo. Unless you want it to be."

"I have to shower and change. I'm still in my pigtails."

"Awwwwwww. Is it too much to ask that you wear those again?"

"Yes."

We both laugh.

"Two hours."

"I'm holding my breath. Don't be late or I'll die."

I hang up because I cannot stand how adorable he is.

And then waste ten whole minutes replaying his voicemail until I have the entire thing memorized.

I choose a short, loose-fitting, summer dress with revealing cold-shoulder sleeves. It's yellow, and has a flirty skirt, and says casual summer evening. Yellow looks fantastic with my dark, wavy hair and the sun I got yesterday really makes my skin glow. I accent it with a pair of strappy silver wedges and a little silver bag for lipstick and phone.

When I look in the mirror everything about me says beach.

That's what I'm going for. I want Jesse to think of our day together yesterday. I'm kinda proud of myself for planning that whole experience. Yes, I did it out of spite, and revenge, and maybe a little bit of hate.

But it kinda backfired on me. Because by anyone's standards it was pretty damn perfect. Even my family. That was a move meant to put him in his place and make him uncomfortable. Let him know I'm protected by these big Dumas men and he should never fuck with me or hurt me again.

And now he has a standing Saturday night dinner invitation.

Life is so weird.

I drive the Huracán because sure. I bought it to show off and show him up, but I kinda like that monster. It definitely sends the right message pulling up to the Boston Brothers' building.

Now that building is a character in its own right. And not that I stalked the Boston boys when I moved here to the city with the girls for Bright Berry Beach headquarters, but OK, maybe I did stalk them a little. Because I know all about this building.

Called the Bossy Building by locals and built mid-last century, it's a contradiction of sorts. On the one hand it's tall, and flat, and smooth. Very modern in that respect. But it's also made of these almost-white stone blocks and tapers up to a point as it climbs into the sky.

There are open terraces surrounding the top five floors and they used to throw parties up there when the father was still alive. There are also gargoyles. Very creepy gargoyles. You can't see them from the ground, they're way too high up, but I've seen pictures. Weird contorted faces, some half-human, half-animal. A few that are all animals—a bull, a stag, a bear, and a horse. And then there are six that resemble the Boston Boys themselves. Including the father, the uncle, and that cousin of theirs.

No one knows when those were made. There doesn't seem to be a record. But it had to have been in the last forty years because that's when Boston Senior bought the building.

But crazy as that is, the really interesting thing about this building is the land surrounding it like a moat. You can't drive up to the building. The street is a good hundred yards away on all sides. It literally takes up an entire city block.

And in that space there's one of those spurting water sculptures. The kind that shoots water up in a straight line in a random pattern. Only, there's hundreds of those little spouts around the perimeter of the block so they make a walled-in-water courtyard of sorts. And the only way to get past without getting wet is to enter the courtyard on the west side of the building.

It's not the only building in the city with these water fountains, there's a few in other neighborhoods. Kids are constantly running through them and families hang out at those other city water parks during the summer.

But the Bossy Building is deep in the financial district in a neighborhood where people like to work, but not necessarily play. They certainly don't raise families there.

So the whole thing comes off more like a way to keep people out or herd them to the west side of the building than it does a work of city art or park for recreation.

Privacy. Yeah. That's what those water spouts say. Keep out.

Two valets appear immediately when I pull the Huracán up to the west side of the building. One opens my door while the other offers me his hand and says, "Welcome to the Bossy, Ms. Dumas. May I help you out of your car?"

"Sure," I say, taking his hand and stepping out of the low sports car.

"This way, please. Mr. Boston is waiting for you over there."

I walk around the car and stand at the entrance carved out by the wall of water spouts and look down the marked stone path that leads to the front doors to find, not Jesse, but Zach Boston, waiting patiently about halfway between me and the building. Illuminated by spotlights aimed at that particular spot on which he stands. His hands clasped in front of him.

Head up and back straight. Wearing a dark gray suit and silver sunglasses.

I glance up at the building. It's dark out, so the top five floors are also lit up with spotlights and I swear, they are positioned just so, so that the gargoyles cast shadows upward like demons in a horror movie.

Dramatic, right?

These Boston Boys really know how to make an impression.

But why am I surprised?

My first date with Jesse Boston was thirteen years ago and he's been haunting me ever since.

I take a deep breath and walk forward. The valet does not follow me, so I approach Zach Boston alone with more than a little bit of apprehension.

This is what I wanted though, right?

Yes, I tell myself. *This is what I've always wanted.*

Zach waits until I am three paces away before he greets me. "Ms. Dumas," he says, extending a hand. "I'm Zach, Jesse's assistant. Would you like to come with me?"

I shake his hand politely then say, "Yes, thank you."

We walk forward towards the building and there's a cool breeze in the courtyard that seemed to be missing from the rest of the city. A chill runs up my body and I rationalize it by coming up with all kinds of semi-scientific explanations due to the water wall, and the slight mist, and the night air.

But I'm not sure any of that makes as much sense as the real reason I'm chilled.

They are a little bit scary, aren't they? These Boston Boys.

So secretive, so elusive, so rich and powerful.

And dirty, I remind myself.

They're dirty.

But I push those thoughts away when Zach and I pass through the automatic doors and into the lobby.

It's an austere space. No chairs. Not a single one. No reception desk. Just a line of metal detectors—not operational at the moment, since it's Sunday night— and just past those there are dozens of electronic turnstiles that must be activated with a badge before you're allowed to pass through.

There's no security. At least, that's what I think until I look up and spy the cameras.

Zach and I bypass the turnstiles, instead walking through two glass double doors under a large steel archway, which also requires an electronic signature to activate.

These people take their security seriously.

"It's all very dramatic," Zach says, chuckling a little bit to put me at ease. "But the companies who rent space here in the Bossy all require it. The private elevator is this way."

He waves a hand to a little wing of sorts and I go first, stopping in the middle of a bank of elevators. There's four. Which seems excessive when the private floors only house three brothers and an assistant.

But what did I really expect?

This is who they are.

Dark brothers with dark secrets. And that little admission Jesse gave me the other night was just the beginning.

The elevator is as austere as the lobby. Plain stainless-steel box. But it's quick and the floors tick off in rapid succession as we ascend.

Then we're there. The doors open and before me is... not what I expected. At all.

Because it's another lobby. A vast long lobby with floor-to-ceiling windows overlooking the twinkling night skyline of the city.

And standing at the windows, dead center in this lobby, and backlit by the city lights, is Jesse.

He turns to face me as I walk forward, my wedges silent on the shiny black floors.

"Well," he says. "This is me."

264

The elevator doors close and when I glance behind me, I see that Zach has disappeared. Either in the elevator, or possibly down one of the two long, wide hallways that open up on either side of the lobby.

"Does it scare you?" Jesse asks.

"Should it scare me?" I ask.

"Probably," he says.

I smile. Unsure of who he really is. But his tone is light and when he steps out of the shadows I see he's smiling. So I make myself take a deep breath and relax.

It's still him. Same golden boy I spent the weekend with.

Just a little darker now. My fantasy not quite matching up with his reality, but it's OK.

"Well," I say when he stops just two paces away. "It's definitely imposing."

"Which part?" he asks.

"Um." I laugh. "All of it?"

"There's a lot you don't know about me," Jesse says. "About us, actually. What I've told you so far is just… what I know, Emma. And I don't know much either."

"What do you mean?"

He shrugs. "It's all very need-to-know. They never wanted me to know, I guess."

"Who?" I ask.

He's wearing a suit now. Dark gray, from what I can tell in the hazy light. Deep red tie. Hair groomed slick and a little bit of stubble on his chin that looks dark, but can't be. Because I know for a fact that he's blonde. So that golden-boy persona really is gone now and in its place is this... other man.

This mysterious figure with secrets so deep, he doesn't even know them.

"Johnny. My dad. My uncle too, I guess. Though I'm not sure how much blame he's earned, since he died back when I was twenty."

"That day," I say. Picturing our last day together on that very first date.

"Yeah, that day."

He leaves the rest unsaid. The part we're over now. The drugs and disappearing act. And we stand there in awkward silence and hazy, filtered light from the outside world.

"What is this place?"

He looks around, then back at me. "My home, I guess."

"It's a lobby, Jesse."

He nods. "I know. Not very homey. But..." He shrugs and looks a little more innocent and light. More like the man I thought I knew instead of the one I don't. "But it's all I really have left, you know? So I stay, I guess."

"It's not bad," I say, glancing around. There's literally nothing to look at but him and the windows. Or the floor. But the floor is creepy. So shiny and black.

"There's more," he says. "I have a whole floor, remember? You wanna see it all?"

I don't know why I hesitate, but I do.

"Or… you can leave if you're not into it."

And I have to admit. I might want to leave. "I just don't understand what's happening," I say.

"No, me either." Then he closes that short distance between us and places both his hands on my hips as he leans in. Kisses me. The kiss is just as nice, just as perfect, just as sexy as it's always been. But then he whispers, "I won't hurt you, if that's what you're afraid of, Emma. None of us will."

Which implies… what? That they hurt other people?

"Should I take you back downstairs?" he asks. "Or can you find it in yourself to take one more chance with me?"

And I don't know what to say.

I really have no clue what the right choice is. Because that power play game we were playing all weekend was bullshit. The whole thing was bullshit.

I am nothing and no one compared to these people. And it's not about who has more money, or who has a bigger jet, or a better, flashier car.

My influence over him was a carefully crafted illusion.

The last three minutes since I pulled up to this building tell me all I need to know about how different Emma Dumas and Jesse Boston really are.

And how decidedly unequal the division of power would be in a relationship with him.

CHAPTER TWENTY-EIGHT

She's gonna run.

I see it. Picture the whole shit show in my head. Maybe she gives some babbling explanation or maybe she doesn't. Won't matter. I know how this ends. I've lived in this world, in this building, in this skin my whole life. And even I don't know what to think about it. Even I don't fully understand it.

Why do people think I escaped with drugs and alcohol? Why did I run away to sail the world? Why does Joey fly all over the fucking planet partying like an asshole? Why does Johnny lock himself up in that tower of his own making?

This is why.

No one knows this, of course. Because no one knows *us*.

Not even us.

269

So how can I expect Emma to get it?

"Listen," I say. Because I don't know what to do to make her feel better. I don't know how to change something that is so... intrinsic. So much a part of me. But I know I have to at least try. "Just give me ten minutes, Emma. Just ten minutes. That's it. That's all I'm asking for." I look down at her. Have the urge to kiss her again and make this all go away. Pretend it's not happening.

Part of me wishes I didn't invite her over. But if we're going to be together—and I really want to give that a try—then she has to know what she's getting in to. And she has to find a way to navigate her way through this... whatever it is that hangs over our family like a thick, black cloud.

She lifts up her head and meets my gaze. Locks eyes with me. "Who are you people?"

"I wish I had a straight answer for that. I really do. But all I can say is... we're just... us. That's all I know. This is me, OK? And I invited you here so you can know me. The real me, Emma. Not the messed-up guy in the tabloids. Not the drug addict or the alcoholic. Not the guy you thought I was when I left. And not the guy you think I am now."

"So... this whole weekend was what? A lie?"

"It wasn't a lie."

"My family. I brought you to meet my family. Why did I do that?"

I sigh. Long and loud. "That was me. I swear." I know it's not a laughing matter and nothing about this moment has earned a laugh. But I laugh a little. "With you, I'm the real me."

"Then who is this?" She pans her hand around the apartment. "What is this? It's fucking weird, OK? The whole thing is weird. That security downstairs. Who rents a space like this?"

"I mean… that's all public record and—"

"That's not what I'm talking about and you know it. What kind of family lives on four different floors of this creepy fucking building? Why am I standing in a lobby that's supposed to be your apartment? And what kind of businesses need the security you offer?"

"Do you know what I do for a living?"

"You said you're a consultant. For yacht people. Racing, or whatever."

"Yeah." I laugh. "That is pretty much my only job. But I don't work much. I don't need to work."

"Neither do I," Emma says. "So if you're trying to impress me with your money, it's not gonna fly."

"That's not what I'm doing," I say, feeling defensive. "I mean, Jesus Christ. We haven't even had sex yet, Emma."

"Yes, we did. Thirteen years ago."

"That doesn't count."

"Since when?"

"Just… can you listen to me for a minute? We didn't have sex yet because I didn't want to."

"Oh, that's much better."

"I mean, I didn't want to make the same mistake I did before. I wanted to enjoy our weekend getting to know each other. And I feel like we had such a perfect day yesterday that I didn't want to change it. Or take away from it. And when you offered to pick me up I decided… 'OK. Let her in. Let her see the real me. What she's getting into before we take this any further.' And that way, if we did take it further, you'd understand me and wouldn't feel blindsided when you…" I sigh. Throw my hands up in the air. "Saw all this."

She looks around. At the hallway to the left of the bank. Of elevators. To the right, the other hallway. "What is it?"

"It's a fucking office space, Emma. That's it. Just an office space that pretty much looks like every other office space when you get off the elevator."

"When did you move in here? How old were you?"

"Twenty," I say. "I told you that. I didn't grow up alone, if that's what you're asking."

She glances up at the ceiling. Then drops her gaze to the floor. "You grew up down there. One floor below?"

I nod. "Yeah."

She takes a deep breath and holds it for a moment. Thinking, maybe. "OK. Then show me that."

"Why?"

"Because I want to see where you come from."

"This is my home now. Why don't you want to see this?"

"Because I don't understand *this* yet. But if I can start at the beginning, maybe it'll make sense after."

"It doesn't look the same, Emma. No one uses that floor anymore. Not since my uncle died."

"You mean when your father went crazy."

For a second I'm pissed. Because she doesn't even know my father. But then that anger fades, because she's not wrong. "I haven't even been down there in more than a decade," I say. "I don't even know what's down there."

"Show me," she says.

I can feel that this is a hard limit for her but I'm still reluctant. "Johnny's the only one who goes down there." I say that more for my benefit than hers.

Because even though I don't really know what Johnny does with his time, I have an idea. And whatever is left of the family floor below this one, it's probably been claimed by Johnny.

I don't want to start there. I don't want her to see that. Not yet. Not first.

"I want to see it, Jesse."

"It's not me," I say. "This is me. See *this*."

"That first. Why are you so resistant? It's just a place. What are you afraid of finding? What are you afraid I'll see?"

"I don't know." And it's the truth. Mostly. But I have an idea of what *could* be down there. And I don't want to find out for sure this way. Not with Emma next to me. Judging me.

"Take me," she says. "If you like me, you should trust me."

I laugh. "That's funny. Because you sure have jumped to a lot of conclusions about me over the years."

"Maybe that's because you fed me a lot of lies, Jesse. Now's your chance to show me the truth."

"You know what? Fine. Fuck it. Let's go."

I turn towards the elevators and find Zach standing there. "Dude." I laugh. "What the fuck. You snuck up on us."

"What the fuck are you doing?" Zach asks, looking at Emma, then me.

"We're going downstairs."

"Yeah, I heard that part. Why?"

"Because I want to see it," Emma says.

"Who gives a fuck what you want?" Zach says, glaring at her. Then he looks at me and shakes his head. "Don't do it."

"Why?" Emma asks.

He points at her. "Be quiet, Emma. This isn't about you. This is about *him*." And then he points to me.

There's a long moment of silence as Zach and I lock eyes. "Do you know what's down there?" I ask.

"No," he says. "But I can guess. And so can you. And she can't see that."

"Why?" Emma demands.

Neither Zach, nor I, even look at Emma. We just continue to stare at each other. I shrug. "Maybe it's time to know."

He looks at Emma and says, "Go home, Emma."

"No," she says. "I'm not leaving unless Jesse kicks me out." Then she turns to me and says, "If you tell me to leave, I will. But I'll never come back."

Up until this girl, in this moment, I wouldn't have hesitated to say, *Get the fuck out.*

But I think about our day yesterday. Her home town, her family dive shop, her family. My standing invitation for Saturday night dinners. The trimaran, the sailing, the sandbar, the diving, the sunset, and the stars.

What a perfect day.

And I admit, I want more of that. I want her. I think only Emma Dumas, of all the possible women in this world, can handle this. Can handle me. *Us*. My family.

"Zach," I say.

"No," he interrupts. "Not like this, Jesse. We've let it go all these years. We sealed it all up and locked it away and now you want to open up that fucked-up crypt in front of this... stranger? We were gonna do it together. One day. We made a pact."

"What the hell are you two talking about?" Emma says.

"Us," Zach continues. "Baby Bostons, right? We get no truth. We get no explanation. Hell, I didn't even get the damn trust fund. We made a pact."

I look at Emma, helpless. She's shaking her head. "If you don't, I'll leave. I'll walk away. I won't get involved in something... weird after just one weekend, without knowing. Without making that choice for myself."

I look at Zach. He's shaking his head too. "I can't stop you, but I'm going on record that I don't agree. You don't know her. She could be setting you up."

"Setting him up for what?" Emma asks.

"See," Zach says, "if you had any clue what was happening right now, you wouldn't have to ask that."

She turns to me. "Make a choice. We're talking in circles and I'm getting tired of it."

"Do you even have the code?" Zach asks. "Because I sure the fuck don't."

"I don't know," I admit. "I have the old code. But I have no idea if it still works."

"You don't think Johnny changed it?"

"Only one way to find out, I guess." I take Emma's hand and start leading her down the north hallway.

She resists, planting her feet in place. "Where are you going?"

"To the entrance," I say. "You can't get to that floor from this elevator bank. It's been bricked up. We have to go this way."

She still hesitates when I tug on her hand. And I give her a minute to change her mind.

But then she relents and follows me down the hallway. Zach follows us, his footsteps echoing behind me, but he doesn't make any more protests.

My heart begins to beat faster as we approach the end of the hallway. There's nothing down here but one set of double doors.

They open up to another elevator hallway. This time just one. And it only goes down one floor.

I press the code to call the elevator and part of me hopes it won't work. It's an old code so there's a high chance I'll be saved from whatever revelations are awaiting me downstairs.

But did I really think Johnny would change it?

Never.

The doors open and the three of us walk inside, then turn around as they close. Zach presses the button on the panel marked with an X and we descend for exactly one second.

The elevator dings our arrival and the doors open.

CHAPTER TWENTY-NINE

It's dark, so at first I can't see anything except the faint outline of the floor-to-ceiling windows covered with some kind of translucent paper.

Why did I insist on coming down here again?

"Where's the lights?" Zach whispers as the three of us walk forward. And for a guy who was totally in alpha-asshole prick mode upstairs, he sure is reverent and quiet now.

"Over here," Jesse says. He lets go of my hand and walks away, disappearing into the shadows. A few seconds later the lights come on in the little lobby. It's not a lobby like upstairs and I realize that this is on the other side of the building. So somewhere on this floor is that lobby like upstairs, but this is some side entrance, I guess.

There are built-in cabinets on every wall. But more like cupboards, because it's not open shelves. So what's in there? I have no clue. I'm just about to ask when I notice what's covering the windows. "Oh, what the fuck?" I say. "Newspaper? That's not creepy. Not at all."

I catch Jesse and Zach trading a look, but they don't say anything.

"What?" I ask. "What am I missing?"

"Nothing," Jesse says. "There's nothing to see here. So—"

"Oh, no," I say. "We're here now, buddy. And I know this place is huge. Let's go."

They trade another look and this time Zach just shrugs. "Up to you," he says.

"Fine," Jesse says. "I guess…" He looks around, chooses a hallway, and says, "This way."

I follow him to a door and Zach brings up the rear. I'd be lying if I said having him behind me wasn't making me nervous. But when Jesse opens the door it's just a big room. A massive room, actually. But a normal room.

He lets out a breath, which I interpret as relief. "OK," he says, panning his arms wide. "Living room."

And it does look like a living room. If said living room was say, maybe, the size of a hotel lobby. It has seven separate seating areas. Couches and chairs artfully arranged in clusters for talking. Except they are all covered in white sheets. Like this is not just any hotel lobby, but a haunted one.

I get past that and notice there's no newspaper on the windows and instead of being clear, uninterrupted glass like upstairs in Jesse's lobby, these have panes. Lots of them. So many, in fact, the window looks like a freaking checkerboard.

There's a whoosh of fabric and a swirling of dust as Jesse removes one of the sheets over a long, pale-green, velvet couch.

He smiles down at it. Then looks at me. "I slept here all the time."

Zach laughs. Then pulls off another sheet across the room to reveal a pale-gray velvet couch. "This one was mine, wasn't it? Shit, I remember that now." He points to another couch and Jesse walks over and pulls off the sheet. Another gray couch. "That was Joey's, right? And this one"—he pulls off yet another sheet off yet another couch, pale green this time—"was Johnny's. He said—" Zach laughs. "He said no one could shoot him from this one, because it was behind this beam. He's such a dumbass. But that's why he slept here."

"You guys slept in here?" I ask.

"For fun," Zach says. "We all had bedrooms too. I wonder if mine looks the same." And then he walks off down a dark hallway to go look.

"That's where we put the Christmas tree," Jesse says, pointing to the massive expanse of paned windows. "When we used to get them. And here," he says, pointing to the closest fireplace, because now that I notice, there's three of them in here. "This is where we hung the stockings. God, this place, man. It was fun living here. I know you think it's weird, but I didn't know any better. It was fun."

"Dude," Zach yells from somewhere far away. "My fucking bedroom is a riot." He walks back towards us. "There's a crib in there. Why don't I remember there being a crib?"

Jesse squints his eyes at his cousin. "I don't remember that either. What's mine look like?"

"I don't know where yours is anymore," Zach says. "Were you on this side? Or the other side?"

"This conversation is weird," I say.

Jesse looks at me and shrugs. "You wanted to come down here. We can leave any time you want."

"Are you kidding? And miss my only chance to see Jesse Boston's childhood bedroom? Forget it. Lead on."

As we make our way through a hallway, into a library, then a billiards room, another living space, and finally to another hall with lots of closed doors, I realize it's set up like a circle. But if that's so, then... "What's in the middle?" I ask.

"What do you mean?" they both say at the same time.

"The space doesn't make sense."

Jesse looks confused for a moment, then says, "Yeah, you're right. It doesn't. I never thought of that." We share a moment. Then he points to a door and says, "This was me. That one was Joey, and Johnny was on the other side of the building."

"Why?" I ask, just as Zach opens up Jesse's door to reveal a large, but fairly normal teen boy's bedroom. Posters on the wall. Guitar and amp in one corner. Huge TV and sound system. Outdated, of course. And a king-sized bed.

"No," Jesse says.

I glance at him. "What?"

"No," he says again, shaking his head. "I never had any girls up here. We weren't allowed. They had to meet us in the lobby."

"I bet that was fun."

Zach laughs, then walks away and starts opening all the doors.

"So there you go," Jesse says. "Normal enough for you?"

I back out of the room and follow Zach, peeking into all the other rooms.

"Yeah," I say. "I guess so. If you can overlook the size of this place."

Zach reaches the end of the hallway and opens up a set of massive double doors to reveal the main lobby.

Jesse and I walk that way and meet him in the center of the room. It's bare, like the others. But there's another hallway on the other side and Zach keeps going, so we follow him.

A huge industrial kitchen, a long, elaborate dining room with seating for twenty. Then another hallway with offices and finally, the last few bedrooms.

"This was Johnny."

"Why was he so far away from you and your brother?" I ask.

Jesse and Zach trade that look again. Like they know why, but they're not gonna tell me.

"Why were you guys so afraid to come down here? It's not that crazy."

Again with the traded looks.

"What am I missing?" I ask.

"Nothing," Jesse says. "Can we go back upstairs now? I'd rather show you my place."

I take one more look around and sigh. "OK, I'm satisfied. Is there a shortcut back to that secret elevator?"

"This way," Jesse says, continuing down the hallway. It turns a corner and we end up right where we started. A big circle.

The newspaper room.

But that's when I notice one of the articles printed on the newspaper and walk over to the window.

"Elevator," Zach calls.

"What the hell?" I say, reading the headline. Then the next one, and the next one, and the next one. I turn back to Jesse and find him right behind me.

We lock eyes and he says, "Don't." It's not an order. It's not hard at all, in fact. It's more like… a plea.

But I look back at the headlines. All of them. And begin to read out loud. "'Son of pharmaceutical mogul killed in car crash on the coast.' 'Head of oil company drowns in the Gulf of Mexico.' 'Son of publishing CEO killed in freak plane accident.' What is this?"

I turn to Jesse and he's shaking his head.

"Time to go," Zach says.

That's when I notice the built-in cabinets again. I walk over to one, grab the handle, and I'm just about to pull it open when Zach says, "Don't do it, Emma."

"Why?" I say, whirling around to look at them. "What's in here?"

"We don't know," Zach says. "We don't want to know."

I look at Jesse. "Is that how you feel too?"

He nods. "Yeah. I do. I'm not gonna stop you. So if you wanna know, look. But I'm telling you right now, this isn't me. This is Johnny. So whatever you find in there, that's him. I've got nothing to do with it and neither does Zach. They left us out on purpose, Emma. I told you this. And if you know this secret, whatever it really is, then…"

He shrugs with his hands.

"Then what?" I ask. "He'll come after me and I'll end up a headline on a newspaper taped to a window?"

"No," Zach says. "That's not Johnny. All that was our fathers."

I look at him. "They were assassins?"

They both shrug.

"You're telling me they killed those people and in the same breath you're telling me you don't know?"

Nothing but blank stares.

I open the cabinet.

CHAPTER THIRTY

It's empty. She opens all of them, and all of them are empty.

But it doesn't even matter. She saw more than she should've. And she knows. At least she knows as much as we do.

"Can we go now?" I ask. "Did you see what you needed to see?"

And suddenly I'm angry with her. No, I'm _pissed_ at her.

So I don't wait. I just walk away.

"Jesse," she calls.

But I can't even wait long enough to call the elevator. I just punch the code for the fire stairs, open the door so hard it smashes against the wall with a bang, and take the steps three at a time back up to my floor.

"Jesse, wait," Emma calls, following me. Her footsteps are soft, in stark contrast to my loud ones.

When I reach the landing I whirl around to face her. "You know what, forget it, Emma. Just…go on. Think what you want. Judge me, hate me, whatever. I brought you here because I thought we understood each other. I thought we had something. I thought, at the very least, you'd give me a fucking chance. Why? I don't know. I should've known better. That little drugging and kidnapping stunt should've told me just how understanding you are. I didn't leave you, OK? My fucking uncle died. I was a mess. My brother came and got me. Maybe I am a liar. Fine. I lied to your business partners when I fucked them. I told them whatever they wanted to hear to get what I wanted. How was I supposed to know a few days later I'd meet you? And then when I said all those things to you, I meant them because it *was you*."

I pause and take a breath. See if she's got anything to say.

She doesn't.

But I'm not done yet.

"We're good. OK? Everything that happened Friday night is forgotten. I never went to the hospital. Zach Photoshopped that toxicology report. I was lying.

Again. So just go back to your life. Forget about me, and my family, and my fucked-up house."

She's three steps below me and she recoils back as I rant, so that I suddenly feel like a mountain of rage as I hover over her.

Her brown eyes are wide and there is no innuendo in her raised brows.

She's conflicted. I see that. Maybe she wants to get on this ride with me. Maybe she doesn't.

I point up the stairs. "You know what's up there? At the top?"

She says nothing.

"Johnny. That's who. Those cabinets were empty but that doesn't mean anything."

"What?"

I back up until I hit the wall of the landing and lean against it. So fucking tired of carrying this burden. She can still opt out. But if I tell her the rest, then she can't opt out. She's just in… whether she wants to be or not.

"Forget it," I say. I want to walk away and leave her behind. But I don't know if I could live with myself if I did that.

"Why?" she says.

"Why forget it?" I laugh. "Because trust me, it's in your best interest. You don't want to get involved with me."

"Do you want to get involved with me?"

"It doesn't matter."

"Because you get to decide what's best for me?" she says, taking a step up towards me. "You get the power?" Another step.

"You don't even know what you're talking about."

And then another step and we're both on the landing. "Then explain it."

"I can't."

"Because you don't know? Or because you don't want me to know?"

"Both."

She stomps her foot. And in the echo of that stomp she says, "That makes no sense. Either you know, or you don't."

"I know enough not to tell anyone what I know."

"You're talking in circles."

"Because you keep asking the same damn question. And I keep giving you the wrong answer."

She takes another step towards me and now we're very close. "You look different today. You look... dark. And angry. And maybe a little sad."

I just shake my head but she closes the few inches between us and places her hands on my waist. A safe move. A move that says, *I want more, but I need help to get there.*

There's not going to be an us. There's not going to be any trips down to Key West for Saturday night dinners. There's not going to be any more sailing, or diving, or sandbars, or sunsets, or stars.

She presses forward, her stomach against my cock. "Emma," I say, placing a hand on her arm, fully intending on pushing her away.

"What?" she whispers, leaning up on her tiptoes to kiss me.

I close my eyes and kiss her back. Falling into the feeling of her mouth. Getting lost in the taste of her tongue against mine. She tastes like berries. Like bright berry beaches filled with sun and sand.

God, I want her.

She pulls back from the kiss and takes my hand. "Will you show me your place? Or did I blow it?"

My eyes track up the stairs.

Not to my door, which is right there. But up, in that little gap that lets you see all the way to the top when you stand in just the right place in a stairwell. To Johnny's floor. And the penthouse above it.

Can he hear us? Does he know what I'm doing? Is he even alive?

"Come with me," I say, then lead her up the rest of the stairs and punch in the code to open the fire door into my lobby.

Zach is there waiting for us. Also frowning pretty deeply. "What?" I say. "Why are you looking at me that way?"

"Tabloid story developing."

"What tabloid story?" Emma asks.

"How bad?" I ask.

"Don't know yet."

"What tabloid story?" Emma says again.

"Is she mentioned?"

"Oh, yeah," Zach says.

"What are you two talking about? What's going on?"

I look at Emma. Drugging and kidnapping aside, she's a nice girl. Accomplished woman. Strong, smart, going places… beautiful.

Do I really think she's gonna stick around for the Boston Brothers' Shit Show?

And even if she did, what kind of man would allow her to get involved in a family like ours?

Why did I invite her over here? What was I thinking?

"Here," Zach says. "This is what they're showing right now." He holds his phone out to me.

Emma leans in. "So?" she says, lifting her eyes up to Zach. "It's just me walking into the building with you."

Zach and I trade glances.

"Stop doing that, OK?" Emma says. "It's insulting. If you two have something to say, just fucking say it."

I realize I still have Emma's hand. I give it a squeeze. Then I smile and say, "You're right. It's probably nothing." I glance at Zach. "Hey, why don't you fuck off for a while, eh? I'm gonna show Emma around."

"Whatever," Zach mutters. "You know where I am if you need me."

He disappears around the corner to the left and I lead Emma to the right.

"What's that way?" she asks, glancing over her shoulder.

"That's Zach's side of the floor. I had this place turned into two apartments for us, so this side is mine."

"Hmmm. You really take care of him, don't you?"

"I do my best," I say, stopping in front of the tall, wooden double doors and punching in my key code. The lock beeps, lights up green, and then clicks open. "Well, this is me."

We walk forward into my space. And look, there's nothing weird or creepy about my apartment. It's just a big space well designed with nice high-end furniture. That's all.

I guess that's why I thought having her over would be fine. I didn't factor in the entrance. That's where I fucked up. I didn't see her approach from her point of view.

The building, the water wall, the cement moat, Zach, the metal detectors, every door has a fucking coded lock, my floor lobby, etc., etc., etc.

And it probably didn't help that I had the lights off when she got out of the elevator. I thought she'd like the view. That's the only reason it was dark. I just... thought she'd see the view.

But that's not what she saw.

She saw me.

The real me.

"This is nice," Emma says, letting go of my hand so she can twirl in the center of the space and take it all in.

I don't have much. I'm kind of a simple guy. There's a gray, oversized sectional couch, a huge TV above the fireplace, a few side tables and chairs, and a cozy dining area in front of the windows. The floors are black concrete polished to a slick shine. The walls and rugs are gray and the trim and baseboards are black.

"Very bachelor pad," Emma says.

"Yeah," I say, pulling out my phone to text Zach. "I guess it is."

"What are you doing?"

"Just asking Zach if there's a good bottle of champagne lying around."

"You don't drink," she says.

"Doesn't mean you can't."

"I don't want to drink without you."

"Fine, I'll ask him to bring us some non-alcoholic fizzy." I smile at her as I put my phone away. Then take her hand again and pull her towards me.

She smiles at me. "I'm sorry. I don't know what happened back there. I just… it's weird. Or maybe not. It's just a lot to take in. People don't live like this."

"I know," I say, slipping my arms around her waist until I'm holding her right up against my chest. I gaze down at her. Smile. And it's a real smile. Because she was the one who got away. "Did you get your money's worth this weekend, Ms. Dumas?"

"I did," she says through a small chuckle. "It was fun. A lot of fun, actually. And I'm sorry it started out with you being drugged and kidnapped. I feel so stupid about that now."

I shake my head. "Don't feel stupid. You had feelings. And you took control of them. I can't fault you for that."

"You're not the man I thought you were."

"No?" I ask.

"No. Friday night you were this enigma. This mystery. This bad guy who needed to be trapped and taught a lesson. Until we had that conversation at the Tastee-Freez."

That conversation feels like it happened in another lifetime. But it's been two days. Just two days.

"Then on Saturday you were this player, ya know? This man who wanted to flex his muscles and teach me who was boss."

"You showed me, didn't you?"

She laughs. "I'm really glad I played along. Because yesterday was everything I knew we could be." Her smile drops and she's serious now. "I like you. I've always liked you. Yesterday felt like a do-over. It was the chance to relive that weekend when we first met."

"And today?" I ask. "Who am I today?"

She sucks in a deep breath and lets it out. "I don't know. Some combination, I think. There's definitely more to you than you let on."

I bring her hand up to my lips and kiss her knuckles. "You haven't seen anything yet."

"But I'd like to," she says. She looks down at my waist, places her hand flat on my stomach, then slides it up to my chest as she leans in to kiss me.

It's wrong to kiss her back. But I do it anyway. I kiss her with all the passion she deserves.

Then everything happens at once.

Emma unbuckles my belt while I hold her face and kiss her mouth. Her hands grab my shirt, pull it out of my pants, and then her fingertips hastily unbutton it from the bottom up as I pull down the shoulders of her yellow dress until it reveals her beautiful breasts. It falls to her waist, then past her hips to the floor.

She drags my suit coat down my shoulders and a moment later it joins her dress. She quickly loosens my tie, unknots it, and whips it through my shirt collar.

And I get a little lost after that. Just stare at her as she pops the button on my pants, drags the zipper down, and reaches in to fist my cock.

It's wrong. I do realize that. Because she doesn't know enough to make this decision.

But I don't care.

She starts to kneel, like she's gonna suck my cock, but we've already been there and I'd like to try something new now.

So I take her hand and stop her. She shoots me a look of raised eyebrows. Not innuendo, either. There's no more need for innuendo. It's surprise.

"Come with me," I say, holding her steady as she steps out of the puddle of dress at her feet. "You haven't seen the bedroom yet."

I'm not trying to impress her with my bedroom. It's not even much to look at. Nice furnishings, just like the living area, but nothing more or less than that.

I just want to fuck her in a bed.

When we reach the closed door, I stop for a moment and twirl her around. Push her up against it, then press my body to hers. My shirt is open and I allow myself to get a little lost in the way we make skin-on-skin contact, her soft breasts against my hard muscle.

Then I kiss her hard. I demand that kiss. I own that kiss. I fist her hair and palm her breast, and she moans into my mouth as her hand finds the door handle and then we go crashing through—laughing and finding our balance as we continue kissing.

I push her backwards until she bumps into the bed, and then I make her sit and watch me as I slip my shirt down my arms.

She reaches for the waist of my pants and slips them down my hips as I kick off my shoes and let my pants fall to the floor.

"Commando, huh?" she says with a smirk.

"I come prepared," I say, kicking the clothes away. Then fist my cock and give it a jerk as I bend down and unbuckle her sandals. All the while gazing into her eyes.

I want to memorize this moment so that one day, when I need it, I can pull it out and remember that I did something right. Something good.

Her shoe slips off in my hand, the other one comes off a few moments later.

And now the only thing left is her panties. They're yellow lace. And for a moment I debate the merits of leaving them on. Just pulling them aside and slipping right past them.

I decide no. I'd rather have her completely bare.

So I lean forward as I rise up. Plant each hand on the mattress as I kiss her, forcing her to lie back on the bed. And then I drag those panties down her long legs and toss them over my shoulder.

I could eat her out. I'd like to eat her out. But I'd rather be inside her and I think she feels the same way because she doesn't wait for me to make this decision. She just scoots her way up the bed, forcing me to crawl up her body after her. My cock thick and hard as it drags along the side of her inner thigh.

"Inside me, now," she bosses.

I don't even hesitate.

She spreads her legs, reaches for my cock and places it at her entrance. Everything is suddenly rushed, and desperate, and reckless.

There are no thoughts of birth control, or consequences, or tomorrow.

We are in the here and now. Alive with needs that must be met.

But when I enter her I force myself to slow down and enjoy it. Let her enjoy it too. I prop my arms up on either side of her shoulders and ease my hips forward.

She gasps when I slowly push deeper, clutching the rounded muscles of my shoulders so hard her fingernails dig into my flesh.

"Oh, shit," she moans.

"You feel wonderful," I whisper, lowering my mouth down to hers.

And now everything is slow. Elongated moments and stretched-out seconds. Her legs wrap around my middle, holding me tight as I ease in and out of her with deliberate, careful tenderness.

"Harder," she begs.

"No," I say.

She accepts. Because what comes next is the tenderest lovemaking I've ever experienced.

We are those kids again. Out on my old yacht. Summer of thirteen years ago. And nothing has happened yet. My uncle is not dead, Zach is not an orphan, she was not abandoned, and I never disappointed her.

Innocence was never lost.

I make love to her and rewrite the past in simultaneous moments. Living two lives at once, we stay together and become *that couple*. Only we don't fight, or hate-fuck, or ruin it with bad decisions and hurtful words. We never break up so we never get back together. We never destroy each other from the inside out.

It's possible, I think, as we come together.

It's possible to rise above it when you love someone and only want what's best for them.

I don't know how long we lie in my bed holding each other afterwards. Maybe minutes. Maybe lifetimes. But all things end eventually, so I get up, pull on my pants and head for the door.

"Where are you going?" Emma asks sleepily. It's late now. Probably after midnight.

"To get us that drink," I say. Then I lean down and kiss her on the lips. "Be right back."

I find Zach in his living area, fingers flying as he texts on his phone. "Did you get it?"

He nods. "In the kitchen."

"Thanks," I say.

"It's a dumb idea," he says, only half paying attention to me as he concentrates on his silent conversation.

"It's the only way out of this now," I say, heading down the hallway to his kitchen.

I find a silver tray on the center island with a bottle of sparkling cider in an ice bucket.

Two glasses.

And one pill.

CHAPTER THIRTY-ONE

EMMA

Somewhere something is buzzing. I want it to stop very badly, but I can't open my eyes so I give up and just drift off to somewhere else where there is no annoying buzz.

But again, it comes back. That incessant buzzing won't leave me alone.

What the fuck is it?

I don't know. I don't care. I do my best to drift.

Still, there is more buzzing.

"What the fuck?" I groan. My head is pounding and my mouth is dry. Nothing makes sense.

It takes me a while to remember where I am.

Jesse's place.

Now that wakes me up. I turn over, smiling as I try and force my eyes open. Can't really manage that, so I reach out for him and find... an empty bed.

"Jesse?" I groan.

Nothing but buzzing. And it comes to me what that buzzing is.

My phone.

"Shit," I say, rolling over and propping myself up on my elbows. I crack one eye open and realize… I'm in my bedroom. In my own bed. Alone.

I sit up and regret it immediately when the headache grows to the level of lightning splitting a tree in half, and shield my eyes from the inpouring sun.

My little purse is on the bedside table and the buzzing is coming from inside.

I make an ungraceful mad grab at it, swipe it off the table, then manage to hook my fingertip into the thin chain of a strap and pull it into the bed with me.

A few more seconds go by as I undo the clasp, then finally, I find my phone and press accept.

"Hello," I croak.

"What the fuck, Emma? Just what the fuck? I've been calling you for two goddamn days!"

"Good morning, Mila," I whisper.

"Morning, my ass!" she yells. And holy shit, that really hurts my head. "It's three o'clock in the afternoon! I thought you were dead in a damn ditch somewhere! Why didn't you return my calls?"

"Oh, my God," I moan. "Can you lower your voice? My head hurts."

"Where are you?"

"I'm at home."

"I was just there pounding on your door and you didn't answer."

"I was asleep."

"Well…" She sighs. "Where is you know who?"

"Jesse?"

"Don't say his name on the phone, for fuck's sake! Haven't you seen the fucking internet?"

"What are you talking about?"

"They have footage, you jerk!"

"Oh," I say, flopping back into my pillow. "That."

"Oh, *that*? We're screwed!"

"It's just me walking into his building last night. So what?"

She huffs. "Well, obviously you and I haven't seen the same footage. Because the one I'm looking at shows you, me, Natalie, and Hannah dragging his body into a boat!"

"What?" I say, sitting back up again. My poor head.

"You heard me! They have it all on tape!"

"How?" I ask. "How is this possible?"

"How? Those brothers are out for blood, that's how! It's their security footage!"

"No," I say.

"Yes," she insists.

"No, I mean… he wouldn't do that."

She huffs again, only this time louder. "What the fuck happened this weekend?"

I look around my bedroom and realize I have no idea how I got here. The last thing I remember is… "Shit," I say.

"What?"

"I think he drugged me last night."

"Get your ass in to the office! We need to talk!"

The call drops and I just stare at the screen. A text pops up.

Mila: *Move it! I want you here in less than an hour!*

I don't make it in an hour. I'm pretty sure I spend at least one hour standing under the hot water in my shower. And when I finally do manage to get my shit together and dress, then make my way down to the parking garage, I stand and look at the Huracán for a good ten minutes, trying to piece last night back together again.

It's pretty hazy but I think I got it.

He drugged me.

He fucked me, then drugged me, then took me home in my own car. Somehow he got me upstairs and into bed. I was wearing the yellow dress when I woke up, so he dressed me too.

Then, and this is the most important part as far as I'm concerned, he left me.

Again.

Mila has been texting me constantly wanting updates on my whereabouts and I'm at a red light half a block away from my building when this last one comes in. So I text back: *I'm here. Be there in ten seconds.*

When I pull up in front of the building for the valet, I spy Mila pacing in front of the revolving doors that lead inside, looking like her whole world is falling apart.

Hell, maybe it is?

She stops and stares off at the valet entrance. Just stands there and stares.

I get out of the car and look at her. But now she's texting and my phone dings.

Where are you?

"I'm right here," I say, walking up to her.

"What the—" She whirls around and stares at me. "Where did you come from?"

"My car," I say.

She looks around. There's no car here except for the Huracán. "What car?"

"Mila, my car," I say, pointing at the Lamborghini.

"That's not a car, that's a dick! Why would you buy a new dick? You don't even have an old dick!"

"Are you OK?"

"No, I'm not OK!" Then she looks around and says. "We need to talk. Upstairs."

She grabs my arm and pulls me along to the Bright Berry Beach executive elevator and then spends the entire time inside the glass-walled box with crossed arms and glaring eyes.

But she does not say a word.

When the doors open onto the top floor I follow her out. One of the receptionists stands up, like she has a message for Mila, but Mila puts up a hand and says, "We are all unavailable. Do not interrupt us."

We end up in Mila's office. Hannah and Natalie are already there looking worried and maybe even borderline scared.

"OK," I say, flopping down into a chair in front of Mila's desk. "What's going on?"

"You tell us," Hannah says. "Where the hell have you been?"

"And why didn't you return my calls all weekend?" Mila barks.

"I was..." Shit. There is no good way to explain this weekend. So I decide to keep it simple. "I was on my date."

"Your date?" Natalie says.

"Yup. My ten-million-dollar date."

"Why would you do that?" Hannah asks.

"Well... he called me up on Saturday morning saying he had a toxicology report and..." You know. It goes on like that until it ends with... "And then he drugged me and took me home."

To their credit they didn't say a word as I told them about our weekend. Not one word.

But then Natalie takes a deep breath and finally says, "You left out the part where he sends the lake house security footage to the *Hot Tonight Show* and they run the story about four cosmetic moguls who clearly lost their minds and kidnapped a billionaire after paying ten million dollars for him at a charity auction." She makes one of those curled-lip smiles with raised eyebrows that are very clearly not innuendo, and aims it all at Mila. "This time next year we'll all be in prison and Lifetime will be running a docudrama called *Bright Berry Bitches*."

"He didn't do that, you guys," I say.

But no one is listening to me. Mila starts pacing in front of her window, then says, "We're going on the defensive."

And Hannah says, "I'm calling the lawyers."

And Natalie says, "I'll get in front of it and call a meeting with management."

And then everyone is in motion and everything is moving too fast, so I put two fingers in my mouth and shriek out a whistle so loud they all cover their ears.

"Stop it! Right now! And listen to me!" I pause to let them do that, then stand up and straighten my blouse. "He didn't send that footage. OK? It's not him. And he's not pressing charges. He can't anyway, he drugged me back! He's not the same guy we knew back in Key West. Something is going on with that family and none of it will ever be aired in the courtroom."

"They're going to kill us, you mean?" Hannah says.

"We need more security," Mila adds.

"Stop!" I yell. "You're not listening to me!"

"That's because you're acting insane," Natalie says. "You're crazy if you think this will just blow over. They're running security footage of us dragging Jesse Boston's limp body into a boat, Emma! Get your head in the game! We're about to be ruined!"

"Let me see the footage," I say. "Do you have it?"

Hannah starts tapping on her phone and then holds it out to me. "Here."

I watch it. Several times. Then hand Hannah's phone back. "You can't even tell who that is," I say. "It's all grainy and dark."

"You know what you *can* see," Mila says. "Three women in black cat suits and one in a red gown, dragging a body across the Boston family lake house backyard. It's clearly us!"

"It's not," I say. "Unless we admit to it and we will not admit to it. And if Jesse doesn't corroborate, no one will ever be able to prove it. He has to press charges, you guys. And I'm telling you right now, he won't. Not after what he told me about his family. So just... calm the fuck down and think rationally."

"What is your 'rational plan' then?" Hannah says, making air quotes when she says 'rational plan.'

"We deny it. I'll go back over to Jesse's place and we'll come up with a story. Then we stand together. Us and them. And make a statement to the media denouncing this as... fake news."

"Well," Hannah says with a sigh. "That does usually work." And she's not even being facetious.

Mila stares at me, her face angry and red. "Why do you have so much faith in this asshole? And even if he does go along because he drugged you too, what makes you think his brothers won't push the cops to arrest us?"

I think about this for a moment.

Why *do* I have such faith in him? He drugged me last night. He fucked me, and drugged me, and took me home, and put me to bed. And then he left. And he's not coming back. Not ever. That was an exit. That was... goodbye.

So I'm not sure what to say. I'm not sure I have the words to explain it. But all three of them are looking at me with expectations. They're afraid, I realize. Truly afraid that everything we've built is about to get blown up by the one man who brought us together through mutual hate.

So I have to try.

"You know when you meet someone or do something that changes you forever?"

They all squint at me, not following.

"Like when we met in that bar thirteen years ago. We learned that we were all used in the same way. And that changed us. We banded together, we came up with a plan, and we changed our lives in ways we'd never imagined because of that one chance meeting in a bar. When spring break was over we were changed. We couldn't go back if we wanted to. We couldn't go back if we tried. We were just... different."

I pause to look at them. My three best friends. My three champions. The three people in this world who I know for sure will have my back and stand up for me, no matter what.

"That's what happened to me this weekend, you guys. That's what happened. And I can't explain it, and I don't know what it means, and I did get fucked, and drugged, and sent home—but it's not over yet. I refuse to let it be over. Because I can*not* go back."

I pause again. Expecting them to say something. Mila, at least, to protest and tell me I'm being stupid and silly. But they don't. She doesn't.

So I take a deep breath and say, "Can you trust me to fix this? Just give me one shot at it before we move into things like panic mode, and circling the wagons, and legal defenses? Because if this weekend changed my life then it changed his too."

Hannah shakes her head. "I get it, Emma. But you don't know what he's thinking."

"I know enough to trust him."

"Then maybe you're a fool?" Mila says.

"Maybe I am. But I'd rather know for sure before walking away again. Because I could've made an effort to find him thirteen years ago too. I didn't have to let him walk away. I could've at least come up with a freaking phone number and given it a shot instead of giving up. I'm not going to make that mistake again. Not this time."

Mila throws up her hands. "Fine. Take your shot. But we need to come up with some kind of plan before this day is over."

"OK," I say, standing up. "Thank you."

I turn and walk, realizing… I probably am a fool.

CHAPTER THIRTY-TWO

I sit on the terrace after we drop Emma off at her apartment. Hours pass. The sun rises. Traffic down below in the city gets loud, then louder, and the day passes.

I'm waiting for something to happen, I realize. For Emma to call—she doesn't. For Joey to call—he doesn't. For Johnny to call—he doesn't.

Zach is the only person here with me. He sits on the lounge chair next to me like a faithful little brother should. Talking. Dozing. Getting us glasses of water and ordering us lunch, then dinner. More talking.

Nothing he says is important. Things like, "So you wanna go somewhere this weekend?" As if this will fix anything.

And things like, "Maybe we should really try and make this yacht consulting thing work?"

As if it's just that easy. As if we haven't already tried it.

And finally, sometime after dinner is delivered, he says, "Maybe you should just call her."

I look over at him for the first time today. "I don't think that's a good idea."

He shrugs. "Well, I'm tired of sitting out here. So you gotta do—" His phone rings. He looks at the screen and says, "Fuck."

Out loud I say, "Who is it?" But inside I say, *Thank fuck. Finally, someone gives a shit.* And then I take it back, because maybe it's not about me?

Maybe this world isn't all about me?

"Joey," Zach says.

And then I take back the take-back. Because if Joey's calling Zach, it's definitely about me.

"Yeah," Zach says, answering his phone. He and I lock eyes. He says, "Yup. He's here." Then, "Nope. Hasn't said anything." Another pause as he listens to Joey talk. "OK. See you then."

"What'd he say?" I ask, once the call ends.

"He's home."

"From Tokyo?"

"From wherever he was. Said he got on the jet as soon as Johnny called him with the news and he'll be here in about thirty minutes."

"Why didn't Johnny call me?" I don't know why I bother asking Zach. He doesn't know the answer to that any more than I do.

"Don't worry," Zach says. "I'm sure that call is coming soon."

"Was Joey pissed?"

"Why would he be pissed?"

"Because it's always me, Zach. It's always me they're after. I'm always the one who fucks shit up."

"You didn't do anything wrong. Well, you did drug her last night, but that was for her own good. You really didn't do anything this time, Jess."

"Doesn't matter," I say. "I'm the weak link. I've always been the weak link."

"I don't know. Just wait until Joey gets here and we'll figure it out."

So that's what we do. We wait.

I think about all the other tabloid stories about me. It's been a while since a good one broke. There was one about a year ago chronicling my self-destruction. Some kind of anniversary issue of me going clean. But the only point of the whole thing was to highlight the fact that clean didn't get me anywhere. I had run out of second chances and my life was essentially over.

I kind of agreed with them. It was over. There was nothing to look forward to. This consultant business was going absolutely nowhere. They called me an embarrassment to the family name.

But never once did they mention Joey or Johnny. Who also have no future. Who also live off their trust funds. Who also contribute nothing to the world.

It was always just me they hated.

When Joey finally arrives it's dark and Zach and I are waiting in my living room. I hear the elevator ding on the other side of the doors that lead to my apartment and then they swing open and in he walks.

Joey and I don't look much alike. He's got dark hair and dark eyes. We're the same height and have the same build because we get that from our father, but that's pretty much where the similarities end.

He doesn't say hello. Doesn't acknowledge Zach or me in any way. Simply walks over to the chair across from me, takes a seat, and props an ankle on a knee. All casual, all the time. So cool and unaffected. That's Joey.

He never had the attention I did when we were growing up. And maybe that's because he's the middle child, I don't know. But I have never been sure if he resented me for that, or was grateful I took all the heat.

"Well," I say. "What the fuck do you want?"

He stares out the window. Doesn't even look at me. Then says, "I've been thinking."

I wait for him to continue, but he doesn't. Typical Joey.

"About what?" Zach finally says.

"How maybe we should stop hiding."

"Are we hiding?" Zach asks.

Joey looks at him. Not me, just Zach. "Yeah. We are."

I want to reach over the coffee table and strangle my brother right now. But I take a deep breath and hold it until that urge subsides. When I let it out I say, "It's not a big deal."

I'm not sure what I even mean by that. It's not a big deal that I was drugged and kidnapped by a cosmetic mogul? It's not a big deal that I threatened her so she'd spend the weekend with me after that happened? It's not a big deal that somehow, someone stole the security footage from our lake house? It's not a big deal that *Hot Tonight Show* is blasting it all over the internet?

It could be all of those things.

But it's not any of those things.

So I say, "It's not a big deal because I know what has to be done."

And I do. That's why I drugged her last night. That's why I put her pretty yellow dress back on and took her home. That's why I didn't call her and try to explain today.

"Yeah," Joey says, finally looking at me. "I know you do, Jess. But you know what?"

I shake my head.

"Fuck them."

"Fuck who, exactly?" Zach asks.

"All of them. Everyone. The whole fucking world. I don't think you should toe the line this time, Jesse. I think you should do whatever you think is right. You're not in trouble. She is. That's not our problem."

"Hmm," I say. "Well, I don't know what I was expecting, but this wasn't it. Have you talked to Johnny?"

"No." Joey sighs. "Fuck Johnny too. Sometimes…" He takes a moment to look at me. Like… *really* look at me. "Sometimes you gotta say, 'Enough is enough.'"

I squint my eyes at him. "Are you OK?"

He nods his head. But it turns into a shake pretty quick. "No. I'm not OK."

"What happened?" I ask.

"Nothing you need to worry about."

"What's that mean?" Zach asks.

"It means… I'm gonna handle it."

"OK," I say. "What the fuck are we talking about? Me? Or you?"

"It's not all about you, Jesse. It never had anything to do with you."

Zach and I trade looks. And I'm just about to push Joey for more when the security buzzer rings.

Zach and I trade another look. He says, "I'll get it," then gets up and walks out to see who is downstairs.

"Are you expecting someone?" Joey asks.

"No," I say. Because I'm not. But... I am secretly hoping that's Emma.

"So listen," Joey says, lowering his propped leg, clasping his hands together in front of him, and leaning forward. "I don't think Johnny is ever going to tell you, so I'm gonna do it for him."

"What?"

"Do you know why they love to hate you?"

"Who?"

"Everyone, Jesse. Surely you've noticed that you're the only one they follow around. I've been selling myself at that bachelor auction for years and no scandal ever come out of it even though every date was definitely a scandal. And I'm not blaming you, so before you get defensive, that's not what I'm saying."

"What are you saying?"

"I'm saying it's not your fault. You were just… the deal."

"What deal?"

"The one Dad and Uncle Chuck made when you were born."

"What the fuck are you talking about?" I snap.

"They had to make a trade, OK? Dad and Uncle Chuck. To get this business they had to give something up, and that something was you." He stares at me. "And Mom."

"Mom? Dude, I'm not following."

"You're the black sheep and not because you're the black sheep. You're just… a way to redirect the heat off everyone else." He leans back in his chair again as these words echo in my head. "Not me, of course. I guess I got lucky. No one gives any fucks at all about me as long as I play my part. You are the reason Johnny can do his job. And honestly, he's not gonna be upset about this. He's probably upstairs celebrating right now."

"What. The fuck. Are you talking about?"

"You really don't know, do you? All these years living in this building, underneath the shadow of Dad and Johnny, and you never did figure it out."

I'm not going to repeat myself a third time. So I say nothing.

"Just play along if you want. But I'm here to say, I'm out. I'm done. I'm moving on. I'm not even looking back. Johnny can go fuck himself because I've got a life and I'm gonna stop running, and hiding, and start living it."

It is in this moment that I realize... I don't know my brothers. I don't know a goddamned thing about them.

"The story's good," Joey continues, rubbing his hands up and down his face like he's tired. And he looks tired. He looks like shit, actually. He might've been wearing a suit earlier but right now he's just in dark slacks and a white button-down that's only halfway tucked in. His sleeves are rolled up and he's got several days' worth of stubble on his face.

I'm just about to ask him if he's OK again when he continues. "Deny it, of course. That's expected. But not too hard. Let everyone be suspicious. Let that Dumas woman take your heat and clean it up for you. Just... stay away from her from now on and everything will be fine. You can go back to being..." He waves his hand in the air. "Whoever the fuck you are."

And that's when the doors open and Zach appears with Emma at his side.

CHAPTER THIRTY-THREE

EMMA

The Bossy lobby wasn't empty when I entered. It's Monday now. Late, sure. But it's a work day and there were half a dozen security guards standing between me and Jesse Boston.

They didn't approach me, just glared at me as I approached them. I told them I was here for Jesse, they had a little meeting, and then I guess Zach was summoned, because that's who showed up to escort me upstairs.

Didn't even say hello. Just waved me through that security archway thing and led me to the elevators.

The silence continued as we walked into the lobby and then turned to enter Jesse's apartment.

When I enter I notice two things.

One. Joey Boston is here with Jesse.

And two. They both look like shit. So shitty, in fact, I begin to worry about them and I'm just about to ask if they're OK when Joey stands up and says, "I'll leave you to it. Gonna go get this over with upstairs before I change my mind." Then he looks at Zach and says, "Come with me. I could use the support."

Jesse looks at Zach. Hell, I look at Zach too. And Zach just shrugs and follows Joey down the hallway. There's that telltale beeping sound I remember from when Jesse opened up the fire stairs last night, then the door bangs closed and I take my attention back to the reason I'm here.

"You can't be here," Jesse says.

"Well, I am here," I say, huffing the words out with frustration. "And you're going to listen to me."

"I'm sorry," he says.

But I put up a hand. "Just save it. I don't care that you drugged me. I probably deserved that. Wiping the slate clean now, OK? New day."

He glances at the windows.

"I know it's night. Don't get all specific on me. I have things to say."

Then he smiles. Not a big smile. But it's a charming smile for sure.

I walk towards him and grab him by the shirt. "Listen to me."

He looks down at my hands then up at my eyes. Smirks with raised eyebrows. "You've definitely got my attention. But you never did have a problem doing that."

"Your flirty eyebrow innuendo needs to wait, because I'm being serious now. We're in trouble. We're in a lot of trouble. We did bad things on Friday—which I'm totally sorry for—but the point is, we need to fix this. We need to get in front of this story and change it. And then, once that's done, we're going to date. Really date. For real. Like go out every damn weekend and eat dinner with my parents every other Saturday. Because I lost you once and I'm not gonna let you just get away again, Mr. Boston. You get me?"

"I get you," he says. But then all the charm and possible innuendo fades. And he places both hands on my shoulders. "I'd love all that. I really would. But listen to me, Emma. It's not that easy."

"Of course it's not easy!" I say. Maybe too loud. "Nothing in life is fucking easy. We have no good excuse for why we were dragging your body into a boat Friday night. But we're all smart people. We can make one up. And if you're not pressing charges—you're not, are you?"

"No." He laughs.

"Good. Then we just make something up. What can people do? OK. They're gonna think we're weird, and crazy, and maybe we need therapy. But who cares? And we probably are weird and crazy and need therapy. So fuck it. Why not own it?"

He sighs. "Look, I like you. I'm in. One hundred percent. But there's more you need to know before you decide this is the way forward."

"I know everything. I get you guys. I understand, Johnny is doing… whatever. I'm not gonna say it so I keep my plausible deniability. And it's not about saving my ass, either. Bright Berry Beach will be OK. We'll figure it out. Hell, maybe we need a little scandal in our lives for once. I just…" I stare at him. Memorize him just in case this doesn't go my way. "I just want to give this a shot. That's all I want. Just one more shot."

He steps back. Holds up a finger, and says, "One. This isn't what we think. I don't know what's happening, but there's more to this than I understand at the moment. Two. It doesn't really matter what this is, it's gonna get ugly. Every time something good happens to me, or for me—some tabloid asshole swoops in and ruins it. So if you want that one more shot, you have to go in with the understanding that they're gonna do it to you too. And three." He sighs again. "It's not gonna be easy, Emma. I know this. I've been through it before. You can't understand how much bad publicity can change your life."

"It's gonna suck," I say. "Fine. But I'm the boss of my life. Me. I get to decide how it goes."

"That's not really true, Emma."

I shrug. "I'll make it true. Me, and Mila, and Hannah, and Natalie. We're a powerful force of feminine strength. I have them right behind me. And I have my family too. And you have your brothers and your cousin. So see, we can take it."

"Well, here's the problem," he says. "I don't have my brothers. They're not on my side. They've never been on my side. And I don't really understand that yet, but—"

"Hey."

Jesse and I both look at the hallway to find Zach. "Sorry to interrupt, but Johnny wants to see you, Jesse."

Jesse looks at me, says, "Wait here. I'll only be a minute."

And what can I do? I don't know that I have many choices, so I watch him walk away and disappear down the hallway.

Zach walks over to me. Kinda looks me up and down. And not in the waggling eyebrows innuendo way, either. Kinda sizing me up way.

"It's not what you think," he says.

"Maybe it is," I say. "Maybe it isn't. But I don't care."

"You probably should," Zach says.

"Well… I don't," I say, so frustrated. "I think I could love him, OK? Just put aside the fact that I'm in my thirties with no prospects for a moment. Erase the idea that I might've been obsessed with Jesse Boston for the last thirteen years and that's why I never moved on and found someone else. Forget that I'm a bossy workaholic with control issues. Don't think about the fact that I drugged your cousin and helped tie him to a chair three days ago and then bought a two-hundred-and-seventy-thousand-dollar dick and flew him down to Key West in a private jet to be intimidated by my family just so I could one-up him. He might be my one. Not last chance," I say, holding up a hand. "Let me make that perfectly clear. I'm not desperate."

Zach smiles and it's only now I notice he's got that classic Boston charm. "You're coming off a little bit desperate."

"But in all the right ways," I correct him. "I'm desperate *to save us*." I nod my head. Because that was good. *Very nice answer, Emma.*

A slow clap makes Zach and I turn towards the hallway where we see Joey Boston leaning against a wall and looking like he just got punched in the face because his eye is swelling up.

"Great speech," he says. "But you're wasting your time on this Baby Boston here. He's not the one you need to convince. That guy…" He looks back down the hallway. "He's up there."

Joey walks forward, heading for the set of double doors that lead to the lobby elevators, and then, just as he's about to open the doors, he looks at me over his shoulder. "And just to be clear? I'm not talking about Jesse. I'm talking about the one who bites back." Then he points to his eye as exhibit A, pulls the doors open, and disappears as they swoosh closed behind him.

I start for the hallway but Zach catches me by the upper arm. "Wait. You don't understand. Johnny Boston is—"

"Johnny Boston is a bully, that's what he is!"

And then I shrug him off and head for the fire stairs.

Zach doesn't follow me. He probably thinks I can't get into the stairwell.

But he's wrong.

I'm a numbers girl.

And I've seen Jesse Boston push this code twice now.

331

I could hear them fighting as soon as I opened the fire stairs door. I took the steps three at a time and burst out onto Johnny's floor ready to join the fight.

But I stopped in my tracks when I realized Johnny had a gun pointed at Joey's head.

Joey was face down on the floor. Johnny kneeling beside him.

Johnny looked at me, then back at Joey. Then the gun in his hand.

And he got up and walked away.

I ran over to Joey and pulled him to his feet. He pushed me off him, then glared in the direction Johnny disappeared, and said, "Fuck you all," and left the way he came.

Now I'm standing in Johnny's living room and can I just say... my big brother could really use a maid.

Because this place is a disaster. Newspapers everywhere. Stacks of them. But not only newspapers, files too. Just boxes and boxes of files.

There's furniture here but I can't see most of it, that's how much fucking paper is filling up the huge, expansive space around me. And lined up against the wall are rifles. Dozens and dozens of them. Neatly placed like good little soldiers in formation. The pistol Johnny had pressed to Joey's head is resting on a tall stack of newspapers, forgotten.

This was what I expected down on the family floor, I realize. This was what I thought we'd find in those cupboards, but didn't.

Evidence like this.

Evidence that my brother is something bad. That we are all part of something bad.

The windows are covered with articles he's clipped. And for a moment I assume they're just like the ones downstairs. Death announcements of important people.

But they're not.

Johnny comes back looking put-together. Hair slicked back. Face composed. He's wearing a nice pair of black slacks, a crisp, starched white shirt, a white tie, and a pair of dark, expensive, highly-polished shoes.

He pours two glasses of whiskey, then turns and holds one out to me.

"No, thanks," I say. "I quit that shit a long time ago."

"I know," Johnny says. "Time to start again, brother. Take my word on that."

I can't even manage to laugh. But that was funny. "No, I don't think so, *brother*."

He glares at me.

"So what do you want?" I ask.

"I want to show you something," he says. And then he looks at the windows. Specifically, at the clippings taped to them.

"Yeah, I saw them."

"Did you read them?"

"I read enough to know what they mean."

He smiles at me. "It wasn't personal." Then he frowns. "I want you to know... I did my best, Jesse."

I'm suddenly tired of this. All of it.

Tired of being me. Tired of being part of this family. Tired of... *him*.

I haven't actually seen or talked to my oldest brother in years. If I've ever been in this room, it was so long ago, I can't remember when that was.

"You know who did all this?" he asks, pointing his glass at the windows so fast, whiskey sloshes over the side.

"You," I guess.

He nods. "Me."

"Well… what should I say about that?"

He turns towards me and for a second I think he's gonna fight me the way he did Joey. But he doesn't. He walks over to a door—a door my floor doesn't have—and opens it up. "Come on. What I really want to show you is upstairs."

Upstairs. In the penthouse.

"I asked Joey to come but he's…" Johnny shrugs, trying to think of the right word to describe what my middle brother is, then decides on, "Not being cooperative." He stares at me for a moment. "But you. You won't be able to help yourself. You never did have his control."

I actually laugh at that.

But Johnny doesn't care. And he doesn't wait for me either. Just disappears inside.

I want to go back to Emma. Forget about all of this. But he's right.

I never did have Joey's self-control.

So I follow him. There's no way I'm not going to follow him. I haven't been up in the penthouse since my uncle died thirteen years ago. That's when my father went insane and made all the living arrangement changes. Put us all on separate floors. Compartmentalized us. Why?

I've thought about that a lot over the years. Why did he want us all separate?

There was only one explanation that ever made sense.

So when the day came... when the people came... they couldn't get all of us at once.

And they'd get me first.

Did I believe it?

Maybe not back then when Zach and I first came up with the idea.

But I do now.

The penthouse was my father's office before he died. We never lived up here. We never came up to the very top of the building more than a handful of times.

But I've never been up there through this door. So I have no idea where this will take us.

Emma is right. Living in a building like this is not normal.

Nothing about the Boston family is normal.

Johnny is already throwing open the door at the top of the stairs when I start climbing after him.

Neither of these doors have codes to enter. So whatever this is, it was never a secret from Johnny.

Part of me feels sorry for him.

But after seeing the clippings down there on his windows, most of me doesn't.

When I enter the penthouse I stop short and take in the small room, then look at Johnny and say, "What is this?"

He downs what's left of his drink, then places the glass gently down on a desk. Then reaches for a suit coat hanging reverently—almost ceremonially—on a freestanding valet stand.

When he slips the dark jacket on a chill runs down my spine.

There are white epaulettes on the shoulders. And matching white buttons. I watch him button those and adjust his sparkling cuff links as he adjusts his sleeves. Staring at me the entire time.

I say, "What are you? A fucking general? What the fuck is up with that coat?" Because for a moment… I don't recognize him. He has morphed into something I don't understand. "What's going on?" I ask.

He looks at me and when I meet his gaze straight on, I suddenly see my eyes staring back at me. We are more alike than I remember. Same build. Same muscles. Same hard jaw. Same blue eyes. Same dark-blonde hair.

He opens his mouth to say something. Maybe an explanation. Or maybe just another excuse.

But then we both turn and look at the stairs.

Because someone is coming up after us.

CHAPTER THIRTY-FIVE

EMMA

I run up the stairs because I know Zach is coming after me. Sure enough, when I reach the landing of the next floor up, I hear the door below bang open. "Emma!" he yells. "Don't!"

But I keep running. And when I get to the next floor I stop and punch in the emergency exit code.

0000.

It's dangerous to lock a fire door, isn't it? But less so when the code is easy to remember.

I throw the door open just as another one, far down the hallway, bangs closed.

I pause, aware that Zach is coming up behind me, hear nothing, and then walk quickly forward.

Zach bursts through the fire door just as I reach the end of the hallway and enter the living room.

"What the fuck?" I mutter. Stack and stacks of newspaper and too many guns to count lined up against the wall.

"Emma!" he yells. "Stop!"

I'm stopped. I'm shocked. I'm... "What the fuck?" I say, walking towards the windows. "What the fuck is this?"

"Emma, please," Zach pleads. "Just let them handle this their own way."

"What is this?" I ask, walking up to the window and pointing at the first article.

"I don't know," Zach says. "I swear to God. I've never been up here until a few minutes ago when I came with Joey. I can't even begin to understand what's been happening."

"'Baby Boston caught again,'" I say, reading the closest headline. "'Jesse Boston busted for drugs.' 'Jesse Boston leaves yachting association in disgrace.' 'Jesse Boston—'" I whirl around to face Zach. "What is this?"

He shakes his head, then says, "It's exactly what it looks like."

"Well, it looks like... it looks to me like..."

Zach is already nodding.

"They did this to him? They fed those stories about Jesse to the tabloids?" It hits me then. I know who gave

Hot Tonight Show the security footage. "Johnny did this?"

Zach throws up his hands. "You know as much as I do."

"His brother? Ruined his life?" It's only then I fully realize that neither Johnny nor Jesse are here. "Where are they?"

Zach looks past me and I turn to see what he's fixated on.

Another door. "Where's that go?"

"Upstairs," he says. "I think that's where they are."

I head toward the door, pull it open, and start running up the stairs. It occurs to me that I am so deep inside the innards of this building, no one would ever hear me scream. I could get lost in this place. I could never come out.

There is nothing but silence when I reach the next door. Zach is behind me. Quiet now. We look at each other. Then up. Because there's one more floor above us. Zach shakes his head. *Not up there,* that shake says. Then he sucks in a deep breath of air, reaches for the door in front of us, and pulls it open.

Jesse is the first person I see. He looks at me, open-mouthed. Like he has something to say. But before he can, Johnny says, "Take her somewhere far away." He juts his chin to me. "Get her out of here and never come back. I'll take care of everything, I promise."

"What?" Jesse says. "What the fuck are you talking about?" His voice is loud and it's clear that he's just as confused as I am.

"I'm talking about who we are, Jesse. What we are. What we *do*."

"What do we do?" Zach says.

Johnny looks at him and says, "You don't have to do anything. None of you do."

"Then why did you bring me up here?" Jesse asks. "What does this fucking"—he looks around—"office have to do with anything?"

"You don't remember any of it?" Johnny asks him. "Not even where those lead to?" He motions to the stairs behind Zach and me.

Jess stares at the darkness behind me, squinting his eyes. "The… spire," he whispers.

I glance at Johnny quick enough to see him nod. "The spire. We were up there once, remember? Dad told us to go up there and watch." Johnny takes a few steps closer to Jesse and I have a sudden urge to stand between them. There's something wrong with him. Something deeply disturbing. And what is up with his outfit? He looks like… he looks like a cross between a general and… an evangelist.

"You want to know?" Johnny says. "You really want to know?"

I glance at Jesse as he nods. "Yes," he says. "Tell me."

But Johnny shakes his head. "I have to show you."

"OK," Zach says, "Maybe he's right, Jesse. Maybe we should just leave. I mean"—Zach shakes his head—"maybe not knowing is better."

"You don't know anything yet," Johnny says. "You can walk away. Just... be who you are, Jesse. And you too, Zach," he says, looking at Zach. "But if you go up there, there's no turning back. Once you know, you can't un-know."

Jesse hesitates. Looks at me, then Johnny, then Zach. Then back to me. He reaches for my hand, like we're gonna leave, but I say, "No," and take a step backward. "No way."

All of them look at me. But I'm talking to Johnny now. That's what Joey said to do. Tell it to the one who bites.

"We're not running. Fuck that. Do you even know who I am?"

Zach lets out a small laugh.

"I am the goddamned *numbers girl* for the fifth largest cosmetics company on the planet Earth! That's the entire planet of Earth! And I have friends, OK?

Powerful friends. Bossy friends who aren't afraid to drug and kidnap for revenge. I drive a motherfucking Lamborghini Huracán in *matte black*. I am one-fourth owner of the biggest pink jet ever made and… and I have three massive brothers who know how to… *fish*. You get me?" I say, pointing my finger at them. "This bullshit ends now."

No one says anything. And Johnny just blinks at me a few times.

So I sigh and give Jesse my full attention. "Look. OK, I will admit that this is all totally weird and I'm pretty sure I don't understand any of it. But I love you, OK? There. I said it. I love you and I see that this family is ruining you." I point to Johnny. "You're the one who sent that footage to the tabloids. And I want answers, motherfucker. All the goddamned answers!"

A slow clap echoes out from the stairwell and we all turn our heads to find Joey. Smug and maybe kinda proud, even though his left eye is totally swollen shut. He says, "I was coming up here to say all that and tell everyone I'm in charge now because Johnny has obviously gone insane, just like our fathers. But fuck it. I think the lady has it handled."

I straighten my back and raise my chin. Look directly at Johnny and say, "What is going on?"

He looks at Jesse, then Joey, then Zach, then me. And says, "Go upstairs. Be very quiet. And don't let anyone see you. I'll meet you back down here when it's over."

"When what's over?" Jesse asks. "Who's up there?"

But Johnny is already walking away.

CHAPTER THIRTY-SIX

"*Fuck it,*" *I say*, after watching Johnny walk away. I look at Joey. Then Zach. Then finally, Emma. "Are we doing this or what?"

"We're doing it," Joey says. "I'm fucking sick of this shit. I don't care what's waiting for us up there. I'm getting answers."

Joey turns back to the stairs and starts climbing.

"Zach?" I say, looking at him.

He shrugs. "Up to you, man. You're the boss."

"Emma?" I say, turning to her next. "You can leave. This has nothing to do with you."

She scowls at me. Points her finger in my face. "Did you just not hear me? I love you. I have always loved you. Since the first time I laid eyes on you. I was in then and I'm in now. You'll have to drag me out of here kicking and screaming to make me leave now."

"OK." I sigh. "Then follow me."

We quietly enter the stairwell and climb. I stop at the door, looking back over my shoulder at Zach and Emma like, *Last chance.*

But Emma pushes me on the shoulder and whispers, "Open it."

So I do. There's an immediate murmur. Like somewhere ahead there's a large crowd of people.

But I'm distracted when I glance up and see the glass spire above us.

This is the top of the building. We are seventy-five stories above the city right now.

And I feel every bit of that distance. I feel like I just walked into another world.

"Over here," Joey whispers, peeking his head out from the edge of a hallway. "They're down there."

The three of us walk towards him like a team and I have a flash of memory.

I have been up here before.

Once.

Joey and Johnny were there too. I don't know how old I was. Very young. And now that I think back this might even be my first memory.

This spire. My brothers. The murmur of a crowd down below us.

And once we turn the corner it becomes very clear that this spire isn't a floor like the rest of them. It's more like a catwalk around the interior of the penthouse below us. Like a choir loft in a church.

Floor-to-ceiling beams are evenly spaced around the catwalk. Joey gets down on his hands and knees and crawls across the catwalk, stopping behind each beam to peek down below, then continues on until he finally stops at the fourth beam and motions for us to follow him.

Emma drops to her knees and immediately begins to crawl. I follow, then Zach follows me.

She stops to hide behind the beam closest to Joey, I continue forward and join her, and Zach ends up at the beam behind me.

Down below is a fancy dining room. Like you'd see in a banquet hall. Maybe three dozen tables. I count the place settings at each table and do a quick count. A little over two hundred men and women below us. All dressed up in black suits and white ties, like Johnny. But unlike Johnny, these men do not have the white epaulettes on the shoulders.

The women are all wearing white dresses and small white hats with a short veil that covers their faces.

For a second I think it looks like a wedding.

But there's too much... *wrongness* here, for it to be a wedding.

"What the fuck?" Zach whispers.

No one answers him. We have no answers. Only more questions.

Then suddenly everyone down below goes quiet. The hushed murmurs stop and everyone stands.

Johnny appears at the head of the room and the people clap. Not like... applause, exactly. But polite clapping.

Johnny stands at the top of the room under a spotlight that coats him in an eerie white haze.

Then, without anyone speaking a word, a woman at the top of the room stands and walks forward towards him.

I realize that whatever this dinner is, it's over. Everyone has already eaten.

The woman approaches Johnny, stops in front of him, then does a little bow, and hands him a white envelope.

"What the fuck?" I mumble.

Joey shushes me and when I look over at Zach, he's just shrugging.

A man is now standing next to Johnny. He takes the envelope when Johnny offers it, and places it in a large metal box on wheels. While all that was happening a line has formed along the side of the banquet hall. And the whole thing repeats itself.

They approach Johnny, bow, hand him the envelope, and Johnny hands it off to be placed in the box.

It takes me several minutes to realize that people are leaving. That the room is emptying out. One by one, as they hand over whatever is in that envelope, they exit through doors directly below us.

We watch as every single person in the room hands him an envelope. And by the time it's done my legs are cramping and everyone is getting restless.

But we stay. Because surely Johnny will say something, right?

He has not said a word this whole time.

But when the last person hands over their envelope Johnny places it inside the box himself, flips the large trunk lid closed, and turns to leave, pulling the box behind him.

No comment at all.

And that makes sense. Because there's no one left to talk to.

Joey crawls over to us, still being quiet and stealthy, even though there's no one left down below to hide from. "Let's go," he says.

353

We all crawl back the way we came, then stand, walk down the hallway in silence, and then enter the stairs and descend back to Johnny's floor.

He's waiting for us in the office. The box beside him. He opens it up to reveal more than two hundred white envelopes.

"Dude," I say. "What the fuck was that?"

He just hands me an envelope and says, "Open it and see."

I take the envelope. It's sealed with black wax. And imprinted in the wax is a monogram with the initials WAY. I shoot Johnny a questioning look, but he just says, "Open it."

I crack the wax and pull the flap up. Inside is... "A card?" I say, once again looking at Johnny for some kind of explanation. He says nothing.

The card says:

Promissory note in the amount of one hundred million dollars for The Way from Member Number Two Hundred Nine.

"Who the fuck is The Way?" I ask, just as Joey comes over and takes the check from me.

"Apparently," Johnny says, "I am."

"What?" Zach says, taking the card from Joey. "A hundred million dollars? Jesus."

"Every one of those cards promises the same amount," Johnny says.

"Why?" Emma asks.

Johnny looks at her, then Zach, then Joey, then me. "Because... I'm the boss?" He says it like a question.

"You're the boss?" I say.

"I'm the boss."

"Of what?" Joey says.

He laughs. "I have no fucking clue."

"What do you mean?" Joey asks. "How could you be the boss of something like..." He looks back at the stairwell, then points to Johnny's suit coat. "Something like that... shit show... and not even know what it is?"

Johnny takes off the suit coat, places it reverently back on the valet stand, then walks around to the other side of the large desk and takes a seat. He leans back in his chair and smiles. "I have looked through every fucking file in the upper-floor vaults."

"Wait," I say. "What vaults?"

Johnny sighs. Like he doesn't want to talk about any of this and now that he started, he realizes there's even more to explain than he realized. "All our floors have an inner vault filled with documents that chronicle the... business, I guess you'd call it. The

Way. But it's just accounting. All those files down on my floor. That's five years of searching for answers. And I have none, you guys."

"So wait," Emma says, holding up a hand. "You don't kill people for a living?"

"What?" He laughs and leans forward.

"All those fucking guns," Zach says.

"Well. Call me paranoid. But if you were me and every month you went out into that banquet hall and collected twenty billion dollars and you had no idea why, you'd collect guns too."

Truth.

"Where does the money go?" Joey asks.

We all look at Johnny. He shakes his head and lets out a long, tired breath.

Then he says, "Us. It all goes to *us*."

There's a long moment of silence as we all think about that statement.

"Wait," Joey says. "I don't understand."

Johnny swivels his chair to the right to face Joey and says, "I don't either, Joe. Dad came to me after Uncle Chuck died and he made me watch, just like I made you. We've been up there before. Do you remember?"

"I do," I say. "Barely, but I do."

"It was after Mom disappeared," Joey says.

"He told me that day too, but I was what? Four?" Johnny shakes his head. "It didn't make any sense. I knew the ceremonies happened every month because he made sure I knew. But I didn't do anything other than sit up in the loft where you guys were and watch until Dad died."

"And then what happened?" Zach asks. "Did someone come and tell you to take his place?"

"No," Johnny says. "I just… put the fucking suit on and carried on."

"Why?" Joey asks. "Why the fuck would you do that?"

Johnny looks at Joey and makes a face of *don't-be-an-asshole*. "You know why, Joe."

"Wait, hold on," Emma says. "I don't know why. Fill me in!"

"Why are you *here*?" Johnny snaps at her.

"I don't know either," I say. Not because I want to know. I have decided maybe I don't need to know this shit. I say it because I don't want Johnny looking too close at Emma. She's the one who started this night. She's the one who opened the can of worms. She's the reason…

"Hey," I say. Narrowing my eyes at Johnny. "What the fuck is up with you and me? Do you fuckin' hate me or something?"

"Yeah," Emma says. "Whatever with your creepy money ritual. You're the reason why the tabloids are talking about us right now. You gave them that footage."

"I had to," Johnny says. "I needed…" He pauses to take a deep breath and look me in the eyes. "I needed the cover."

"Cover for what?" Zach asks.

Johnny swivels his chair around, gets up, and starts walking away. I grab him by the arm and grip it tight. "Where the fuck are you going?"

"Yeah, answer the question," Joey says. "Cover for *what?*"

He glares at Joey. Joey glares back. His eye almost swollen shut. And it hits me that for a moment there, I forgot who Johnny is. I only saw him for who he was.

But he had a gun to my brother's head when I walked in.

Was he going to kill him? Or was it just a threat?

"That… you really do not want to know." And then he shrugs me off and disappears down the hallway.

The rest of us stand there and look at each other. Emma is taking breaths like she's about to have a panic attack. Zach is shaking his head and Joey grits his teeth.

"Come on," I say. "Show's over. Let's go."

"Go?" Joey says, grabbing me by the arm. "We need to set him straight. Like… now."

"What do you want to do?" I ask. "Kill him?"

"No," Joey says.

I shrug. "Then what? What are we gonna do? We don't have any leverage and even if we did—"

I stop, because Emma is suddenly walking through the door and heading back downstairs.

"Shit." I look at Joey and Zach and say, "Hey, if you two are stupid enough to confront Johnny again tonight, be my guest. But I'm not gonna lose one more goddamn thing because of that asshole."

I brush past Joe and follow Emma down the stairs. She's already pulling the fire stair door open when I catch up to her. Heading down to my floor.

"Emma wait," I call.

But she doesn't wait.

Her feet fly down the stairs and she disappears inside my apartment.

CHAPTER THIRTY-SEVEN

I rush down the hallway, no idea where I'm going. The tour yesterday is all a bit blurry from the drugs, I guess. And my heart is beating fast with panic because I need to do this before Jesse catches up with me and tries to talk me out of it.

But the doors are all closed. I start opening them, quickly peeking in, then rush off to the next one.

The fire stair door slams open, hitting the wall with a bang. "Emma!" Jesse calls. "Wait!"

"No," I say. Rushing towards the next door and pulling it open.

This. This is what I need. I go in and the sound of Jesse's shoes slapping on the shiny black floors echoes in my head like bad omen.

I go over to the closet and open it up just as he comes sliding to a stop in front of his bedroom door.

361

"What the hell are you doing?" he asks, all out of breath. Which is kinda sexy.

And it's so inappropriate that I think this, but I can't help it. This man… he just does it for me. When I fell for him back when I was eighteen, I fell all the way to the bottom.

"You know what?" I say, whirring around to face him as I hold the closet door open.

"What?" he says. He's got a very serious, worried look on his face. And hey, I do not blame him one bit. His family is *psycho* with a capital S sounding P.

"I don't want to get back up."

He juts his head back a little. "What?"

"When I fell for you, Jesse Boston, I fell hard. And it hurt. I'm not gonna lie. It fuckin' hurt. And taking a chance on you is a huge risk. And people are gonna ask me, "Why, Emma? Why are you doing this?" And you know what I'm gonna say?"

He swallows. "What?"

"I'm gonna say we're just that couple, you know."

He cracks a smile.

"We're that couple that comes from two totally crazy families. In two totally different ways. Let's just make that clear now. That's how I'm gonna start it. Every time people ask me why I chose Jesse Boston

362

I'm gonna say "We're two very different people. But it works and you know why it works?""

He's smiling big now and I feel a little better. "Why," he asks, crossing his arms and leaning against his bedroom door.

"Because I'm in charge."

He chuckles. "Is that right?"

"That's right. These people?" I point up with a finger. "Fucking. Nuts. OK? Nuts with a capital N. And I'm not gonna let you stay here one more second. You're coming home with me."

Zach has appeared in the doorway now too.

"You," I say, snapping my fingers at Zach. "Pack your shit, buddy. You're coming too."

"Wait? What?" Zach says.

"Pack. Your. Shit. You can't live here. None of you can live here." I say that because Joey has now appeared too. "You don't live here, right?" I ask him.

"Fuck no," he says.

"See," I point at Joey. "Listen to me, Jesse. You can't choose your family. But you can choose to walk away from them. Any time you want. But let me also make this very clear. You don't have a choice. I'm packing your shit and you're moving in with me. That's the end of it so if you have objections, then I suggest you keep that crap to yourself, OK? Because I don't want to hear them. This place is a… a… a fucking shit show of a nightmare. I don't know how any of you are sane. But from now on," I point to Zach again. "You have dinner in Key West on the first and third Saturdays of every month. You can come too," I offer to Joey. "But… whatever. I'm gonna assume you have some sane people on your side already, because you had the good sense to get out early. But you two?" I point to Jesse and Zach. "Key West. Every other fucking Saturday until the day you die. Because this is not what a family looks like."

Jesse walks towards me and I suck in a deep breath of air. I don't care what he says. He's coming with me. He's leaving this life behind. He's not staying here.

"Emma Dumas," he says. Reaching up to gently place his hands on my cheeks.

"Jesse Boston."

"You had me at 'I'm in charge.'" And then he leans in and his lips touch mine. His kiss is soft. And filled with something new. Something I never felt with him before now.

Trust.

And everything I just saw, and all the weird confusing things that come along for the ride by loving this man, *disappear.*

None of it matters.

"We're that couple," he whispers. "We're that couple who sticks together because we know who's side we're on."

"Ours," I say.

"Ours," he agrees. "I would go anywhere with you. I would do anything you ask. You know why?"

"Why?" I whisper, looking up in his blue-blue eyes.

"Because you're the best boss ever."

A miniature Barbie and Ken cinnamon roll hits me in the head and I turn to find Emma staring at me from across the top deck of our new yacht. She looks radiant and sexy in her teal-green bikini that really sets off her pigtails. The sun is just setting to the west. A long tail of orangey-pink stretches out across the ocean and lights her up like some kind of celestial angel.

"What was that for?" I laugh, plucking the mini-roll out of my lap and popping it into my mouth.

"Stop it right now, mister. I can practically read your mind. We made a pact when we came down here."

"We did." I sigh. We handled shit. We all went on Hot Tonight Show the day after Zach and I moved in with Emma and did an interview.

Me, Emma, Joey, Mila, Hannah, Natalie, and Zach. Everyone but Johnny. And we told them the story we made up.

It was a murder mystery date. I played the victim, the girls were the kidnappers and then we made up this whole plot about Joey being the detective and Zach was his sidekick.

It's a stupid excuse but we can't tell the truth.

Not because there was actual drugging and kidnapping happening that weekend, but because the whole reason Johnny was tipping off the tabloids about me all these years and encouraging Joey to party around the globe was so that no one would take us seriously.

No one would see us as a threat.

I called him from the jet on the way down here. I wasn't expecting him to pick up. He never picks up. But it was eating away at me. Joey went back to... wherever the fuck he's staying. But he didn't go home. I guess Tokyo is home. Just learned that about him, actually. He stayed and it feels good to have him here. Because this is home. I know he's moved on, but I'm not quite there yet.

I know I should walk away from Johnny. Hell, he wants me to walk away. He's done everything he could think of to save me from the life he's stuck in.

Joey and I are the laughable, the ridiculous, the foolish Boston Brothers. We waste money. We do drugs and drink. We will never amount to anything but this.

Harmless fuck-ups. No threat to this secret society called The Way. Which I do not understand at all.

But fine. I'll play that role. I'll be that guy in public if that's what it takes to keep everyone safe.

But I'm not ready to give up on Johnny. He's still my big brother. And I get Emma's point about how he fucked up my life with the tabloid stories.

But sometimes things should be forgiven without question.

I know this better than anyone.

Johnny didn't make me a drug addict. He didn't make me do all those things when I was younger.

I did that all on my own.

So I called him up and we talked a little. For the first time in decades, we talked like brothers. He even apologized. I, of course, used to being the one who always needs to apologize, forgave him. I even invited him down to Saturday dinners. I don't think he'll come. Ever. But the invitation is there. Maybe one day we'll figure this all out and it'll make sense. Maybe one day Johnny can stop whatever it is he's doing and find a nice girl like Emma to be with.

I have that same hope for Joey as well. There's something going on in his life right now. I'm not sure what it is, because he's not talking much. But I'm here for him too.

When the day comes that Joey Boston needs me, I'll be there.

Emma and I came back down to Key West to forget. *One week,* we said. *One week to forget and then we'll deal.* We'll start looking into The Way thing. It's a cult, maybe. Or a secret society. Or hell, it could be a sanctioned government entity for all I know.

"Jesse," Emma says.

"Emma?" I smile at her.

"I'm giving you an order. Stop. Thinking."

She reaches behind her back and a few seconds later her bikini top falls to the ground at her feet.

I stare at her perfect breasts in awe, her nipples perky and tight when she bends over—eyes locked on mine—and wiggles her bottoms over her hips. They join the top on the deck at her feet.

She waggles her eyebrows at me.

"Are you innuendo-ing me?" I laugh.

She stalks towards me like a lioness on the prowl. And when she reaches me she climbs into my lap— one knee dipping down into the cushions of the top-deck couch—and places her forearms on my sunburned shoulders.

I gaze up into her brown eyes and smile.

"What do you think?" she asks.

"I think you're trying to distract me. Make me bend to your will."

She grins, reaching for my board shorts. Deftly untying them with one hand.

She's practiced that move a lot over the last week. She's practically an expert now.

"I'm gonna make you forget, Jesse Boston." She pulls my cock out and mouths, "Blow your mind." Then winks and whispers, "And your cock too."

I can't hold in the laugh. Because Emma Dumas is my *jam*.

"But first," she coos, lifting her hips up as she guides my cock to the entrance of her pussy, "I'm gonna let you blow mine."

She sinks down on me and the world turns.

The sun disappears and the stars start to twinkle above us.

And when she kisses me we travel backwards thirteen years and become that couple.

The one that falls in love after one weekend.

The one that drifts apart and finds their way back.

The one we knew we'd always be.

It just took us longer than most to find our way home.

Welcome to the End of Book Shit where I get to say whatever I want about the book. This is always done after editing and I barely proofread it, so... you know. Don't judge me. Or I guess you can if you want, but I give no fucks about typos because it's nine o'clock at night, I've been up working since 5 AM and the only reason I'm writing this right now is because I would like to hold this paperback in my hand on release day and I need to get it uploaded tonight to make that happen with two-day shipping. That's all I'm saying.

I'm gonna warn you ahead of time - this one's got a rant theme.

373

So three things to start:

One – this is book one of a series. At least three books, probably four, and possibly seven. But I reserve the right to change my mind about pretty much anything I want. So could just be three.

Two – this is a romantic suspense because that's what I write. That means it's got a mystery.

And **Three** – this should go without saying since it is a clearly marked series, but again, this is a series, so no. You're not going to get all the answers to the mystery revealed at the end of book one at the end of book one.

And I only preface this EOBS with these clarifications because I've seen some *really strange* reviews for other authors lately. I mean... you know. If you pick up a dark book and then bitch about it being dark in the review – go away. OK. Go read something else. This wasn't my book, BTW. It was someone else's book and I didn't read it but I didn't have to in order to deduce that this reader had a problem. Either they were A) a complete asshole or B) They don't know how to choose a book they actually like. I know this because I made the mistake of clicking over to see ALL of this person's reviews and it was just one-star, after one-star, after one-star. Just… choose another genre. OK? Don't read every dark book out there and then one-star them for being too dark. Take some responsibility for your book choices. If every book you read is a one star you're kinda bringing that on yourself.

I mean here's the reality for me. I almost never finish a book. I DNF just about everything. But it's not the author's fault. They wrote their book, I didn't get in to it because I'm kinda picky and I like a very particular kind of story, so I move on. There's no drama. Just move on. I don't return the book and I don't complain about it. Ever. I bought it, I tried it, I moved on. It's just that simple.

And then there was one that said "No character development of this random tertiary character". Hmmm… I mean. This isn't literary fiction. It's romance. There's really only a few characters in the book who really count and this was a series so it's very possible that the author has big plans for that random tertiary character in a future book and revealing all that stuff in this particular book is not actually beneficial.

Sometimes the author really does know what they're doing. I saw this tweet on Twitter a couple months ago. This tweeter is a blogger and "aspiring author" but has not actually written a book. She is one-hundred percent "mean girl". I know this because she's been around for years and the things she has said about people who actually "write and publish books" in the past were just quite despicable. And this tweet said something like… "Just FYI – using ellipses to indicate emotion doesn't actually qualify as good writing."

And I just laughed. Because… lol yeah. It can. Especially if you've ever written a book and didn't think about what your audiobook would sound like as you were writing it. Because those ellipses actually convey a whole fucking lot to the narrators. But this "writer" doesn't know that yet because not only has she never written a book, she's never made an audiobook before either.

Some authors really do know what they're doing. And sometimes you don't know what you don't know. You only have opinions about it. Because you've never actually fucking done it before. I've done this about 70 times now. I know what the fuck I'm doing. Some people might not LIKE what I'm doing—that's totally cool. But I know what the fuck I'm doing. And that "dark author" knows what the fuck she's doing too. This isn't her first rodeo. So when that reader says things like "childish" and "juvenile" and "not even worth reading if free" in this woman's review? Just go away, dude. Just go the fuck away.

Back when I first started writing fiction in 2012 EVERYONE had an opinion about indie writers. Who were we? What right do we have to tell stories? Where were our qualifications? Who did we think we were?

WHO DID WE THINK WE WERE? That's what everyone with a fucking MFA, or a job in publishing, or a book blog that read "serious fiction" wanted to know about us back then.

Who did we think we were?

(answer: We're women with stories in our heads, motherfucker. That's who we are. And we're gonna write them down, OK? And you can just piss off and go read something else if you don't like it.)

I mean, that was the "tone" in so many reviews when I first started. Things have calmed down a lot since then. Probably because those of us who are still around really do know what we're doing. You don't write and publish the number of books like I have without learning a thing or two in the process.

But this mentality has been creeping back. I see it a lot more now than I did last year. And it's starting to piss me off.

There was another one that said, "No feelings for these characters." That was for that same book the "I hate dark shit" reader one-starred. I mean, OK. That's valid. But again, not really the author's fault. She wrote her book, her loyal fans all loved it to death, and so you know. Probably that was the reader. And that review would've been just fine if this reader didn't go on and on about how everyone needed to click over to such and such website to read her "full review" of how much she hated this book because she couldn't swear on Amazon.

Here's the bottom line for me. I just don't get **mean people**. I don't understand the "mean-girl mentality". There were no "mean girls" in my schools growing up. Every once in a while we got into arguments but there was no troop of cheerleaders walking around like they owned the place. And I went to five different high schools so I had a decent sample size compared to most people.

My daughter and I were talking about this recently. She's twenty-eight this year and I asked her if there were mean girls at her schools. She said no. So I'm not sure when this "mean girls" stuff became a "thing". Because it wasn't like that for me or her.

And that's why I made this particular team of women in Jesse's book act like adults. They could've very easily went in a different direction once they found out they were crushing on the same guy during spring break. But they didn't. They bonded over it and lifted each other up.

So I just don't understand mean people. Especially mean people in the age of social media. Facebook didn't turn us into a "global community" BTW. It turned us against each other. That's the truth. It might not be written yet, but a hundred years from now there will be a slew of academic papers on the negative impact of social media on the personalities of anonymous people.

And I probably lean a little bit mean myself. I'm definitely on the anti-social side. But I don't bash people in public. Almost never. I have to be really riled up to call someone out in public. Like that #cockygate shit? Remember that? I did say something in public because that was outrageous and people were getting threatening letters for something that wasn't even legal. And three were a few incidents a couple months back where readers would message authors after a signing to complain that they "weren't what they expected" and "didn't fulfill their in-person expectations" and "how about you make yourself look good next time".

Are you fucking kidding me? Say that to my face, OK? lol. Not on social media. Because if you said that shit to my face I'd make you feel so small and insignificant for trying to make ME feel that way first, you wouldn't know what to do with yourself.

No one says that shit to my face. But if they did they'd be telling the story of my reaction to their great-grandchildren until the day they died.

I leave pretty much everyone alone until I'm confronted. I mostly just ignore everything and everyone and move on. Life is too short.

So I just want to make it crystal clear that this is book one. This is a series. This series has a mystery. And by the time I'm done with the series all the pieces of said mystery will fall into place. And if anyone thinks I owe them all the mysterious answers at the end of book one they should probably check their expectations.

BTW – this is the first time I've ranted in an EOBS in YEARS. It's been years since I had an opinion like this at the end of a book. Probably goes all the way back to Social Media Book One: Follow. And that was summer 2014. Most of the time I just want to talk about my book. But this shit has been piling up for some time now and so there you go.

Julie writes a "classic EOBS" and puts it all out there.

Be nice to each other. That's my real message here. Especially if you're having a bad day. Don't put someone down to make yourself feel better because that never works. Never, ever, ever. Build someone up for once. You never know. That person just might turn into your best friend and you might become independent cosmetic company sales-bosses one day.

So, OK. Back to the Bossy Brothers. These guys went through quite the evolution since I came up with the idea back in January 2019. It started out pretty typical JA Huss. And by that I just mean – I started with one thing in mind and it came out the other end completely different!

It was gonna be more office-romance-y. Kinda like Mr. Perfect. The father was there. I knew he was dead and I knew the boys has some bone of contention, but beyond that, I had no clue. And I knew this first book about Jesse had a bachelor-auction trope. I just really had no idea these crazy ladies were gonna kidnap him until I got done with chapter one.

And then I was like… well… that wasn't in the plan. Almost none of it was in my original basic outline. I didn't even have Bright Berry Beach Cosmetics when I sat down to write that first paragraph – it just popped up out of nowhere when Emma started making her speech. Writing is weird like that. And this is just my most favorite part about the whole process.

In fact, thinking back on it, I had almost none of this book down in my outline. Why do I outline again? There was no pink jet, there was no trip to Key West, there was no dive shop, no three Dumas brothers. All of it just came out of nowhere.

I should know better by now. Of course there was going to be something creepy at the end. Of course there's gonna be secrets. Of course this mystery will only get bigger as we go. I just like that stuff and that's why they all end up like this.

But I tell you what, this book was fun to write.

Jesse Boston is the charmer of the three brothers. Joey is the tortured middle boy. I just finished book two. Today, actually. And Johnny, who will have the starring role in book three, is the real dark, broody one.

What I really like exploring in Jesse's book was the idea of this "reverse dream date" thing. Emma and her friends got dumped and they were hurt, and sad, and mad, and all those emotions we're all familiar with when we're more invested in a relationship than the other party.

Three of them managed to move on. Their idea of revenge is "success".

(That's mine too. Now. I will admit I did enact a pretty fucking amazing revenge plan back in my thirties. I mean... yeah, bitches. I got even *so hard*. I should write *that book*! Haha But I digress...).

But Emma didn't move on. Probably because she was the only who truly fell in love with Jesse. She truly felt that connection with him when they met and she spent all those years in between wondering if her "one" got away. She probably asked herself over and over again if she would ever feel that way about someone again.

Thus, her crazy revenge plan was born. And because these ladies are a team (not to mention super rich and powerful now) this almost felt like a good idea. *Almost*.

I loved their crazy revenge plan from the start, but what I really loved most was the way Emma took charge after she knew she was falling for him again, but he wasn't gonna let her off the hook for the kidnapping.

And that car scene in front of her building just came out of nowhere and from that point on Emma drove the show right up to the very end.

She didn't need him. She wanted him.

In fact, it was really Jesse who needed rescuing. So Emma stepped in to be his knight. She gave him the happily ever after. And OK, I'll just be honest with you right now, there's a whole lot more to this story coming in the next few books. So this is more of a HEA for now kind of ending.

Joey's book—releasing in late July—also started out with a basic trope. Surprise baby! I've never really written a surprise baby before. I'm thinking back right now... trying to find a story where there was a surprise baby in my backlist... some of them are pregnant at the end, but I've never based a story on a baby before (and Kate in Ford's book doesn't count, because she wasn't *his* baby.)

Also, it's funny that I'm writing this EOBS and book two is already done. Because that's not usually how I release books. But I'm ahead this year. And now that Joey's book is done it's so NOT your typical "surprise baby" trope. At all. For one, it's a ménage… lol

Didn't plan that either. Like AT ALL. But you know, when the guy comes home from fucking off in Tokyo with his two best friends and he's got no steady girl, what did I really think THAT was gonna turn in to?

Anyway, no one is pregnant in that book. Just warning you now. I don't seem to be able to follow the trope rules very well. So is it really a surprise baby? Yes. JA Huss style. And there's another trope in there too. The one I actually planned and does kinda follow the rules. If said trope involved a MMFM reverse harem… which… I dunno… not sure I've seen these two together before. :)

And Johnny's book was originally planned as another very familiar trope, which I'm not gonna reveal just yet, because I might find a way to twist this one all up and still use it, but I'm not sure yet. But of course, now Johnny's is gonna be darker and more dangerous.

But he's a dark and dangerous guy, anyway. Can't wait to meet the woman who can tame his antisocial ass.

So… welcome to the Bossy Brothers series.

At least three books, probably four (Zach might need to tie up some loose ends) and then *maybe maybe* there's a few more bothers down in Key West who would like a super sexy HEA when I'm done with these guys. We'll see about those Dumas boys.

I might not have time because I have a VERY DARK story brewing in my head that I am aching to write. And I will. I'm planning a January release for book one. This one is a little Meet Me In The Dark… just a little. Maybe a little more than a little. It's dark, for sure. But the dynamics are different than they were with Merc and Sydney. I am in to the girls driving the story right now and this girl for this book definitely drives the story. She will not be kidnapped, she will not be captive, she will not be submissive. And neither will he.

So if you're up for something emotionally dark, erotically sexy, and has all the feels—look for that. I'll announce a pre-order in October and this one will release wide. (at first). Then probably go into KU after release.

I haven't written one of these "genuinely dark books" in a long time. The Dirty Ones is the only thing that comes close. And I'd call that book more twisted than dark.

OK, well, it's nine-thirty now and I gotta go get this paperback uploaded. I hope you had fun on Emma's dream date. I hope you fell for Jesse. I hope you'll come back and read Joey's story too. Because believe me, it's **_dirty, and heart-melty, and the mystery continues!_**

Thank you for reading, thank you for reviewing, and I'll see you in the next book.

Julie
AKA JA Huss
June 12, 2019

JA Huss never wanted to be a writer and she still dreams of that elusive career as an astronaut. She originally went to school to become an equine veterinarian but soon figured out they keep horrible hours and decided to go to grad school instead. That Ph.D. wasn't all it was cracked up to be (and she really sucked at the whole scientist thing), so she dropped out and got a M.S. in forensic toxicology just to get the whole thing over with as soon as possible.

After graduation she got a job with the state of Colorado as their one and only hog farm inspector and spent her days wandering the Eastern Plains shooting the shit with farmers.

After a few years of that, she got bored. And since she was a homeschool mom and actually does love science, she decided to write science textbooks and make online classes for other homeschool moms.

She wrote more than two hundred of those workbooks and was the number one publisher at the online homeschool store many times, but eventually she covered every science topic she could think of and ran out of shit to say.

So in 2012 she decided to write fiction instead. That year she released her first three books and started a career that would make her a New York Times bestseller and land her on the USA Today Bestseller's List twenty-one times in the next five years.

In May 2018 MGM Television bought the TV and film rights for five of her books in the Rook & Ronin and Company series' and in March 2019 they offered her and her writing partner, Johnathan McClain, a script deal to write a pilot for a TV show.

Her books have sold millions of copies all over the world, the audio version of her semi-autobiographical book, Eighteen, was nominated for a Voice Arts Award and an Audie Award in 2016 and 2017 respectively, her audiobook, Mr. Perfect, was nominated for a Voice Arts Award in 2017, and her audiobook, Taking Turns, was nominated for an Audie Award in 2018. In 2019 her book, Total Exposure, was nominated for a Romance Writers of America RITA Award.

Johnathan McClain is her first (and only) writing partner and even though they are worlds apart in just about every way imaginable, it works.

She lives on a ranch in Central Colorado with her family.